INHALTSVERZEICHNIS

1ST *CONDITIONAL* – BEDINGUNG 1

A Erklärung

Ein ***Conditional*** ist ein **Bedingungssatz**. Er besteht – wie der Name sagt – aus einer **Bedingung** und einer **Folge**. Man nennt sie deshalb auch „wenn-dann-Sätze" – oder auf Englisch **„*if*-Sätze"**, weil sie meistens mit dem Wort ***if*** (**wenn, falls**) eingeleitet werden.

REGEL

Wenn du anrufst, werde ich dir alles erklären.
If you call, I will explain everything.

↓ **Bedingung** (*If you call,*)
↓ **Folge** (*I will explain everything.*)

B Anwendung

1st Conditional ist der **„Fall der Wirklichkeit"**. Du beschreibst damit die tatsächlichen Folgen einer Bedingung: Wenn die Bedingung erfüllt wird, dann tritt die Folge auch (wirklich) ein.

REGEL

Wenn du die Schachtel öffnest, wirst du eine Überraschung erleben.
If you open the box, you'll get a surprise.

↓ **Bedingung** (*If you open the box,*)
↓ **Folge** (*you'll get a surprise.*)

Wir werden uns einen Film ansehen, **wenn** es regnet.
We'll watch a film if it rains.

↓ **Folge** (*We'll watch a film*)
↓ **Bedingung** (*if it rains.*)

C Bildung

Bedingung *if*-Satz	Folge Hauptsatz	Folge Hauptsatz	Bedingung *if*-Satz
*If we **run**,*	*we **will catch** the bus.*	*We **will catch** the bus*	*if we **run**.*
present simple +	***will-future***	***will-future*** +	***present simple***

1 ✱

Finish the sentences with will-future. – Vervollständige die Sätze mit *will-future*.

1 If I lose my bus pass, I *(get)* __________________ into trouble.

2 If Lydia invites me to her party, I *(come)* __________________.

3 If we ask Dad to help us, he *(do)* __________________ it.

4 If you break a mirror, you *(have)* __________________ bad luck for seven years.

5 If an asteroid hits the Earth, many people and animals *(die)* __________________.

6 I *(tell)* __________________ you a funny story if you want to hear it.

7 Lenny *(come)* __________________ with us if we wait a minute.

8 My parents *(be)* __________________ disappointed if I don't pass the test.

9 We *(stay)* __________________ in the house if it rains or snows.

10 Aunt Natalie *(earn)* __________________ a lot of money if she gets the new job.

Bedingung und/oder **Folge** können auch **negativ** (mit **Verneinung**) sein:

REGEL

*If you **don't open** the box, you **won't know** what's in it.*
*If Malcolm **isn't** at home, we'll leave the present at his door.*
*You **won't miss** the bus if you run.*
*We will leave without John if he **doesn't come** soon.*

2 ✱✱

Finish the sentences with present simple. Some sentences are negative. – Setze die Verben in *present simple* ein. Achte auf Verneinungen.

1 If you *(read)* __________________ in the dark, you'll ruin your eyes.

2 If Hannah *(make)* __________________ another mistake, she'll lose the match.

3 If Adrian *(not be)* __________________ at home, we'll leave him a message.

4 If the weather *(not change)* __________________, we'll go sailing tomorrow.

5 If I *(not feel)* __________________ better soon, I won't go to school this week.

6 You'll miss your bus if you *(not leave)* __________________ now.

7 Our neighbours won't like it if we *(play)* __________________ loud music.

8 It'll get very cold in here if you *(not shut)* __________________ the window.

9 Everything will be fine if you *(do)* __________________ what I say.

10 Nobody will know that we're here if we *(not make)* __________________ a noise.

11 If Sophia *(not get)* __________________ Lenny a birthday present, he'll be very sad.

Quest 1.1

Üben

3 ✱✱ *Match the conditions with the consequences – and the other way round*.* – **Welche Folgen passen zu welchen Bedingungen – und umgekehrt?**

If you come after 10 o'clock,	1		A	if you don't apologise to him.
If Philip falls asleep now,	2		B	if she isn't more careful.
If the sun shines tomorrow,	3		C	he won't see the end of the film.
If I don't find my glasses,	4		D	if you don't eat any vitamins.
If we don't go to bed now,	5		E	the party will be in the garden.
Lily will have an accident	6		F	if you make fun of them.
You'll get sick	7		G	if you don't put any petrol in it.
Joe will be very disappointed	8		H	I will be asleep.
Nobody will like you	9		I	we'll be very tired in the morning.
The engine won't run	10		J	I won't see anything.

**other way round* – umgekehrt

4 ✱✱ *Cross out the wrong form.* – **Streiche die falsche Form durch.**

1 If you *visit / will visit* us next time*, we *go / will go* skiing with you.
2 We *take / will take* a taxi if it *rains / will rain*.
3 If I don't *see / won't see* you tomorrow, I *phone / will phone* you.
4 Nothing *happens / will happen* to you if you *tell / will tell* the truth.
5 If you *read / will read* these stories, you *know / will know* more about superstitions.
6 If Grandpa *wins / will win* the lottery, he *buys / will buy* a new and bigger car.
7 We *visit / will visit* Ground Zero if we ever* *go / will go* to New York City.
8 You *don't see / won't see* who is in the room if you *don't / won't* switch on the light.
9 Veronica *gets / will get* a headache if she *doesn't / won't* wear a hat.
10 You *don't / won't* lose weight if you *sit / will sit* in front of the computer all day.
11 Penny *comes / will come* to my party if she *isn't / won't* be busy.
12 The vase *breaks / will break* if you *drop / will drop* it.
13 If you *don't / won't* behave, you *don't / won't* get any presents.
14 Antonia *is / will be* sad if we *don't / won't* invite her.
15 If the sun *will shine / shines* tomorrow, we *will go / go* for a walk.

**next time* – nächstes Mal **ever* – jemals

Quest 1.2

5 ✱✱✱ *Present simple or will-future? You decide! Write the correct tense and remember: 'if' goes with present, not with future.* – *Present simple* oder *will-future*? Du entscheidest! Setze die richtige Zeit ein und vergiss nicht: auf *if* folgt die Gegenwart, nicht die Zukunft.

*You **will have** good luck all year if you **find** a horseshoe.*

*If you **break** a mirrow, bad luck **will be** with you for seven years.*

1 If you *(find)* __________________ a penny and pick it up, you *(have)* __________________ good luck all day.

2 If a black cat *(cross)* __________________ your way, something bad *(happen)* __________________.

3 If you *(walk)* __________________ under a ladder, you *(get)* __________________ bad news.

4 If you *(carry)* __________________ a rabbit's foot with you, everything *(be)* __________________ fine.

5 If you *(see)* __________________ a shooting star* and make a wish, your wish *(come)* __________________ true.

6 Bad things *(not come)* __________________ your way if you *(knock)* __________________ on wood.

7 Things *(go)* __________________ well if you *(cross)* __________________ your fingers.

8 You *(succeed*)* __________________ with your plans if you *(spit*)* __________________ on a coin*.

9 You *(be)* __________________ lucky all year if you *(see)* __________________ a chimney sweep* on New Year's Day.

10 Things *(turn out*)* __________________ badly if you *(do)* __________________ them on Friday, the 13th.

**shooting star* – Sternschnuppe **succeed* – gelingen, Erfolg haben **spit* – spucken
**coin* – Münze **chimney sweep* – Rauchfangkehrer **turn out badly* – schlecht ausgehen

Üben

6 ✱✱✱ *Same as before – present simple or will-future? You decide again.* – Wie bei der vorhergehenden Übung – *present simple* oder *will-future*? Du entscheidest wieder.

1. If somebody *(see)* ________________ us here, we *(get)* ________________ into trouble.
2. If you ever *(go)* ________________ back to Canada, we *(be)* ________________ very sorry.
3. If Charlie *(not get)* ________________ up now, he *(not get)* ________________ breakfast.
4. If you *(not learn)* ________________ English, you *(not understand)* ________________ the people in England.
5. If you *(study)* ________________, you *(not fail*)* ________________ the test.
6. If Gina *(come)* ________________ to my birthday party, I *(be)* ________________ the happiest boy on Earth.
7. You *(feel)* ________________ hungry if you *(not finish)* ________________ your breakfast.
8. Everybody *(laugh)* ________________ at us if we *(wear)* ________________ these silly costumes.
9. The bus driver *(not wait)* ________________ if we *(be)* ________________ late.
10. You *(catch)* ________________ cold if you *(not put on)* ________________ a warm coat today.
11. We *(go)* ________________ to the cinema tonight if Maria *(come)* ________________ with us.
12. You *(know)* ________________ where I am if you *(read)* ________________ my emails.
13. If you *(wear)* ________________ a mask, people *(not recognise)* ________________ you.
14. If we *(meet)* ________________ Elsie in town, we *(say)* ________________ hello.
15. Joe *(buy)* ________________ these sneakers if they *(not be)* ________________ too expensive.
16. Chloe *(not keep*)* ________________ the dress if she *(not like)* ________________ it.

**fail* – durchfallen, nicht bestehen   **keep* – hier: behalten

Üben

Quest 1.3

D *if not = unless*

- Anstatt *"if … not"* kannst du auch ***"unless"*** schreiben.
- Dabei gilt dieselbe „Zeitenfolge" wie zuvor:

if / unless + ***present simple*** — **Hauptsatz** + ***will-future***

REGEL

Elena will miss the bus ***unless*** *she hurries.*
Elena will miss the bus ***if*** *she* ***doesn't*** *hurry.*

7 ✱ *Use unless instead of if … not in the following sentences.* – Verwende *unless* anstelle von *if … not* in den folgenden Sätzen.

1 If you don't do your homework first, Mum won't let you watch TV.

2 Please don't call me today if it's not really important.

3 If Liam doesn't leave right now, he will miss his train.

4 Dad will work in the garden all week if it doesn't rain.

5 If Mum's bus isn't late, she'll be back in an hour.

6 Your friends won't know about your concert if you don't tell them.

7 If you don't wear a mask, people will recognise you.

8 I will pass* the exam if I'm not too nervous.

9 If the firefighters don't come soon, the house will burn down.

10 Miranda will be very disappointed if you don't dance with her.

11 If Dad doesn't find a petrol station soon, we'll be in deep trouble.

**pass* – durchkommen

2nd *CONDITIONAL* – BEDINGUNG 2

A Erklärung

- Ein ***Conditional*** ist ein **Bedingungssatz**. Er besteht – wie der Name sagt – aus einer **Bedingung** und einer **Folge**. Man nennt sie deshalb auch „wenn-dann-Sätze" – oder auf Englisch „***if*-Sätze**", weil sie meistens mit dem Wort ***if*** (**wenn, falls**) eingeleitet werden.

REGEL

Wenn ich könnte,	würde ich dir alles erklären.
If *I could,*	*I would explain everything.*
↓	↓
Bedingung	**Folge**

B Anwendung

2nd Conditional ist der ***„Fall der Möglichkeit"***. Du beschreibst damit, was geschehen könnte, wenn die Bedingung tatsächlich erfüllt werden sollte – was nicht sicher, aber möglich ist.

REGEL

Wenn ich die Antwort wüsste, würde ich sie dir sagen.
If *I knew the answer, I would tell you.*
↓ **Bedingung** ↓ **Folge**

Wir würden zuhause bleiben, **wenn** es regnete (regnen würde).
We would stay at home ***if*** *it rained.*
↓ **Folge** ↓ **Bedingung**

C Bildung

Bedingung *if*-Satz	**Folge** Hauptsatz	**Folge** Hauptsatz	**Bedingung** *if*-Satz
If I ***knew*** *the answer,*	*I* ***would tell*** *you.*	*I* ***would tell*** *you*	*if I* ***knew*** *the answer.*
short form: I'd tell, you'd tell, he'd tell			
past simple +	***would + base form***	***would + base form*** +	***past simple***

8 ✱

Finish the sentences with would + base form. Use short forms if possible. – Vervollständige die Sätze mit *would + base form*. Verwende Kurzformen, wo es sinnvoll ist.

1 I *(give)* ________________ you Jenny's phone number if I knew it.

2 Alex *(come)* ________________ with us if he had more time.

3 Grandma *(be)* ________________ disappointed if I forgot her birthday.

4 We *(play)* ________________ outdoors* if it stopped raining.

5 Brian *(earn)* ________________ more money if he had a better job.

6 If I missed the train, Dad *(drive)* ________________ me to school.

7 If Camilla spoke Chinese, she *(understand)* ________________ the tourists.

8 If we asked Dad to help us, he *(do)* ________________ it.

9 If I found a wallet, I *(take)* ________________ it to the nearest police station.

10 If electric cars were cheaper, my dad *(buy)* ________________ one.

**outdoors* – draußen, im Freien

Wissen
Üben

Bedingung und/oder **Folge** können auch **negativ** (mit **Verneinung**) sein:

REGEL

*You **wouldn't get** bad marks if you worked harder.*
*We would stay here longer if the weather **wasn't** so bad.*
*If Tim **didn't like** the food, he **wouldn't eat** eat it.*

9 ✱✱

Finish the sentences with past simple. Some sentences are negative. – Setze die Verben in *past simple* ein. Achte auf Verneinungen.

1 If you *(do)* ________________ your homework, everything would be fine.

2 If Jeremy *(make)* ________________ another mistake, he would lose the match.

3 If Adrian *(not be)* ________________ at school, we would notice* it.

4 If they *(not speak)* ________________ so fast, we would understand them.

5 I would go to the party if I *(not study)* ________________ for the Maths test.

6 You would miss your bus if I *(not drive)* ________________ you to the bus stop.

7 Felix wouldn't like it if we *(play)* ________________ with his game console.

8 Mum *(not worry)* ________________ so much if we phoned her.

**notice* – bemerken

Quest 2.1

10 Cross out the wrong form. – Streiche die falsche Form durch.

1 If you *asked / would ask* me nicely, I *lent / would lend* you my bicycle.
2 We *took / would take* a taxi if it *rained / would rain*.
3 If you *wrote / would write* your homework on the computer, it *was / would be* easier to read.
4 Nobody *believed / would believe* you if you *told / would tell* them this story.
5 Daniel *didn't / wouldn't* play today if he *didn't / wouldn't* feel well.
6 If pigs *had / would have* wings, they *flew / would fly*.
7 This soup *tasted / would taste* better if it *had / would have* more salt in it.
8 I *called / would call* Evelyn today if I *knew / would know* her phone number.
9 We *went / would go* swimming if it *wasn't / wouldn't be* so cold.
10 You *found / would find* your things if you *tidied up / would tidy up* your room.
11 Vivian *wasn't / wouldn't be* so nervous if she *didn't / wouldn't* drink so much coffee.
12 You *didn't / wouldn't* make so many mistakes if you *listened / would listen* to me.

11 Match the beginnings and ends of the sentences in the grid. – Ordne die Satzbeginne den Satzenden zu.

If there was more snow,	1	A	we'd watch a movie together.
I would take my dog for a walk every afternoon	2	B	you'd be a better player.
If Gerald was here,	3	C	he wouldn't be so tired in the morning.
We'd get to school in time	4	D	if it didn't cost so much.
If Kevin didn't go to bed so late,	5	E	we'd build a snowman.
Eva would have more friends	6	F	if we took an earlier bus.
I'd see a dentist	7	G	if she wasn't such a gossip*.
If you practised three hours every day,	8	H	if I had a toothache.
Dad would buy a bigger car	9	I	if I didn't have so much work to do for school.

**gossip* – Klatschmaul

Üben

Quest 2.2

ACHTUNG

If I ***were*** *you …* Wenn ich du **wäre** …

If I ***were*** *you, I* ***would*** *stay a little longer.*
I ***wouldn't*** *talk back to Ms Jones if I* ***were*** *you.*

12 ✱✱✱ *Cross out the wrong word – will / won't or would / wouldn't? present simple or past simple?* – Streiche das falsche Wort durch – *will / won't* oder *would / wouldn't*? *present simple* oder *past simple*?

> *If the sun shines, we* **will** / ~~would~~ *have a picnic.*
> *George* ~~won't~~ / **wouldn't** *be so cheeky if he knew how strict Mr Smith is.*
> *If we* **finish** / ~~finished~~ *first, we will get a medal.*
> *You would see the mountains if the fog* ~~isn't~~ / **wasn't** *so thick.*

1. Fred *will / would* sell his stamp collection if he needed the money.
2. If you *break / broke* my glasses, you will have to buy me new ones.
3. If Tony *invites / invited* me to his party, I would go.
4. I *won't / wouldn't* open the door if I were you.
5. Charlie wouldn't help us if he *doesn't / didn't* want to.
6. If you go out with Sandra, I *won't / wouldn't* be your friend anymore*.
7. What *will / would* you do if you don't find your keys?
8. If Connor *doesn't / didn't* answer the phone, we'll have to text* him.

**not anymore* – nicht mehr, nicht länger **to text* – eine SMS senden

Quests
2.3
2.4
2.5

Wissen
Üben

ABILITY & PERMISSION – „KÖNNEN" & „DÜRFEN"

A Ability – Fähigkeit, Können

REGEL

can und ***(be) able to*** + ***base form*** drücken Fähigkeit und Können aus.
Verneinung: *cannot / can't*; *(be) not able to* + *base form*

present	
*I **can speak** three languages.* *She **can walk** on her hands.* *We **cannot answer** this question.*	*I **am able to speak** three languages.* *She **is able to walk** on her hands.* *We **aren't able to answer** this question.*
past	
*I **could swim** when I was a baby.* *He **could read** when he was four.* *They **couldn't vote** before 1918.*	*I **was able to swim** faster than my friends.* *He **was able to read** my handwriting*.* *They **weren't able to find** their passports.*
future	
–	*I'**ll be able to drive** Dad's car in a few years.* *You **won't be able to go** to the dance.*
present perfect	
–	*We'**ve been able to solve** the problem.* *He **hasn't been able to open** the box.*

**handwriting* – Handschrift

*I **can** see that you've got a problem with your bike, but I'**m not able to** help you.*

PRESENT

- Beide Formen haben die **gleiche Bedeutung**:
  *I **can play** the piano.* = ***I'm able to play** the piano.*
- **Beim Sprechen** verwendet man aber fast immer ***can***.

REGEL

*They **can't stop** the fight.* = *They **aren't able to stop** the fight.*
*We **can help** you.* = *We**'re able to help** you.*

13 ✱✱ *Use can and (be) able in the following examples.* – Verwende *can* und *(be) able* in den folgenden Sätzen.

> Vicky _can_ tap dance*. – Vicky _is able_ to tap dance*.
> I _cannot_ move my feet! – I _'m not able_ to move my feet!
> _Can_ you hear me? – _Are you able_ to hear me?

1 Who ______________ translate this sentence into German?
Who ______________ to translate this sentence into German?

2 I ______________ not come to the gym with you.
I ______________ not ______________ to come to the gym with you.

3 We ______________ beat the other team.
We ______________ to beat the other team.

4 ______________ Justin answer these questions?
______________ Justin ______________ to answer these questions?

5 Sarah ______________ 't come to my birthday party.
Sarah ______________ not ______________ to come to my party.

6 What ______________ the police do about* the traffic jams*?
What ______________ the police ______________ to do about the traffic jams?

7 Nobody ______________ look into the future.
Nobody ______________ to look into the future.

8 Mum is the only* person who ______________ help us now.
Mum is the only* person who ______________ to help us now.

**tap dance* – Stepptanz **do ... about* – (etwas) dagegen tun/unternehmen
**traffic jam* – Stau **only* – hier: einzig

Quest 3.1

PAST

- Du sagst und schreibst ***was / were able to* + *base form***, wenn jemand in einer bestimmten Situation etwas tun konnte oder zu etwas in der Lage war.

REGEL

*I **was able to speak** with Oliver yesterday.*
*We **were able to finish** the project in time.*

- Du sagst und schreibst ***could* + *base form***, wenn etwas im Allgemeinen möglich war.

REGEL

***Could** you **read** and **write** when you were in kindergarten?*
*Nobody **could imagine** smartphones in the 1980s.*

- In einem **verneinten Satz** – wenn also jemand etwas nicht tun konnte oder dazu nicht in der Lage war – kannst du sowohl ***couldn't / could not*** als auch ***was / were not able*** verwenden.

REGEL

*Simon **couldn't / wasn't able to** come last week.*
*In the past, people **couldn't / weren't able to** read and write.*

Wissen
Üben

14 ✱✱ *Cross out the wrong words: could or was / were able to?* – Streiche die falschen Wörter durch: *could* oder *was / were able to*?

1. It rained last night, but we *could / were able to* finish the tennis match.
2. Carol played well, but I *could / was able to* beat her in two sets.
3. In the Middle Ages*, more people *could / were able to* ride horses than today.
4. Every evening I *could / was able to* watch lions come to drink water.
5. *Could you / Were you able to* ride a bike when you were six?
6. In 1911, Amundsen *could / was able to* reach the South Pole before Scott.
7. When Dad was in school, he *could / was able to* choose between Latin and French.
8. Our neighbours' cat ran away, but they *could / were able to* catch it again.
9. Last week was so hot that we *could / were able to* go swimming every day.
10. From my room in the old house, I *could / was able to* see a big park.

**Middle Ages* – Mittelalter

Quest 3.2

15 ✱✱✱ *could (not) or was / were (not) able to? Fill in the correct form.* – *could (not)* oder *was / were (not) able to*? Allgemein oder eine bestimmte Situation? Setze die richtige Form ein.

> **After some minutes,** *Dad was able to start the car.* → *bestimmte Situation*
> **When I was a child,** *I could stand on my head.* → *allgemeine Situation*
> *Marty broke his model plane, and he couldn't / wasn't able to repair it.* → *Verneinung*

1 I ____________________ answer all the questions in yesterday's test.

2 Doris wasn't at home, but I ____________________ talk to her on the phone.

3 After two days on the slopes*, Anthony ____________________ ski.

4 Dad had nothing to do all day, so he ____________________ play with us.

5 My little brother ____________________ walk when he was 11 months old.

6 I spoke very slowly, but they ____________________ not understand me.

7 After her accident, Lucy ____________________ walk for two weeks*.

8 It was terribly hot in the room, but we ____________________ not open the windows.

**slope* – Hang   **for two weeks* – zwei Wochen lang

16 ✱✱ *What happened at the weekend? Fill in could (not) or was / were (not) able to.* – Was geschah am Wochenende? Setze *could (not)* oder *was / were (not) able to* ein.

1

We ____________________ play outside.

2

Max ____________________ finish his model ship.

3

Amy's parents ____________________ buy a new car.

4

Sue ____________________ ride her bike.

FUTURE

- Du verwendest **für alle Personen der Ein- und Mehrzahl** ***will be able to + base form***. ***Can*** in irgendeiner Form ist **nicht möglich**.

REGEL

*I, you, he, we, they ... **will be able to meet** interesting people.*

- Die **Verneinung** lautet ***will not / won't be able to + base form***.

REGEL

*I, you, she ... **will not be able to see** the movie tonight.*
*I, you, he ... **won't be able to get** up early in the morning.*

- Und so bildest du **Fragen**:

REGEL

***Will** I, you, it, we ... **be able to walk** again soon?*
*When **will** you, she, they ... **be able to read** the books?*
*Who **will be able to show** us the way?*

17 ***

What will these people be able to do tomorrow or next week or next time ... ? (–) means won't. – Was werden diese Menschen morgen, nächste Woche, das nächste Mal … tun können? (–) bedeutet Verneinung *(won't)*.

1 Little Tommy ______________________ ride a bike when he's older.

2 You ______________________ speak with my parents tomorrow.

3 I hope they ______________________ repair our car soon!

4 The doctors say Nick ______________________ leave the hospital soon.

5 If it gets really warm, you *(–)* ______________________ see our snow castle.

6 Callie ______________________ finish first, I think.

7 The girls *(–)* ______________________ remember what you said.

8 If you don't read the book, you *(–)* ______________________ talk about it.

9 I'm sure you ______________________ find your tickets again!

10 ______________________ we ______________________ visit Central Park in New York City?

PRESENT PERFECT

- Du sagst und schreibst ***have / has (not) been able to* + *base form***.

REGEL

I, you, we, they ***have been able to skate*** *for years.*
He, she, it ***hasn't been able to sleep*** *since Sunday.*

- Und so bildest du die **Frage**:

REGEL

Have *you* ***been able to ask*** *your parents?*
Has *Joe* ***been able to solve*** *the problem?*
Who has been able to answer *all the questions?*

18 ✱✱ *What have they (not) been able to do?* – Was habe diese Menschen (nicht) tun können?

1

Jake ______________________ fix his broken kite.

2

I'm sorry, I ______________________ come sooner!

3

Grandma ______________________ find her glasses yet.

4

The bank robbers ______________________ ______________________ escape the police.

19 ✱✱

Complete the mini dialogues using the correct form of present perfect: have(n't) or has(n't). – Vervollständige die Mini-Dialoge. Verwende dabei die richtige Form von *present perfect*: *have(n't)* oder *has(n't)*.

> A: *Has your father finished the garden shed yet?*
> B: *No, he* <u>*hasn't been able to*</u> *get the right kind of wood.*

1 *A:* Have you done your homework, Julie?

B: Yes, and I ______________________ answer every question!

2 *A:* Where's Violet?

B: No idea. We ______________________ phone her.

3 *A:* Has your father sold his car yet?

B: Oh yes, and he ______________________ get a good price for it.

4 *A:* Are we going to the concert next week?

B: Yes! I ______________________ buy some tickets.

5 *A:* Is Uncle Joe's car running again?

B: No, he ______________________ find a mechanic who can fix it.

6 *A:* Has your suitcase arrived?

B: No, they ______________________ deliver* it yet.

**deliver* – liefern, zustellen

20 ✱✱✱

past or present perfect or future? Cross out the wrong words! – *Past* oder *present perfect* oder *future*? Streiche die falschen Wörter durch.

> *Nate* **wasn't** / ~~**hasn't been**~~ *able to buy the jeans because they were too expensive.*
> *Kylie* ~~**was**~~ / **has been** *able to swim since she was three years old.*
> *You* ~~**were**~~ / **will be** *able to meet my friends tomorrow.*

1 Joe Smith *was / has been* able to speak Spanish since his visit to Spain.
2 Grace *will be / was* able to visit us again next month.
3 The Coopers *weren't / haven't been* able to sell their house yet.
4 We *were / have been* able to catch the last bus yesterday.
5 You *won't be / haven't been* able to see anything. It's too dark outside.
6 Hailey *hasn't been / won't be* able to get an A in English since last year.
7 I *have been / will be* able to help you if you ask me.
8 Nobody *was / has been* able to find their shoes after the party.
9 Helen had a broken finger, so she *wasn't / hasn't been* able to play the violin.
10 Jason *wasn't / hasn't been* able to run and jump since his accident.

Quest 3.3

21 ✱✱✱ *Look at the pictures and say what they will or won't be able to do. Use the words from the box.* – Schau dir die Bilder an und sage, was die Leute (nicht) werden tun können. Verwende *will / won't be able to* mit den Handlungen aus dem Rahmen.

play basketball ▪ go to the dance ▪ buy a camera ▪ cook dinner
visit us this year ▪ see different sights

1

2

3

4

5

6

1 Theo ______________________________.

2 Lilly is ill. She ______________________________.

3 In the holidays, we ______________________________.

4 Richard ______________________________.

5 Mum ______________________________.

6 My grandparents ______________________________.

22 ✱✱ *What have they been able to do this year? Write sentences with have / has been able to.* – Was haben die Menschen heuer schon erledigen können? Schreibe Sätze in *present perfect*: *have / has been able to*.

win – football cup

sell – her painting

grow – a huge pumpkins

1 We ____.

2 Nora ____.

3 Mr Frederick ____.

Üben

23 ✱✱✱ *And now all tenses – present, past, future and present perfect. Cross out the wrong options.* – Und jetzt eine Übung mit allen Zeiten: *present, past, future* und *present perfect*. Streiche die falschen Möglichkeiten durch.

> *Look, we **can** / ~~**could**~~ see the ocean from our hotel room!*
> *Dad ~~**couldn't**~~ / **wasn't able to** find his car key this morning.*
> *I hope I ~~**have been**~~ / **will be** able to give you an answer tomorrow.*
> *Jimmy needs a new mobile, but he ~~**wasn't**~~ / **hasn't been** able to buy one yet.*

1 Reading English is easy, but I *couldn't / am not able to* speak it very well.
2 Hundreds of people *can / were able to* watch the concert live last night.
3 Are you still looking for your glasses, Hannah? – Yes, I am. I *haven't been / won't be* able to find them yet.
4 I've hidden the Easter eggs so well you *aren't / won't be* able to find them.
5 Why *couldn't / won't* you answer the phone when I called you?
6 We were so tired that we *won't / weren't* able to stay awake* during the film.
7 Max is very clever. He *can / could* play the guitar and the saxophone.
8 *Were / Are* you able to hear me or is it too loud here?
9 Nobody *will be / is* able to contact Mrs Jones. Where can she be?
10 Last week we *could / can* play outdoors, this week we *couldn't / can't*.

**stay awake* – wach bleiben

B *Permission* – Erlaubnis & Verbot

- Mit ***can(not)*** und ***be (not) allowed to*** + ***base form*** sagst du, dass etwas **erlaubt** oder **nicht erlaubt** ist.

REGEL

Mum, can I watch a film now? – Yes, but you ***can't stay*** *up too late.*
We ***weren't allowed to leave*** *the room during the concert.*
*When I'm 16, I****'ll be allowed to drive*** *a car.*
Joe ***has never been allowed to eat*** *junk food.*

- Anstelle von ***am / is / are not allowed*** – also nur in *present* – kannst du in allen Personen der Ein- und Mehrzahl auch ***mustn't*** sagen und schreiben.

REGEL

We ***aren't allowed to stay*** *up late.*	=	*We* ***mustn't stay*** *up late.*
Mila ***isn't allowed to speak*** *with Liam.*	=	*She* ***mustn't speak*** …
*I****'m not allowed to watch*** *TV in my room.*	=	*I* ***mustn't watch*** …

24 ✱ *Match the pictures and the sentences.* – Ordne die Bilder den Sätzen zu.

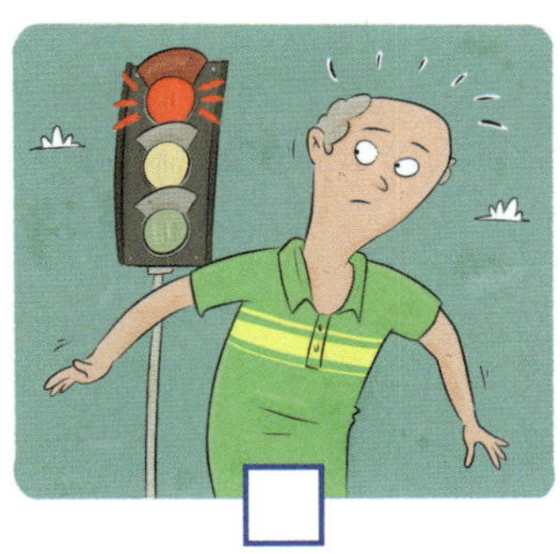

1 People aren't allowed to feed the ducks.
2 We aren't allowed to ride our bikes here.
3 The man isn't allowed to cross the street.
4 You aren't allowed to fish here.
5 I'm not allowed to drive Dad's car.
6 A child isn't allowed to drink beer.

25 ✱ *Re-write the sentences in exercise 24 with mustn't.* – Schreibe die Sätze von Übung 24 mit *mustn't* anstelle von *not allowed to*.

1 ______.

2 ______.

3 ______.

4 ______.

5 ______.

6 ______.

26 ✱✱ *Read the dialogue between Alice and her mother and replace can and can't with (not) be allowed to. Take the first sentence as an example.* – Lies die Unterhaltung zwischen Alice und ihrer Mutter und ersetze *can* und *can't* durch *(not) be allowed to*. Nimm den ersten Satz als Beispiel.

1 *Alice:* Why can't I go to Gina's party, Mum? Betty can go!
2 *Mother:* Yes, but …
3 *Alice:* All my friends can do what they want!
4 *Mother:* That's not true. Betty can't go out during the week and she can bring friends home only at the weekend. So she can't do what she wants.
5 *Alice:* Maybe, but she can watch TV in her room. I can't even have my own TV set!
6 *Mother:* That's because …
7 *Alice:* Why? Why can't I do what Betty does?
8 *Mother:* Because 12-year-old girls can't do the things 18-year-olds do! And that's the end of the discussion!

1 Why *am I not allowed to go* to Gina's party, Mum? Betty *is allowed to go*!

2 Yes, but …

3 All ______

4 ______
______

5 ______
______

6 That's because …

7 Why? ______

8 Because ______
______

Üben

27 ✱✱ *Match the questions and answers.* – Ordne die Antworten den Fragen zu.

Am I allowed to speak?	1		A	Oh no! Look, there's a 'no smoking' sign.
Is Tim allowed to stay longer?	2		B	It's okay if he or she is nice.
Are the girls allowed to watch the boys dance?	3		C	No, everyone must be quiet during the lesson.
Are people allowed to smoke in this bar?	4		D	Yes, all costumes are possible.
Am I allowed to dress up as a Chinese?	5		E	I don't know. Mia usually sits here.
Is Emma allowed to bring a friend to the party?	6		F	No, sorry, he must leave in ten minutes.
Am I allowed to sit here?	7		G	No, we must leave them in our lockers*.
Are you allowed to wear shoes in the classroom?	8		H	Of course, but the boys won't like it.

**locker* – Spind, versperrbarer Schrank

28 ✱✱ *Mark the correct tense: present, past, future or present perfect.* – Kennzeichne die richtige Zeit: *present, past, future* oder *present perfect*.

> *Marc and I* ***will be / were*** *allowed to ride Benny's motorcycle yesterday.*
> ***Are / Were*** *we allowed to use a dictionary, sir?*
> *Alfie* ***has been / will be*** *allowed to drive the family car since his 17th birthday.*
> *I* ***am / will be*** *allowed to invite more friends for my next birthday party.*

1 Every year, Martin *is / was* allowed to choose a place for the summer holidays.

2 I *won't be / haven't been* allowed to hold my sister's new baby yet.

3 The girls *were / are* allowed to have earrings and piercings in our school.

4 We *aren't / won't be* allowed to make so much noise next time*.

5 Afro-Americans *aren't / weren't* allowed to ride at the front of the bus.

6 Ms Miller says we *will be / have been* allowed to go on a school trip next year.

7 In our English lessons we *won't be / aren't* allowed to speak German.

8 *Are / Were* you allowed to use your brother's mountain bike? – Yes, sometimes.

**next time* – das nächste Mal

Quests 3.4 3.5

Üben

29 ✱✱✱ *Look at the picture of people at the zoo and say what's wrong. Use the words from the box.* – Schau dir das Bild mit den Menschen im Zoo an. Was machen sie falsch? Was dürfen sie nicht tun? Verwende die Wörter aus dem Rahmen.

~~break rules~~ ▪ bring a dog ▪ climb, fence ▪ climb, trees ▪ feed
have picnic ▪ litter ▪ play music ▪ smoke ▪ tease

1

2

3

4

5

6

7

8

9

You're not allowed to break the rules.

1 You mustn't ______________________________.
2 You're not allowed ______________________________.
3 You mustn't ______________________________.
4 ______________________________.
5 ______________________________.
6 ______________________________.
7 ______________________________.
8 ______________________________.
9 ______________________________.

LET

- ***let*** heißt **lassen, zulassen** oder **erlauben**.
- Damit sagst du, dass dich jemand etwas tun lässt oder es dir erlaubt.
- Frage und Verneinung bildest du mit ***do, does, did*** und ***will***.

REGEL

*Mum and Dad **let** me ride Dad's scooter sometimes.*
They allow me to ride it.

*They **won't let** me see the photos of the accident.*
*They **don't** allow me to see the photos.*

*Does your sister **let** you wear her T-shirts?*
***Does** she allow you to wear them?*

30 ✱ *Re-write these sentences using let instead of be allowed to.* – Schreibe diese Sätze neu. Verwende *let* anstelle von *be allowed to*.

> *Martin **is allowed to** choose a place for the summer holiday.*
> *Martin's parents **let him choose** a place for the summer holiday.*

1 Sometimes I'm allowed to sleep in my parents' bed.

My parents sometimes ______________________________ in their bed.

2 Sylvia is always allowed to use my pen.

I always ______________________________.

3 Are you allowed to dye your hair purple?

__________ your parents ______________________________?

4 We weren't allowed to listen to loud music.

They didn't ______________________________.

5 You will be allowed to go home soon.

They ______________________________.

6 I wasn't allowed to watch the late night movie.

My parents ______________________________.

Quest 3.6

COMPARATIVES: A REVISION – VERGLEICHE: EIN RÜCKBLICK

A Zur Erinnerung

- Du verwendest **Adjektive** (Eigenschaftswörter), um Dinge oder Menschen zu vergleichen.

- **Adjektive** haben **drei Stufen**:

Grundstufe *adjective*	Mehrstufe *comparative*	Meiststufe *superlative*
long	*long**er***	*the long**est***
big	*bi**gger***	*the bi**ggest***
ugly	*ugl**ier***	*the ugl**iest***
attractive	***more** attractive*	***the most** attractive*
good	***better***	***the best***

- **Einsilbige** Adjektive und zweisilbige, die auf ***-er, -le, -ow,*** und ***-y*** enden, bilden die Mehr- und Meiststufe (*comparative and superlative*) mit ***-(e)r*** und ***-(e)st***.

ACHTUNG

RECHTSCHREIBUNG!

- **Verdoppelung** des Konsonanten am Wortende:
  *bi**gg**er – bi**gg**est; ho**tt**er – ho**tt**est …*

- Wandel von **y** zu ***-i*** nach einem Konsonant:
  uglier – ugliest; happier – happiest …

- **Drei- und mehrsilbige** Adjektive und die restlichen zweisilbigen bilden *comparative* und *superlative* mit ***more*** und ***most***.

  ***more** attractive – **most** attractive; **more** comfortable – **most** comfortable …*

- **Unregelmäßige Formen**: ***good*** – ***better*** – ***best***; ***bad*** – ***worse*** – ***worst*** …

31 *

Find the adjectives in the wordsnake. Write them down and find their comparative and superlative. – Finde die Adjektive in der Wortschlange. Schreibe sie auf und bilde für jedes die Mehr- und Meiststufe.

MADYOUNGNARROWWONDERFULPRETTYUSEFULTHIRSTYRUDESUCCESSFULQUIET

adjective	comparative	superlative
narrow		

Quest 4.1

Wissen

Üben

B Vergleiche

MIT DEM ADJEKTIV (Grundstufe)

The dog is ***as big as*** *the cat.*

The cat is ***not as big as*** *the dog.*

MIT DEM KOMPARATIV (Mehrstufe)

*The dog is **bigger than** the cat.*

*The cat is **smaller than** the dog.*

MIT DEM SUPERLATIV (Meiststufe)

*The horse is **the biggest**.*

*The cat is **the smallest**.*

32 **

Match the expressions on the left with those on the right. Which mean the same? –
Ordne die Ausdrücke rechts denen links zu. Welche bedeuten das Gleiche?

faster	1
more expensive	2
hotter	3
sweeter	4
lazier	5
more interesting	6
worse	7
more modern	8

A	not as bitter as
B	not as boring as
C	not as good as
D	not as cold as
E	not as traditional as
F	not as slow as
G	not as cheap as
H	not as hardworking as

Quest 4.2

33 * *

Look at the pictures and complete the sentences with the given adjectives. – Schau dir die Bilder an und vervollständige die Sätze mit den gegebenen Adjektiven.

1

2

3
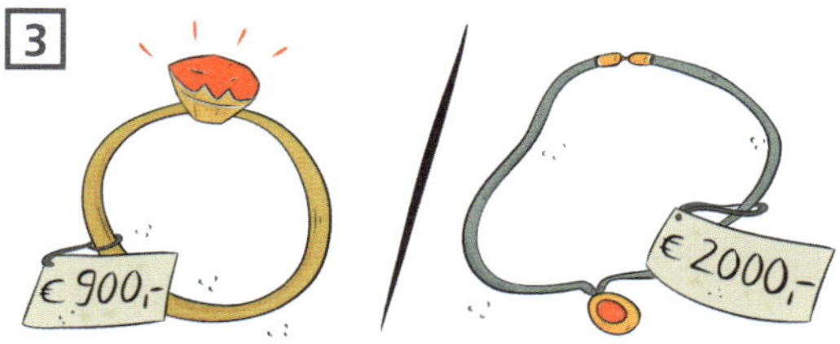

4

5

6

1 Monday was *(cold)* ____________________ Tuesday.
2 Pineapples are *(cheap)* ____________________ papayas.
3 The necklace is *(expensive)* ____________________ ring.
4 A helicopter is *(fast)* ____________________ jet plane.
5 Elephants are *(exotic)* ____________________ sheep.
6 A supermarket is *(impressive)* ____________________ a castle.

Quest 4.3

34 *

Complete the sentences with the comparative of the adjectives. – Vervollständige die Sätze mit der Mehrstufe (*comparative*) der vorhandenen Adjektive.

> *Mike is **clever**, but Suzie is* cleverer _____.

1 Golf is an expensive sport, but polo is ____________________.
2 Cookies are good, but donuts are ____________________.
3 A headache is painful, but a toothache is even* ____________________.
4 This is an incredible story, but my story is ____________________.
5 'Dracula' was frightening, but 'Frankenstein' was ____________________.
6 You're early, but we were even* ____________________.

**even* – sogar

Üben

35 ✱ *Complete the sentences with a superlative. Use the given adjectives.* – Vervollständige die Sätze mit der Meiststufe (*superlative*) der vorhandenen Adjektive.

Quest 4.4

1 Table tennis is faster than tennis, but squash is ______________________.
2 Dad is older than me, and Grandpa is ______________________.
3 San Marino is smaller than Liechtenstein, and Monaco is ______________________.
4 Simon's sisters are really pretty, but my sister is ______________________.
5 Peaches and cherries are sweet, but grapes are ______________________.
6 Rick and Tony are talented players, but I am ______________________.
7 Zoe's and Nora's hats are elegant, but Emma's is ______________________.
8 Purple and orange are popular colours, but pink is ______________________.
9 I get angry sometimes, but Mr Black is ______________________ person I know.
10 Biology and History are cool subjects, but Physics is ______________________.
11 The Browns and the Nelsons have new cars, but ours is ______________________.
12 'Buddy' and 'Molly' are cute dogs, but 'Coco' is ______________________.

Üben

36 ✱✱ *Complete the text with the correct form of the given adjectives.* – Setze die richtigen Formen der Adjektive in Klammer ein.

Hi, I'm Ethan – Ethan Cole. I'm 13, and I live in San Francisco, the *(lovely)* ________________ city on Earth. No other city is as *(beautiful)* ________________ San Francisco! And here's my family. I'll start with Tracy, my *(young)* ________________ sister. She's only 3, and she's really the *(cute)* ________________ little girl. Then there's Mia. She's one year *(old)* ________________ me. We are *(good)* ________________ friends, but sometimes she can be quite *(touchy*)* ________________. Then it's *(good)* ________________ to get out of her way as *(fast)* ________________ you can! My dad's name is Owen. He's forty. He's a policeman. My mum, Esther, is forty, too, so she's *(old)* ________________ my dad. She's an IT expert. My parents are really *(nice)* ________________. Mum is *(patient*)* ________________ than Dad, but I think this has to do with his job. We've also got a cat named Tiger. He's the *(lazy)* ________________ cat in the world! He sleeps most of the day and only gets up to eat. So he's also *(fat)* ________________ cat in the world!

**touchy* – zickig, launisch **patient* – geduldig

37 ✱✱

Which word is correct? Cross out the wrong option. – Welches Wort passt in den Satz? Streiche die falsche Option durch.

1 The *taller / tallest* building of the world is in Dubai.
2 Last Friday was the *worst / baddest* day of my life.
3 A foot (30.3 cm) is not *long / as long as* a yard (91 cm).
4 The *richest / richer* person of the world lives in the USA.
5 Jeff is *nicer as / as nice as* his twin brother David.
6 Your hands are *as cold as / the coldest* ice.
7 Melissa is *as intelligent / more intelligent* than all the other girls.
8 Wood is *not as heavy as / heavier as* gold.
9 Our dog isn't *as cute / cuter* as our cat, but he's *the cleverest / cleverer*.
10 Winter holidays are usually *expensiver / more expensive* than summer holidays.

38 ✱✱✱

Look at the pictures of the three famous buildings and study the facts. Then read the sentences and tick true or false. – Sieh dir die Bilder und Informationen über die drei berühmten Gebäude an. Lies dann die Sätze und kreuze an: richtig (*true*) oder falsch (*false*).

Washington | London | Vienna

Washington	London	Vienna
built: 1792–1800	built: 1703	built: 1775–1780
132 rooms	775 rooms	1441 rooms

		True	False
1	Buckingham Palace is older than Schönbrunn Castle.	☐	☐
2	Schönbrunn Castle is bigger than Buckingham Palace.	☐	☐
3	The White House is the youngest building.	☐	☐
4	The White House is bigger than Buckingham Palace.	☐	☐
5	Buckingham Palace is the oldest building.	☐	☐
6	The White House is the biggest building.	☐	☐

Quest 4.5

Üben

(BE) GOING TO – DIE „NAHE" ZUKUNFT

A Zur Erinnerung

Mit ***(be) going to* + *base form*** bildest du die „nahe" Zukunft.

Du verwendest ***(be) going to***,

- wenn du über **etwas** sprichst, **das sehr bald** (und sehr wahrscheinlich) **geschehen wird**;
- wenn du über **Handlungen** sprichst, die **für die nahe Zukunft geplant** sind;
- wenn du **Fragen über Handlungen** stellst, die **für die nahe Zukunft geplant** sind.

REGEL

*Look at those dark clouds! It**'s going to rain soon**.*
*We**'re going to watch** 'War of the Worlds' **tonight**.*
Do you want to join us?
*What**'s** Joe **going to do** with his old comic books?*

- Die **Verneinung** bildest du mit ***am not*/*is not*/*are not going to* + *base form***.

REGEL

*We **aren't going to watch** TV tonight; we**'re going to** a concert.*

- Achtung beim Verb *go*: ***We're going** to a concert*
  und nicht … *~~We're going to go~~ to a concert.*

39 ✱✱ *What are they going to do? Look at the sentences and write their number into the correct picture.* – Schau dir die Bilder an und schreibe die Zahl in das richtige Bild.

1 Don't worry, this isn't going to hurt.
2 Your snowman is going to melt*.
3 What are you going to do now?
4 The cat is going to catch the mouse.
5 I'm not going to find the Easter egg.
6 You're going to miss the bus.

**melt* – schmelzen

40 ✱✱ *Complete the questions with the correct form of (be) going to.* – Vervollständige die Fragen mit der richtigen Form von *(be) going to*.

1 __________ Allison ____________________ sing and dance tonight?

2 __________ you ____________________ tell me about your plans?

3 __________ I ____________________ get an answer to my question?

4 What __________ you ____________________ say to your parents?

5 __________ Michael ____________________ fix his bike or not?

6 When __________ you ____________________ tidy up your rooms?

7 __________ it ____________________ rain today? – I think so. Look at the clouds!

8 __________ they ____________________ visit Salzburg or Innsbruck first?

9 Who ______________________________ take the dog for a walk today?

Quest 5.1

Üben

41 ✱ ✱ *Make sentences with (be) going to.* – Bilde Sätze mit *(be) going to.*

I ▪ dance ▪ only with Maria	→ *I'm going to dance only with Maria.*
We ▪ solve ▪ this problem	→ *We are going to solve this problem.*
When ▪ you ▪ phone me ▪ ?	→ *When are you going to phone me?*
George ▪ not come ▪ today	→ *George isn't going to come today.*
they ▪ not visit ▪ us ▪ ?	→ *Aren't they going to visit us?*

1 Mr Hicks ▪ sell ▪ his car ▪ ? → ______________________________?

2 you ▪ hear ▪ a funny story → ______________________________.

3 I ▪ not invite ▪ Joe ▪ again → ______________________________.

4 you ▪ help me ▪ ? → ______________________________?

5 When ▪ we ▪ visit ▪ Granny ▪ ? → ______________________________?

6 Liz ▪ move ▪ to another town → ______________________________.

7 Jackie ▪ not like ▪ this → ______________________________.

8 you ▪ not open ▪ the box ▪ ? → ______________________________?

9 Linda ▪ study ▪ in Vienna ▪ ? → ______________________________?

10 we ▪ go to England ▪ next week → ______________________________.

Üben

42 ✱ ✱ *Find the questions to the answers. Use (be) going to.* – Finde die passenden Fragen zu den gegebenen Antworten. Verwende dabei *(be) going to.*

Why aren't they going to stay longer? – Because they have not enough time.

1 What ______________________ do this afternoon? – I'm going to watch TV.

2 Who ______________________ clean the bird cage today? – Not me!

3 When ______________________ finish your model ship? – Next week, perhaps.

4 Why __________ you ______________ come to my party? – Mum says I can't.

5 __________ your father ______________ help us? – He is if we ask him.

6 How ______________________ get to Joe's house? – We're going to take a taxi.

7 Where ______________________ meet next time? – Let's meet at the gym.

8 __________ I ______________ see you again? – Of course! I'll be back soon.

Quest 5.2

B Future with going to or with will?

- Wann du ***(be) going to*** verwendest, kannst du auf Seite 36 nachlesen.
- Die **Zukunft mit *will*** verwendest du …

REGEL

- für zukünftige Ereignisse, die (noch) nicht geplant sind, z. B. **Erwartungen**, **Hoffnungen** oder **Befürchtungen**:
  *We all **hope** that Joe **will be** well again soon.*
  ***I'm afraid** we **won't come** back in time.*
- für **Vorhersagen** und **Versprechungen**:
  *I **promise** I'**ll give** you the money tomorrow.*
- für **plötzliche Entscheidungen**:
  *You don't look well, Joe. **I'll make you a cup of cocoa!***

43 ✱✱ *Finish the text with will-future or (be) going to.* – Setze *will-future* oder *(be) going to* richtig ein.

Emilia: Hi, Felix! What are you doing this weekend?

Felix: Hi! I *(see)* ____________________ the new play tomorrow.

Emilia: Have you got the tickets yet?

Felix: I *(get)* ____________________ them later today. Would you like to come?

Emilia: Oh, thanks! That would be wonderful.

Felix: I *(get)* ____________________ you a ticket, too.

Emilia: Great! What time does it start?

Felix: Seven thirty, but we *(all meet)* ____________________ at the 'Burger Bar' at 6 o'clock.

Emilia: Okay, I *(meet)* ____________________ you there, but I *(be)* ____________________ there a little later.

Felix: No problem! I *(phone)* ____________________ the others and tell them that you *(come)* ____________________ with us.

Emilia: Thanks a lot, Felix! This *(be)* ____________________ great fun!

Quests
5.3
5.4

PASSIVE – PASSIV (LEIDEFORM)

A Erklärung

- Du kannst einen Sachverhalt aktiv oder passiv ausdrücken.
- **Aktiv** heißt, **jemand tut** (oder tat) etwas. **Passiv** heißt, **etwas geschieht** (oder geschah) mit jemandem. Dieser „jemand" ist dabei das Subjekt des Satzes.
- Es ist nicht immer wichtig zu wissen, von wem die Handlung ausgeführt wird.

REGEL

aktiv: ***They speak*** *English all over the world.*

passiv: ***English is spoken*** *all over the world.*

*The dog **bites** the postman.*
*The postman **is bitten** by the dog.*

44 ✱ *Active or passive? Does the subject do something or does something happen to the subject? Tick active or passive.* – Aktiv oder passiv? Tut das Subjekt etwas oder geschieht etwas mit dem Subjekt? Kreuze *active* oder *passive* an.

		active	passive
1	The old hospital was opened in 1965.	☐	☒
2	Avalanches kill many people every year.	☐	☐
3	Cheese is made from milk.	☐	☐
4	People called the firefighters and the police.	☐	☐
5	The man was taken to hospital in an ambulance.	☐	☐
6	Many tourists visit our country every year.	☐	☐
7	I found a wallet on my way home from school.	☐	☐
8	These letters were found in an old book.	☐	☐

Quest 6.1

45 ✱ *Active or passive once again! Read these sentences and cross out the wrong form.* – Noch einmal *active* oder *passive*! Lies die Sätze und streiche die falsche Form durch.

> They **make** / ~~are made~~ excellent ice cream here.
> The first car ~~built~~ / **was built** in Germany.

1 Wood and coal *use / are used* for making fire.
2 Many of my friends *love / are loved* football.
3 The USA *celebrates / is celebrated* Independence Day on July 4th.
4 A lot of wine *produce / is produced* in Italy.
5 St. Paul's Cathedral *build / was built* in the 17th century.
6 The Vikings *discovered / were discovered* America long before Columbus.
7 A volcano *destroyed / was destroyed* the city of Pompeii in 79 AD*.
8 Pompeii *buried / was buried* under 4 m of ash.

**79 AD* – 79 n. Chr. (nach Christi Geburt) [AD = Anno Domini; lateinisch für „im Jahr des Herrn"]

B Bildung von *passive*

REGEL

subject* + *be* + *past participle

present simple passive	***I***	***am***		
	you, we, they	***are***	***sent***	*to the headmaster.*
	he, she, it	***is***		

past simple passive	***I, he, she, it***	***was***	***sent***	*to the headmaster.*
	we, you, they	***were***		

46 ✱ *Complete with present passive.* – Setze das Passiv in der Gegenwart ein.

1 Opel cars *(make)* ______________________ in Germany.
2 At the airport, every passenger *(ask)* ______________________ for an ID.
3 A lot of fish *(catch)* ______________________ in the North Atlantic.
4 Chopsticks *(use)* ______________________ for eating in China and Japan.
5 Excellent food *(serve)* ______________________ in this restaurant.
6 Fresh vegetables *(sell)* ______________________ at the market all day.

47 ✱ *Complete with past passive.* – Setze das Passiv in *past tense* ein.

1 Many important things *(invent)* ______________________ in the 19th century.

2 The New Testament *(write)* ______________________ in Latin.

3 Gold *(find)* ______________________ in California in 1849.

4 The boys *(pay)* ______________________ some money for mowing the lawn*.

5 The bank robbers *(arrest)* ______________________ very quickly.

6 In 1066, a big battle* *(fight)* ______________________ near Hastings in England.

**mow the lawn* – den Rasen mähen **battle* – Schlacht

Quest 6.2

C *By-object*

Wenn du angeben willst, von wem eine Handlung durchgeführt wird (oder wurde), verwendest du das sogenannte ***by-object***.

REGEL

England and Denmark ***are ruled**** ***by queens****.*

Quidditch ***is played by the young magicians*** *of Hogwarts.*

The electric light bulb ***was invented by Thomas A. Edison****.*

The biggest pyramids ***were built by the Egyptians****.*

**rule* – regieren

48 ✱ *Put the words into the correct order.* – Bringe die Wörter in die richtige Reihenfolge.

1 the ▪ heard ▪ by ▪ explosion ▪ was ▪ everybody

____.

2 hit ▪ was ▪ I ▪ a tennis ball ▪ by

____.

3 many ▪ spoken ▪ by ▪ is ▪ English ▪ people

____.

4 bill ▪ my parents ▪ the ▪ paid ▪ by ▪ was

____.

5 painted ▪ were ▪ these ▪ by ▪ pictures ▪ my mother

____.

Quest 6.3

49 ✱✱ *What was going on here? Write passive sentences in past.* – Was geschah hier? Schreibe *passive*-Sätze in *past*.

1 our car ▪ stop ▪ police ______________________________.

2 treasure ▪ bury ▪ pirates ______________________________.

3 houses ▪ damage* ▪ storm ______________________________.

4 UFO ▪ see ▪ many people ______________________________.

5 ruins ▪ discover ▪ explorers ______________________________.

6 these photos ▪ take ▪ Mrs Clark ______________________________.

**damage* – beschädigen

50 ✱✱ *How tea is made in England. Fill in the verbs in present simple passive.* – Wie man „Englischen Tee" zubereitet. Ergänze den Text mit den Verben in *present simple passive*.

First, the kettle *(fill)* ____________________ with water. Then the kettle *(put)* ____________________ on the heater and the heat *(turn)* ____________________ on. In the meantime*, the teapot *(rinse*)* ____________________ with hot water and the water *(pour*)* ____________________ out again. Then some spoonfuls of tea *(put)* ____________________ into the pot, one for each cup and one for the pot. When the water boils, it *(pour*)* ____________________ on the tea in the pot. After 3 to 5 minutes, the tea is ready. It *(drink)* ____________________ with or without milk and sugar. Tea *(enjoy)* ____________________ by many people in England.

**in the meantime* – inzwischen **rinse* – spülen **pour* – gießen, schütten

51 ✱✱✱ *Match the two sentence halves and choose a verb from the centre. Then write the full sentences. Get your information from the Internet.*– Verbinde die zusammengehörenden Satzhälften mit Hilfe eines Verbs aus der Mitte. Schreibe dann die fertigen Sätze auf. Hole dir die nötige Information aus dem Internet.

1 Basketball *was played for the first time in 1891*.

1	Basketball	begin	by Leonardo da Vinci.
2	Iceland	bring	by a meteor 60 million years ago.
3	The dinosaurs	compose	by Conchita Wurst in 2014.
4	The Great Wall of China	discover	for the first time in 1891.
5	The 'Mona Lisa'	found*	by Vikings in the 10th century.
6	The Winnetou stories	kill	to Austalia by European settlers*.
7	Penicillin	nominate	over 2,500 years ago.
8	The Eurovision Song Contest	paint	by Alexander Fleming.
9	Rabbits	play	by Karl May.
10	The United Nations	settle*	for the 'Oscar' 15 times.
11	More than 150 songs	win	by Lennon and McCartney.
12	Steven Spielberg	write	in 1945.

2 Iceland ______________________.

3 The dinosaurs ______________________.

4 The Great Wall of China ______________________.

5 The 'Mona Lisa' ______________________.

6 The Winnetou stories ______________________.

7 Penicillin ______________________.

8 The Eurovision Song Contest ______________________.

9 Rabbits ______________________.

10 The United Nations ______________________.

11 More than 150 songs ______________________.

12 Steven Spielberg ______________________.

**found* – gründen **settle* – besiedeln **settlers* – Siedler

Üben

52 ✱✱ *Complete the text about the Statue of Liberty. Use past simple – active or passive.* – Ergänze den Text über die New Yorker Freiheitsstatue mit *past active* oder *passive*.

The Statue of Liberty *(give)* ________________ to the United States by France. It *(be)* ________________ a present on the 100th 'birthday' of the USA. The statue *(design)* ________________ by a French artist named Frederic Bartholdi. It *(complete)* ________________ in France in 1884. Then it *(transport)* ________________ to America in 350 pieces. They *(arrive)* ________________ in New York in 1885. There the pieces *(put)* ________________ together and the statue *(open)* ________________ in October 1886.

53 ✱✱ *Correct the statements with the words in brackets. Use the Internet for information. Use past passive.* – Stelle die Behauptungen richtig mithilfe der Wörter in Klammer und des Internets. Verwende *past passive*.

> Paul Allen founded* Amazon®. **(Jeff Bezos)**
> No, Amazon® was founded by Jeff Bezos.

1 The Americans sent the first satellite into space. *(the Russians)*

No, the first satellite ____.

2 An avalanche destroyed Pompeii. *(a volcano)*

No, ____.

3 Ferdinand Magellan discovered Australia. *(James Cook)*

No, ____.

4 Steven Spielberg created* 'Indiana Jones'. *(George Lucas)*

No, ____.

5 Alan Turing invented the World Wide Web in 1989. *(Tim Berners-Lee)*

No, ____.

6 Beethoven wrote 'Don Giovanni' and 'The Magic Flute'*. *(Mozart)*

No, ____.

**founded* – gegründet **create* – erschaffen **flute* – Flöte

Quest 6.4

Üben

PAST CONTINUOUS

A Bildung

REGEL

was / were + ***ing-form*** *(present participle)*

I, he, she, it	*was* ***waiting*** *…*
you, we, they	*were* ***waiting*** *…*

B Anwendung

REGEL

Du verwendest ***past continuous*** (auch *past progressive* genannt) immer dann, wenn du über **eine Handlung** sprichst, **die zu einem bestimmten Zeitpunkt in der Vergangenheit stattfand und / oder noch nicht beendet war**.

- Dabei kann dieser **bestimmte Zeitpunkt direkt oder indirekt genannt** werden …

Yesterday at 3 p.m. I *was* ***doing*** *my homework.* → **Uhrzeit**
When Dad came home**, we* ***were watching *TV.* → **Als** …

↓ bestimmter **Zeitpunkt in der Vergangenheit** (Uhrzeit) (**Als** Dad nachhause kam)

↓ **zu** diesem **Zeitpunkt** gerade **stattfindende Handlung**

- … oder der **bestimmte Zeitpunkt** wird nicht genannt, aber **angenommen**; dabei geschehen **zwei oder mehrere Handlungen gleichzeitig**.

My sisters ***were watching*** *TV* ***while*** *I* ***was doing*** *my homework.*

↓

Während
zwei Handlungen gleichzeitig
zu einem bestimmten Zeitpunkt

54 *

Complete the sentences. Use the continuous forms from the box. – Ergänze die Sätze. Verwende die *continuous forms* aus dem Rahmen.

was living ▪ was reading ▪ was shining
were sitting ▪ was snowing ▪ was walking

1 When we left the restaurant, it ______________________.
2 We ______________________ in the garden when the phone rang.
3 When I woke up this morning, the sun ______________________.
4 Bill ______________________ home from school when he found a wallet.
5 When Joe met Marylin, he ______________________ in London.
6 Jason and Jill ______________________ a book when the lights went out.

Quest 7.1

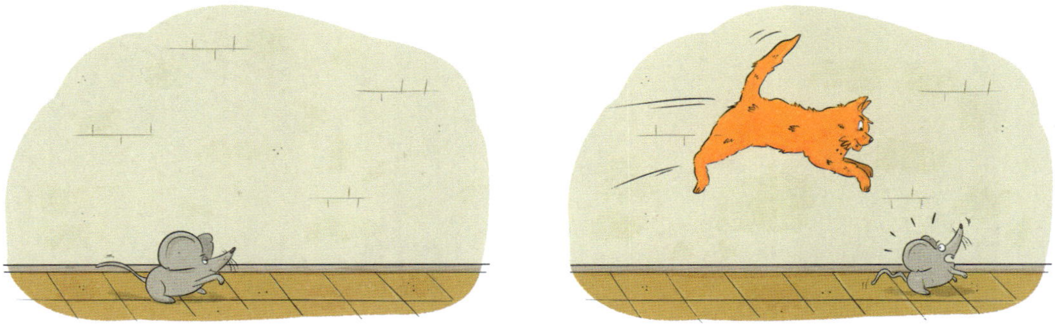

The mouse **was running** across the room when the cat **caught** it.

55 *

What was everybody doing at 9 a.m. last Sunday? Complete the sentences with past continuous. – Was haben die Menschen (und Tiere) letzten Sonntag um 9 Uhr früh gemacht? Ergänze mit *past continuous*.

At 9 o'clock last Sunday morning, …

1 Dad *(make)* ______________________ breakfast for the family.
2 My sisters *(help)* ______________________ him.
3 Mum *(read)* ______________________ the newspaper.
4 Our dog *(run)* ______________________ around in the garden.
5 The cats *(sleep)* ______________________ in their baskets.
6 I *(brush)* ______________________ my teeth.
7 My little brother *(play)* ______________________ with his toys.
8 Outside, the birds *(sing)* ______________________ …
9 … and the sun *(shine)* ______________________.
10 We all *(have)* ______________________ a good time.

Üben

Üben

56 ✱✱ *Look at the picture and write down what was going on when Alice took this photo. Use the words from the box.* – Schau dir das Bild an und schreibe auf, was alles gerade vor sich ging, als Alice dieses Foto schoss. Verwende die Wörter aus dem Rahmen.

chase ▪ climb ▪ come ▪ fly ▪ jump ▪ look
ride ▪ run ▪ sit ▪ watch

When Alice took this photo, …

1 The ice cream man ______________________________ along the street.

2 Joe and Mia ______________________________ towards the ice cream man.

3 Adam ______________________________ his skateboard down the sidewalk*.

4 Lilly ______________________________ for her bicycle in the garage.

5 Simon ______________________________ onto* the roof of the garage.

6 Little Annie ______________________________ in the pool.

7 Archie ______________________________ into the pool.

8 The cat ______________________________ the butterflies across the lawn*.

9 Some birds ______________________________ through the air.

10 Mrs Smith ______________________________ the kids from the upstairs window.

**sidewalk* – Gehsteig   **onto* – hinauf   **lawn* – Rasen

Quest 7.2

57 ✱✱✱ *Look at the pictures and words and write sentences with past continuous and past simple. Use when and while.* – Schau dir die Bilder und Wörter an und schreibe Sätze mit *past continuous* und *past simple*. Verwende *when* und *while*.

1 while

fall asleep ▪ watch TV

2 while

climb up ladder ▪ fall

3 when

read a book ▪ phone ring

4 while

walk to bus stop ▪ meet some friends

5 when

play in the park ▪ start raining

6 when

work in the garden ▪ cut finger

1 *I fell asleep while I was watching TV* ______.

2 Brian ______.

3 Sandra ______.

4 The girls ______.

5 The boys ______.

6 Dad ______.

Quest 7.3

58 ✱✱ *Can you find all the ing-forms and past forms?* – Kannst du alle *ing-forms* und *past forms* finden?

S	L	E	P	T	F	G
A	E	A	U	D	I	D
S	A	T	T	O	O	L
W	R	I	T	I	N	G
E	N	N	I	N	E	H
N	E	G	N	G	O	T
T	D	B	G	C	D	I

past forms

1 ______
2 ______
3 ______
4 ______
5 ______
6 ______

ing-forms

1 ______
2 ______
3 ______
4 ______

Üben

59 ✱✱✱ *Past simple or past continuous? Fill in the correct form. – Past simple* oder *past continuous?* Setze die richtige Form ein.

> When I **(leave)** left the house this morning, a cold wind **(blow)** was blowing.
> Nobody **(listen)** was listening while the teacher **(speak)** was speaking.
> While Joe **(run)** was running, he **(fall)** fell and **(break)** broke his leg.
> Mrs Jenkins **(feed)** was feeding the chickens when she **(see)** saw a fox.

1 When I *(walk)* ________________ into the classrooms, all my friends *(stand)* ________________ by the windows, looking out.

2 Eric *(watch)* ________________ a horror movie when he *(hear)* ________________ a strange noise from the next room.

3 We *(play squash)* ________________ when I *(slip*)* ________________ and *(hurt)* ________________ my elbow.

4 Dad *(drive)* ________________ home in the evening when a rabbit *(jump)* ________________ across the road in front of him.

5 My mother *(live)* ________________ in Vienna when she *(meet)* ________________ my father.

6 While we *(playing)* ________________ games with our parents, our cat *(sleep)* ________________ on my lap*.

7 I *(play)* ________________ tennis when a ball *(hit)* ________________ me.

8 We *(drink)* ________________ tea in the warm living room while outside a terrible storm *(howl)* ________________.

9 The Coopers *(have)* ________________ dinner when somebody *(knock)* ________________ on their door.

10 I *(pack)* ________________ my bags while Dad *(get)* ________________ the car ready.

**slip* – ausrutschen **lap* – Schoß

Üben

60 ✱✱

Read the report of a person who was there on 9/11 when the World Trade Center was attacked. Complete the report with past simple or past continuous. – Lies den Bericht einer Zeugin/eines Zeugen über den Angriff auf das World Trade Center, bekannt als „9/11". Ergänze den Text mit *past simple* oder *past continuous*.

I *(hear)* ________________ a terrible explosion while I *(walk)* ________________ into my office on the 24th floor of the north tower, so I *(look)* ________________ out the window. Lots of paper *(fall)* ________________ from the sky. A voice on the loudspeaker *(say)* ________________ we should leave the building, so we *(start)* ________________ walking down the stairs. As we *(go)* ________________ down, we saw some firefighters. They *(run)* ________________ up the stairs. When we *(get)* ________________ to the ground floor, we *(run)* ________________ away from the building as fast as we could, and after about ten minutes we *(stop)* ________________ in a small park. That's where we *(stand)* ________________ when the second tower *(fall)* ________________.

61 ✱✱✱

Read the two short texts and complete the 'stories'. Use past simple or continuous. – Lies die zwei Kurztexte und schreibe die „Geschichten" fertig. Verwende *past simple* oder *continuous*.

Rick and his friends *(play)* ______________________ basketball in the gym when Rick's friend Tony *(stumble*)* ______________________ and *(hurt)* ______________________ his wrist. While one of the boys from the team *(look)* ______________________ for help, Rick *(phone)* ______________________ Tony's parents and *(tell)* ______________________ them about the accident.

Last evening, I *(read)* ______________________ a book while my parents *(watch)* ______________________ a show on TV. My little sisters *(play)* ______________________ with their toys and Tiger, our dog, *(sit)* ____________ by the door. I think he *(want)* ______________________ to go for his walk!

**stumble* – stolpern

Quest 7.4

- **Frage und Verneinung** von *past continuous* bildest du so:

REGEL

Verneinung	→	*wasn't / weren't + ing-form*
Frage	→	*Was / Were + subject + ing-form*

The sun ***wasn't shining*** *when we left the house this morning.*
The birds ***weren't singing*** *when I looked out of the window.*
Was the baby sleeping *when you came back?*
Were the children doing *their homework when the light went out?*

62 ✱ *Make these sentences negative.* – Bilde die Verneinung der folgenden Sätze.

They were taking pictures of us. → *They weren't taking pictures of us* .

1 Sarah was snoring* in her sleep. → ____________________.
2 We were waiting for you. → ____________________.
3 I was daydreaming. → ____________________.
4 You were listening. → ____________________.
5 The boys were playing games. → ____________________.
6 Dad was listening to Queen*. → ____________________.

**snore* – schnarchen   **Queen* – eine 1970 gegründete britische Rockband

63 ✱✱✱ *Find the suitable sentence from exercise 62 to complete the sentences.* – Finde zu jedem Satz den passenden Satz aus Übung 62.

They weren't taking pictures of us . *They wanted to photograph the old castle!*

1 ____________________. He doesn't like rock music.
2 ____________________. She was having a bad dream.
3 ____________________. They were working on their PCs.
4 ____________________. I was thinking about what you said.
5 ____________________. We were just standing there.
6 We told you the whole story, but ____________________.

64 ✱ ✱ *Ask questions with past continuous (Was ... ? / Were ... ?).* – Bilde Fragen mit *past continuous (Was ... ? / Were ... ?).*

> *Jack was learning to play the drums.*
> → *Was Jack learning to play the drums?*
> → *Who was learning to play the drums?*
> → *What was Jack doing?*
> → *What was Jack learning?*
>
> *The girls were riding their horses this morning.*
> → *Were the girls riding their horses?*
> → *Who* **was** *riding their horses this morning?*
> → *What were the girls doing?*
> → *What were the girls riding?*
> → *When were the girls riding their horses?*

1 The farmers were milking the cows.

(a) Were ______________________? *(c)* What ______________________?

(b) Who ______________________? *(d)* What ______________________?

2 James was living in Manchester.

(a) Was ______________________? *(c)* What ______________________?

(b) Who ______________________? *(d)* Where ______________________?

3 The girls were laughing because they were happy.

(a) Were ______________________? *(c)* What ______________________?

(b) Who ______________________? *(d)* Why ______________________?

4 Dad was driving to work at 8 a.m.

(a) Was ______________________? *(c)* What ______________________?

(b) Who ______________________? *(d)* When ______________________?

PRESENT PERFECT WITH FOR & SINCE

A Zur Erinnerung

- Du verwendest ***present perfect*** für Handlungen, die vor kurzer Zeit geschehen sind und/oder bis in die Gegenwart andauern.

REGEL

*It **has rained**. The streets are wet.*
Der Regen ist vorüber, aber die **Folgen** – die nassen Straßen – sind noch da.

*I **have known** Bettina since kindergarten.*
Die **„Handlung"** begann in der Vergangenheit und **dauert noch an**.

B Bildung

I, you, we, they	***have***	+	***past participle*** (3. Stammform)
he, she, it	***has***		

65 ✱✱ *Find the past participles of the verbs in the box and write them into the crossword.* – Finde die *past participles* der Verben im Rahmen und trage sie an der richtigen Stelle ins Kreuzworträtsel ein.

Quests 8.1 8.2 8.3

A	J	C	L	O	T	S	R
B	F	O	R	G	E	T	E
D	G	M	A	M	G	E	T
B	R	E	A	K	I	A	V
Y	E	B	U	A	V	L	H
C	A	T	C	H	E	K	O
U	D	L	F	I	N	D	L
T	O	V	S	T	A	N	D

across →	down ↓
______ / ______	______ / ______
______ / ______	______ / ______
BREAK / BROKEN	______ / ______
______ / ______	HIT / HIT
______ / ______	______ / ______
______ / ______	______ / ______
	______ / ______

66 ✱✱ *Look at the pictures and fill in the present perfect of the words in the box.* – Schau dir die Bilder an und setze die passenden Wörter aus dem Rahmen in *present perfect* ein.

arrive ▪ bake ▪ buy ▪ go ▪ have ▪ lose
sleep ▪ spend ▪ win

1 I ______________________ my keys! I can't get in!

2 Melanie ______________________ the tennis tournament.

3 Ryan ______________________ a skiing accident.

4 Grandma ______________________ our favourite cake.

5 Oh no, I ______________________ all my money!

6 Dad looks tired. He ______________________ only four hours.

7 Look, the guests ______________________!

8 The children ______________________ to bed.

9 Mum ______________________ new shoes for me.

Quest 8.4

C Frage und Verneinung

Have you ever seen this film?

No, I haven't seen it yet, but I've already read the book.

REGEL

(Fragewort) ***have / has*** **+** ***past participle***
oft mit ***ever*** oder ***yet***

haven't / hasn't **+** ***past participle***
oft mit ***never*** oder ***not … yet***

Have you done your homework yet?
Have we ever been to this place?
Has Benjamin finished his project?
What have you told your parents?
Who has opened the window?

I haven't done my homework yet.
We've never been here before.
Benjamin hasn't started on his project yet.
I haven't told my parents anything.
We haven't been in the room.

67 ✱✱ *Ask questions and negate.* – Bilde Fragen und die Verneinung.

The guests have gone to bed.
(a) Have the guests gone to bed ?
(b) Who has gone to bed ?
(c) The guests haven't gone to bed .

1 The baby has woken up.

(a) ____________________? (b) ____________________?

(c) ____________________.

2 They have built a snowman.

(a) ____________________? (b) ____________________?

(c) ____________________.

3 You have tidied up your room.

(a) ____________________? (b) ____________________?

(c) ____________________.

Quest 8.5

4 Our dog has eaten the sausages.

(a) ____________________? (b) ____________________?

(c) ____________________.

68 ** *Find the present perfect and cross out the wrong word.* – Finde die *present perfect tense* und streiche das falsche Wort in jedem Satz durch.

Üben

1 Dad *will fix / has fixed* my bike.

2 *Have you ever touched / Did you ever touch* a snake?

3 I *have never thought / never think* about this problem.

4 Who *ate / has eaten* my snack?

5 You *haven't thanked / didn't thank* Uncle Harry for the present yet!

6 We *have stayed / will stay* long enough.

7 What *did you bring / have you brought* with you?

8 *Has Joe answered / Did Joe answer* your email yet?

9 Who *painted / has painted* this beautiful picture?

10 *Have you heard / Will your hear* from Julia yet?

11 Andy *will drop / has dropped* the vase.

12 Tina *has fed / fed* the hamster.

11

12

D *for & since*

Beide Wörter bedeuten **„seit"**, aber …

- mit ***for*** gibt du an, **wie lange** eine Handlung/ein Zustand schon andauert → **Zeitdauer**
  Auf Deutsch kannst du dafür auch „lang" sagen, z. B.
  for a week = **eine Woche lang** oder eben seit einer Woche.
- mit ***since*** gibst du an, **ab wann** eine Handlung/ein Zustand schon andauert → **Zeitpunkt** oder **Beginn**
  Hier sagst du auf Deutsch z. B. **seit** meinem Geburtstag.

REGEL

for	*a week, three days, some time …*
since	*last Thursday, 2010, you arrived …*

69 ✱ *For or since? Write the phrases from the box in the correct column.* – *For* oder *since*? Schreibe die Begriffe aus dem Rahmen in die richtige Spalte.

ten days ▪ midnight ▪ 2011 ▪ half an hour ▪ January
many months ▪ Christmas ▪ a short time ▪ May 1st
we arrived ▪ hours ▪ more than a year ▪ a little while ▪ 7 o'clock
I met you ▪ for a few seconds

for		since	

Quest 8.6

70 ✱

For or since? Underline the correct word in each sentence. – For oder *since*? – Unterstreiche in jedem Satz das richtige Wort.

Quest 8.7

1 Gina hasn't read a book *for / since* she left school a year ago.
2 Mum hasn't slept *for / since* three nights in a row*. She looks really tired.
3 I haven't been shopping with my friends *for / since* Ellie's birthday.
4 Grandma hasn't watched a movie *for / since* 1989.
5 Harry hasn't spoken with me *for / since* our silly fight last week.
6 My computer hasn't properly* worked *for / since* a week.
7 Mum hasn't made pizza *for / since* a long time.
8 I haven't heard from Melissa *for / since* over a year.
9 We haven't had ham and eggs for breakfast *for / since* our trip to England.
10 Dad hasn't played hockey *for / since* many years.

**in a row* – in Folge, hintereinander   **properly* – richtig

71 ✱✱

Match questions and answers. – Welche Antwort passt zu welcher Frage?

How long have/has …

… you lived in this house?	1		A	For 15 years. I was born soon after.
… you been in love with Alexa?	2		B	For a week, and now he's got a fever.
… Timmy had this cold?	3		C	Since 2001, when he left school.
… you known the Smiths?	4		D	Since I was born.
… your parents been married?	5		E	For 24 hours.
… your Dad worked for J&P?	6		F	Since I first saw her.
… it rained?	7		G	For half a year, and she likes it.
… Jane done yoga?	8		H	Since they bought the flat next door.

Üben

72 ✱✱

Write the words in the correct order. – Schreibe die Wörter in der richtigen Reihenfolge, damit sich *present perfect*-Sätze ergeben.

1 Jim ▪ I ▪ kindergarten ▪ known ▪ since ▪ have

____.

2 days ▪ eaten ▪ for ▪ Mila ▪ hasn't ▪ two

____.

3 fallen ▪ the ▪ from ▪ apples ▪ the ▪ have ▪ tree

____.

4 has ▪ three ▪ Diego ▪ Durchstarten ▪ years ▪ for ▪ learned ▪ with

____.

PRESENT PERFECT OR PAST SIMPLE

A Erklärung des Unterschiedes

Im Deutschen ist es egal, ob wir **„Tim kaufte sich ein Fahrrad"** oder **„Tim hat sich ein Fahrrad gekauft"** sagen. Die Bedeutung ist die gleiche.

Im Englischen ist das anders:

- *Tim **bought** a bicycle last month (yesterday, last year, half an hour ago ...).*
  Tim hat **irgendwann** einmal ein Fahrrad gekauft (vielleicht gestern, vielleicht voriges Jahr, vielleicht vor einer halben Stunde). Wir wissen nicht, ob er das Fahrrad noch immer hat.

- *Tim **has bought** a bicycle.*
  Wir wissen nicht, wann Tim das Fahrrad gekauft hat, aber wir wissen, dass er es noch immer hat. Denn ***present perfect*** hat **Folgen auf das „Hier und Jetzt"**.

past simple für alles, was abgeschlossen und vorbei ist		***present perfect*** für alles, was auf das „Hier und Jetzt" hinweist	
Signalwörter für *past simple*		**Signalwörter** für *present perfect*	
yesterday	gestern	***for, since***	seit
last week, year ...	letzte Woche ...	***so far***	bisher, bis jetzt
in (2015)	im Jahr (2015)	***just***	soeben, gerade
on (April 1st)	am (1. April)	***already***	schon, bereits
(an hour) ago	vor (einer Stunde)	***not ... yet***	noch nicht
when (we left)	als (wir weggingen)	***... yet?***	schon (in Fragen)
		Look! Listen!	als Hinweis auf Folgen oder Auswirkungen auf „Hier und Jetzt"

Wissen

73 ✱✱

Read the sentence pairs. If the first sentence is true, can you say that the second sentence is true, too? Tick off yes or can't say. – Lies die Satzpaare. Wenn der erste Satz stimmt, kannst du dann auch mit Sicherheit sagen, dass der zweite Satz ebenfalls stimmt? Kreuze *yes* oder *can't say* an.

	yes	can't say
Jeremy has gone to the gym. He's not at home right now.	☒	☐
Jeremy went to the gym. He's still there.	☐	☒

		yes	can't say
1	It has rained. The streets are wet.	☐	☐
	It rained. The streets are wet.	☐	☐
2	Ben hurt his elbow. He can't move his arm.	☐	☐
	Ben has hurt his elbow. He can't move his arm.	☐	☐
3	We have lived here for two years. We still live here.	☐	☐
	We lived here for two years. We still live here.	☐	☐
4	The bell rang. Somebody is at the door.	☐	☐
	The bell has rung. Somebody is at the door.	☐	☐
5	Somebody opened the window. It's cold in here.	☐	☐
	Somebody has opened the window. It's cold in here.	☐	☐

74 ✱✱✱

Look at the underlined verbs. Which tense are they – past simple (PS) or present perfect (PPF)? Circle the correct letters. – In welcher Zeit stehen die unterstrichenen Verben – *past simple (PS)* oder *present perfect (PPF)*? Kreise die richtigen Buchstaben ein.

> *Last week, I kicked (PS) (PPF) my football over the neighbour's fence and I haven't got (PS) (PPF) it back yet.*

1 I've had *(PS) (PPF)* a terrible headache all day. – Oh no! When did it start? *(PS) (PPF)*

2 I had *(PS) (PPF)* a phone call from Larissa last night. – How is she?
I haven't heard *(PS) (PPF)* from her for weeks.

3 When Mum was *(PS) (PPF)* 17, she spent *(PS) (PPF)* a year at an American high school. She has been *(PS) (PPF)* back to the USA many times since then.

4 Look at this mess! What have you done? *(PS) (PPF)* – I'm sorry.
When I opened *(PS) (PPF)* the drawer, everything fell *(PS) (PPF)* to the floor.

Quest 9.1

75 ✱✱

Match questions (present perfect) and answers (past simple). – Welche Antwort *(past simple)* gehört zu welcher Frage *(present perfect)*?

Has Elsie gone home?	1
Have you ever eaten snails*?	2
Has the concert started yet?	3
Have the guests arrived?	4
Has Joe got a new bicycle?	5
Have you made your bed?	6
Has Jenny found her bracelet?	7

A	Yes, I did it this morning.
B	Yes, she left some time ago.
C	Yes, last year in France.
D	Yes, it was under her pillow*.
E	Yes, they came while you were gone.
F	Yes, they shut the doors a moment ago.
G	Yes, he got it for his birthday.

**snails* – Schnecken   **pillow* – Polster

76 ✱✱✱

Past simple or present perfect? Complete the sentences with the right tense. – *Past simple* oder *present perfect*? Setze die richtige Zeitstufe ein.

A: I **(see)** saw 'Transformers 3' last weekend. **(you, see)** Have you seen it yet?
B: No, not yet, but I **(want)** 've wanted to see it for a long time.

1 *A:* I *(have)* ________________ this camera since 2017.

B: *(you, buy)* ________________ it or *(be)* ________________ it a present?

A: I *(buy)* ________________ it with my birthday money.

2 *A:* I *(text)* ________________ Sue some days ago, but so far she *(not answer)* ________________. I hope she's alright.

B: I *(speak)* ________________ to her yesterday. She *(have)* ________________ a fever since Tuesday, but she's getting better.

3 *A:* Do you know Andy Miller?

B: Of course. I *(know)* ________________ him since kindergarten. Why?

A: Well, I *(meet)* ________________ him at a party last weekend and I *(like)* ________________ him.

4 *A:* Ah, you're here at last. Where *(you, be)* ________________?

B: I'm sorry I'm late, but the bus *(not come)* ________________ on time and I *(have)* ________________ to wait for twenty minutes.

Üben

Quest 9.2

77 ✱✱ *Fill in the past simple or the present perfect of the verbs in brackets.* – Setze die Verben in Klammer in *past simple* oder *present perfect* ein.

Quest 9.3

1 *(you, ever, hear)* ______________________ of a man called Tenzing Norgay? – I have. He *(reach)* ______________________ the summit of Mt. Everest in 1953.

2 *(you, ever, be)* ______________________ to Japan? – No, I haven't, but my father *(go)* ______________________ there on business last year.

3 What's wrong with Sophie? I *(not see)* ______________________ for a week. – Don't you know? She *(have)* ______________________ an accident last Monday.

4 *(you, like)* ______________________ the movie last night? – It *(be)* ______________________ alright, but I *(see)* ______________________ better films.

78 ✱✱ *Re-write the sentences in the 'other' tense. What's present perfect must become past simple, and what's past simple must become present perfect. Use the words in brackets in the new sentences.* – Schreibe die Sätze um. Was *present perfect* ist, muss *past simple* werden – und umgekehrt. Verwende die Wörter in Klammer in den neuen Sätzen.

> *The last time I saw Martha was last summer.* **(haven't, since)**
> *I haven't seen Martha since last summer* ______________________.

1 How long have you known Alice? *(meet)*

When ____?

2 Uncle Herbert has had his car for 20 years. *(buy, ago)*

____.

3 Rupert arrived a minute ago. *(just)*

____.

4 We moved to this town a year ago. *(live, for)*

____.

5 Diana's plane has just landed. *(ago)*

____.

6 When did you become the number one player of your club? *(how long)*

____?

7 Daniel has been in love with Grace since high school. *(fall in love)*

____.

79 ✱✱✱ *Read this text about a famous actor and decide – should the verbs in brackets be in past simple or in present perfect?* – Lies den Text über einen berühmten Schauspieler und entscheide – stehen die Verben in Klammer in *past simple* oder in *present perfect*?

I think I *(have)* have had a very interesting life. I'm 75 now and I *(not work)* __________ for six years. I *(make)* __________ my last movie at 69. I *(start)* __________ acting at the age of 18. I *(play)* __________ in more than 60 films and I *(have)* __________ some success*.
I *(be)* __________ nominated for the 'Oscar' three times, but I *(win)* __________ it only once, in 2001.
While I was working, I *(visit)* __________ many beautiful places, like Canada, New Zealand and Hawaii, but I never *(go)* __________ to Austria and Switzerland. I *(like)* __________ New Zealand best.
I *(never, play)* __________ a role in a TV series because nobody *(ever, ask)* __________ me, but I *(record*)* __________ a few audio books, so you can hear my voice without seeing me.
I *(met)* __________ many fascinating people and I *(work)* __________ with many great actors and actresses and directors. As I *(say)* __________ at the beginning, my life *(be)* __________ very interesting!

**success* – Erfolg **record* – aufnehmen

80 ✱✱ *What happened then? And what has just happened? Use past simple for the first picture and present perfect for the second.* – Was geschah (damals)? Und was ist soeben passiert? Verwende *past simple* für das erste Bild und *present perfect* für das zweite.

1 Mum *(buy)* __________ a beautiful vase in Rome last summer.
Tiger *(just, knock over)* __________ Mum's beautiful vase.

2 I *(got)* __________ an awfully old-fashioned blouse for my birthday.
I *(not wear)* __________ it yet. It still hangs in my closet.

PRESENT PERFECT CONTINUOUS

A Erklärung

Present perfect continuous

- beschreibt **Handlungen**, die **in der Vergangenheit begonnen** haben und „hier und jetzt" noch andauern oder **noch nicht abgeschlossen** sind.
- bezeichnet sehr oft **Handlungen, die „schon seit …" stattfinden** (und im Deutschen die Gegenwart verlangen).
- tritt daher häufig mit ***for*** oder ***since*** auf.

B Bildung

REGEL

I, you, we, they	***have***	***been***	+	***present participle***
he, she, it	***has***			*(ing-form)*

*I **have been reading for** four hours. My eyes hurt.*
*You **have been watching** TV **since** 3 o'clock. That's enough!*
*Charlie **has been studying** for his exams **since** the summer.*
*We **have been playing** tennis all afternoon.*
*They **have been standing** there **for** hours. What do they want?*

C *for & since*

- ***for*** *a month, some time, five minutes, years …* → **Zeitdauer**
- ***since*** *Friday, December 31st, August, 2012 …* → **Zeitpunkt, Beginn**

*Little Suzie has been sleeping **for** hours.*

*It has been raining **since** Thursday.*

81 *

for or since? Cross out the wrong word. – *for* oder *since*? Streiche das falsche Wort durch.

1 My father has been working for the same company *for / since* 12 years.
2 Isabel and Oscar have been dancing *for / since* the beginning of the party.
3 Mr Zacharias has been teaching at our school *for / since* 2002.
4 That tree has been standing there *for / since* a very long time.
5 Dad has been trying to fix the old radio *for / since* days.
6 My grandparents have been driving their car *for / since* before I was born.

82 **

Complete the sentences with the present perfect continuous of the verbs in brackets. Then write the number of the sentence into the correct picture. – Ergänze die Sätze mit dem *present perfect continuous* der Verben in Klammer. Schreibe dann die Nummer des Satzes in das passende Bild.

☐

☐

☐

☐

☐

☐

1 Oliver *(wait)* ______________________ for Kate for half an hour.
2 The children *(play)* ______________________ in the garden all afternoon.
3 Nigel *(listen)* ______________________ to his favourite music since lunch.
4 Mum and I *(shop)* ______________________ all morning.
5 It *(snow)* ______________________ since yesterday.
6 Olivia *(paint)* ______________________ her fingernails for ten minutes.

Quest 10.1

83 ✱✱ *Match the sentences.* – Welcher Satz passt zu welchem?

Your English is very good.	1		A	It has already damaged many buildings in town.
Nelly has been sleeping for hours.	2		B	She's been dreaming of visiting Disney World for years.
The storm has been blowing for days.	3		C	I've been sitting over it since I came home from school.
You look tired, Dad.	4		D	Yes, she's been studying chemistry since after my birth.
Sally really wants to go to Florida.	5		E	I've been learning the language for three years.
I've almost finished doing my homework.	6		F	Well, I've been working all day.
Where are the children?	7		G	Let's wake her up now.
Is your mother still at university?	8		H	In their rooms. They've been playing games all morning.

84 ✱✱✱ *Present perfect simple or continuous? Complete the sentences.* – *Present perfect simple* oder *continuous*? Ergänze die Sätze.

> We **(wait)** *have been waiting* for hours. Where **(you, be)** *have you been*?
> I **(write)** *'ve been writing* emails all morning, but now I **(finish)** *'ve finished*.

1 Grandpa *(have)* ____________ his driving licence for 50 years, and he *(drive)* ____________ the same old car since I can remember.

2 These trees *(stand)* ____________ next to our school for years and years. I'm glad they *(not cut)* ____________ them down yet.

3 It *(rain)* ____________ for a week, so we *(not be)* ____________ able to play football.

4 The children *(play)* ____________ on the beach for hours, and they *(already, build)* ____________ three lovely sandcastles.

5 *(you, finish)* ____________ tidying up your room yet? – No, not yet, but I *(work)* ____________ since this morning.

6 Our neighbours *(paint)* ____________ their house all week, and they *(already, finish)* ____________ four rooms.

Quest 10.2

Üben

85 ✱✱✱ *Complete the dialogue with the correct form of present perfect – simple or continuous.* – Ergänze den Dialog mit der richtigen Form von *present perfect – simple* oder *continuous*.

Amanda: This is unbelievable*! We *(sit)* ______________________ here for half an hour and nobody *(ask)* ______________________ us what we want to order. I think the waiter *(forget)* ______________________ us.

Melanie: I'm sure he has. He *(walk)* ______________________ past us ten times! Perhaps he thinks we *(already, order)* ______________________.

Amanda: Look at these people over there! They *(be)* ______________________ here for only ten or twelve minutes and they are already eating!

Melanie: The waiter must see that we *(not order)* ______________________ yet. After all*, we *(be)* ______________________ here for half an hour!

Amanda: Well, he *(run)* ______________________ around and taking orders and serving food, but he *(not bother)* ______________________ to ask us yet. Let's call him. … Here, waiter!

Waiter: Just a minute, ladies, I'll be with you in a moment …

**unbelievable* – unglaublich   **after all* – schließlich

Quest 10.3

86 ✱✱✱ *Look at the pictures and put the words into the correct tense – present perfect continuous or past simple?* – Schau dir die Bilder an und setze die Wörter in der richtigen Zeit ein – *present perfect continuous* oder *past simple*?

A: How long *(Joe, sleep)* ______________________?

B: Well, he *(go)* ______________________ to bed at around 8, so that makes it more than twelve hours.

A: How long *(you, play)* ______________________ football?

B: Not very long.

A: When *(you, begin)* ______________________?

B: Only ten minutes ago.

A: How long *(Tina, watch)* ______________________ TV?

B: Since she *(come)* ______________________ home from school.

A: That's four hours! That's too long!

87 ✱✱

Put the words in the correct order and write the sentences. – Bringe die Wörter in die richtige Reihenfolge und schreibe die Sätze auf. (Fortsetzung in Übung 88)

1 Dad ▪ six hours ▪ has ▪ for ▪ been ▪ driving

______________________________. ☐

2 since ▪ looking ▪ been ▪ for ▪ has ▪ Cousin Melody ▪ a flat ▪ May

______________________________. ☐

3 a week ▪ studying ▪ for ▪ been ▪ Simon ▪ exams ▪ has ▪ his ▪ for

______________________________. ☐

4 been ▪ all evening ▪ Mum and Dad ▪ decorating ▪ have ▪ Christmas tree ▪ the

______________________________. ☐

5 practising ▪ has ▪ for ▪ been ▪ months ▪ band ▪ the

______________________________. ☐

6 week ▪ those ▪ last ▪ have ▪ men ▪ watching ▪ our ▪ been ▪ house ▪ since

______________________________. ☐

Emily has been going out with Lucas since the party at her friend Nora's house.

That's why she's so happy.

88 ✱✱

Each of the sentences in this exercise comes after a sentence in exercise 87. Write 1 to 6 into the boxes after the sentences in exercise 87. – Jeder Satz in dieser Übung kommt nach einem Satz in Übung 87. Schreibe 1 bis 6 in dafür vorgesehenen Kästchen nach den Sätzen in Übung 87.

1 That's why we've called the police.

2 That's why he needs a break*.

3 That's why it's been so quiet in the house.

4 That's why she always checks the newspapers.

5 That's why they've locked the door into the living room.

6 That's why they play much better now.

**break* – Pause

PRESENT SIMPLE & PAST SIMPLE

A Bildung

present simple	*past simple*
I, you, we, they + ***base form*** *he, she, it* + ***base form + (e)s***	*all persons* → ***past form***

REGEL

*I **live** in Austria.*
*He **rides** his bike.*
*She **speaks** German.*
*They **spend** a lot of money.*

*Mozart **lived** in Austria.*
*He **rode** his bike.*
*She **spoke** German.*
*They **spent** a lot of money.*

REGEL

Frage → ***Do / Does / Did*** + ***base form***
Verneinung → ***don't / doesn't / didn't*** + ***base form***

REGULAR & IRREGULAR VERBS (past simple)

regular verbs	*irregular verbs*
base form + (e)d	verschieden
arrived – believed – carried – decided – enjoyed – finished – guessed – hated – imagined – jumped – knocked – landed – melted – needed – ordered – painted – reacted – shouted – tried – used – worked	*ate – became – caught – did – found – gave – had – knew – left – met – put – rode – sold – taught – wrote* Du findest eine Liste mit *irregular verbs* ab Seite 144.

ACHTUNG

RECHTSCHREIBUNG!
y → *i* — *cry – cried, say – said, worry – worried …*
Verdoppelung — *drop – dropped, grab – grabbed, plan – planned …*

B Verwendung

present simple	*past simple*
a) für **Tatsachen** b) für **Gedanken**, **Gefühle** und **Meinungen** c) für **Gewohnheiten** und **wiederholte Handlungen**	d) **„Erzählzeit"** e) **abgeschlossene** vergangene **Handlungen**
a) *The sun **sets** in the west.* *Water **freezes** at 0° C.* b) *I really **don't like** cheese.* *Mum **hates** rock 'n' roll.* c) *We often **have** pizza for lunch.* *Joe **walks** to school every day.*	d) *The car **stopped** and two men **got** out. They **looked** around, and then they **went** into the house …* e) *The concert **began** at 9:30.* *The guests **didn't arrive** in time*.*

**in time* – rechtzeitig

C Signalwörter

Diese Wörter weisen oft auf ***present simple*** oder ***past simple*** hin.

present simple	*past simple*
always – every (day, week …) – never – often – sometimes – usually	*yesterday – last (week, month …) – (a week, some time …) ago – in (May, 2015 …)*

89 *

Present simple: cross out the wrong word. – *Present simple*: Streiche das falsche Wort durch.

1 The sun *don't shine / doesn't shine* at night.
2 Ali never *drink / drinks* beer or wine.
3 My parents *don't work / doesn't work* in an office in town.
4 We usually *have / has* pancakes for breakfast on Sunday.
5 Many tourists *arrive / arrives* by plane.
6 The Amazon *empty* / empties* into the Atlantic Ocean.
7 Oranges *don't / doesn't* grow in Austria.
8 Gorillas *live / lives* in the jungle.
9 Trevor *go / goes* to school in Sheffield.

**empty* – hier: münden

D *Present simple*

90 ✱

Present simple: complete the sentences with a verb from the box. – Present simple: Ergänze die Sätze mit einem Verb aus dem Rahmen.

ask ▪ not believe ▪ do ▪ listen ▪ play ▪ stop ▪ take ▪ walk

Quest 11.1

1 Gina always ____________________ her homework at school.
2 Harry and I ____________________ squash every Saturday.
3 The school bus ____________________ across the street from my house.
4 My friends and I usually ____________________ to school together.
5 Ellie often ____________________ to her favourite songs.
6 Young children ____________________ lots of questions.
7 I ____________________ in vampires and ghosts.
8 Mum sometimes ____________________ the bus to work in the morning.

91 ✱✱

Look at the pairs of pictures and write suitable sentences. – Schau dir die Bilder an und schreibe die passenden Sätze dazu.

1

2

3

4

5

6

1 Dad **(walk)** walks ______ to work. He **(not drive)** doesn't drive ______.

2 We *(spend)* ______ our holidays on the beach, but we *(not go)* ______ skiing in winter.

3 The students *(not wear)* ______ uniforms. They *(wear)* ______ jeans and T-shirts.

4 Britney *(live)* ______ in a large flat. She *(not live)* ______ in a house with a garden.

5 I *(have)* ______ two sisters, but I *(not have)* ______ a brother.

6 Margaret *(not like)* ______ dogs, but she *(love)* ______ cats.

92 *

Read this text about Angela and fill in the verbs in present simple. – Lies den Text über Angela und setze die Verben in *present simple* ein.

Angela and her family *(live)* ______ in the country. She *(like)* ______ the country because they *(be)* ______ far away from the noise and pollution of the city. Angela usually *(get)* ______ up early because she *(love)* ______ going for a short walk in the morning. Her father and her brother Freddie often *(go)* ______ with her. Her mother *(stay)* ______ at home and *(prepare)* ______ breakfast. After the walk, they all *(have)* ______ breakfast together. Then Angela and Freddie *(take)* ______ the bus to school, and their father *(drive)* ______ to work. He *(be)* ______ a dentist and he *(work)* ______ in the small town near their village. Angela's mother and a neighbour *(walk)* ______ to the village kindergarten where they *(work)* ______ until 2 p.m. At the end of the school day, the children usually *(not return)* ______ to their house together. Angela *(take)* ______ the bus back but Freddie *(stay)* ______ at school longer because he *(play)* ______ rugby for the school team. Angela's father *(not finish)* ______ working before 5 p.m. Then he *(pick up)* ______ Freddie and they *(drive)* ______ back home in time for dinner.

Üben

Quests
11.2
11.3

E Past simple

93 ✱✱ *Find the past forms of the verbs from the box and complete the puzzle. Who is the 'mysterious person'?* – Schreibe die *past forms* der Verben im Rahmen in das Rätsel. Wer ist die „geheimnisvolle Person"?

1 come	**6** build	**11** cut
2 give	**7** teach	**12** throw
3 ride	**8** arrive	**13** try
4 become	**9** hurt	**14** drive
5 be	**10** ask	

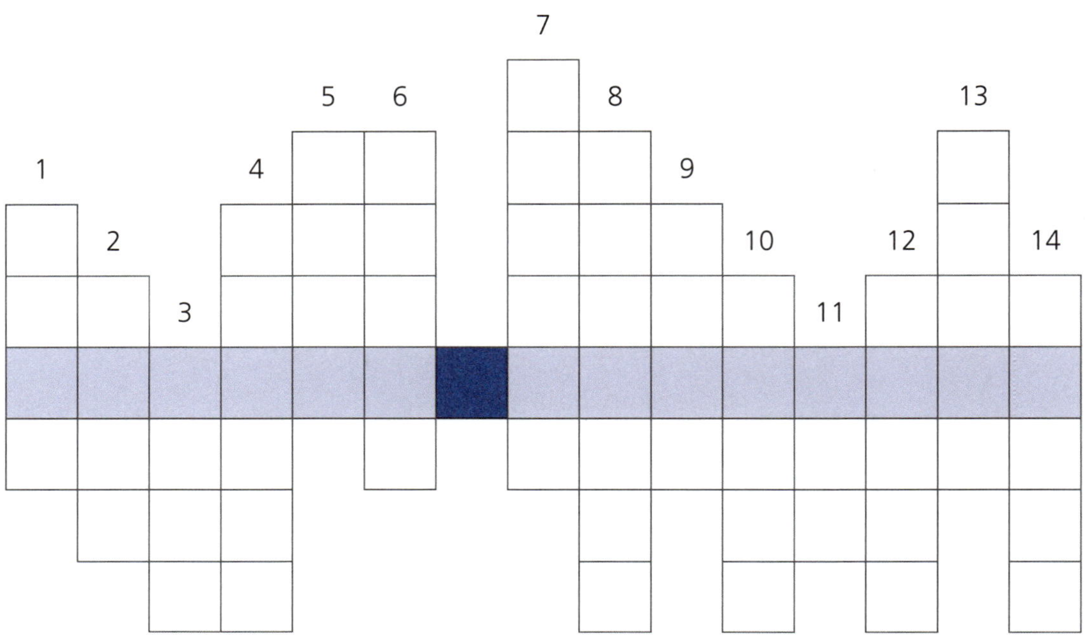

And the 'mysterious person' is __________________________________.

94 ✱✱ *Look at the verbs in the following sentences. Are they regular verbs or irregular verbs? Write **R** for regular and **I** for irregular into the brackets.* – Schau dir die Verben in den folgenden Sätzen an. Sind es *regular verbs* oder *irregular verbs*? Trage **R** für *regular* und **I** für *irregular* in die Klammer ein.

1 We went (__) to Italy last summer, and we visited (__) many beautiful cities.

2 Joe's father liked (__) his car, but then he bought (__) a bigger one.

3 When I was (__) new at this school, I sometimes felt (__) lonely.

4 The men got (__) into the car and drove (__) away quickly.

5 I found (__) a mobile phone in the locker room and gave it (__) to the teacher.

6 The Wright brothers flew (__) the first aeroplane in 1903. It stayed (__) in the air for only twelve seconds.

Quests
11.4
11.5
11.6
11.7

95 **

Write down the base forms of the irregular verbs in exercise 94. – Schreibe die *base forms* der *irregular verbs* aus Übung 94 auf.

1 ______________________ 4 ______________________

2 ______________________ 5 ______________________

3 ______________________ 6 ______________________

96 ***

Look at the pictures and say what they did and didn't do? – Schau dir die Bilder an; was haben die Leute gemacht oder nicht gemacht?

1

visit ride

2

finish drink

3

play tidy up

4

take feed

5

watch read

6

see talk

1 In London, we visited Madame Tussauds, but we didn't ride the London Eye.

2 Rosie ________________ her breakfast, but she ________________ all the milk.

3 You ________________ computer games all afternoon, but you ________________ your room.

4 Lisa ________________ 'Alfie' for a walk, but she ________________ him.

5 Linus ________________ the movie, but he ________________ the book.

6 I ________________ Ruthie today, but I ________________ to her on the phone.

Quest 11.8

97 ✱✱✱ *Read the first part of the story of Aladdin and his magic lamp. Then put the verbs in brackets into past tense.* – Lies den ersten Teil der Geschichte von Aladdin und seiner Wunderlampe und setze die Verben in Klammer in *past tense* ein.

A long, long time ago, in Bagdad, there *(live)* ______________ a boy named Aladdin. One day, an old man *(come)* ______________ to his house and *(say)* ______________ that he *(be)* ______________ his uncle. Aladdin's father *(die)* ______________ many years before, so Aladdin's mother *(be)* ______________ very happy and *(invite)* ______________ the old man into her house.

The next day, the uncle *(give)* ______________ Aladdin nice clothes to wear and *(take)* ______________ him on a tour through the city gardens. All this *(impress*)* ______________ the boy very much, and so he *(say)* ______________ yes when the old man *(ask)* ______________ him to work for him. But this old man *(not really be)* ______________ Aladdin's uncle. He *(be)* ______________ an evil magician, and he *(want)* ______________ to use the boy for his purposes*. Of course, Aladdin and his mother *(have)* ______________ no idea.

So he *(go)* ______________ on long walks with the old man, and on one of these walks they *(come)* ______________ to the foot of a mountain. They *(sit)* ______________ down to rest, and the old man *(light)* ______________ a fire. He *(throw)* ______________ something into the flames* and mumbled* some words. Aladdin *(not understand)* ________________ what his 'uncle' was saying, but suddenly the ground beneath them* *(open)* ______________ and they *(can)* ______________ see a tunnel. Aladdin *(not like)* ______________ this, and he *(be)* ______________ afraid, but the old man *(say)* ______________, "Don't be afraid. Nothing will happen to you. But you must do what I say. Walk through this tunnel until you come to a beautiful garden. In the middle of this garden there is a shining lamp. Bring me this lamp, but do not touch anything!"

Aladdin *(walk)* ______________ through the tunnel, he *(find)* ______________ the lamp and he *(take)* ______________ it with him. When he *(reach)* ______________ the end of the tunnel, the magician *(want)* ______________ to grab the lamp from Aladdin's hands, but Aladdin *(not let)* ______________ it go. The evil old man *(be)* ______________ so angry that he *(close)* ______________ the tunnel before the boy *(can)* ______________ get out. Aladdin *(not know)* ______________ what to do, and in his panic he *(rub*)* ______________ the lamp. Suddenly a genie* *(appear*)* ______________ and *(say)* ______________, "You are my master now and I will do everything you say!" "Take me home," Aladdin *(answer)* ______________. "I want to be with my mother!"

Aladdin's mother *(be)* ______________ happy. Now they *(have)* ______________ everything – enough to eat, nice clothes and a beautiful new house. Every wish *(come)* ______________ true, and for some years everything *(go)* ______________ well.

One day, Aladdin *(see)* ______________ Jasmine, the king's daughter, and he *(fall)* ______________ in love with her at once*. When the king *(see)* ______________ the expensive gifts Aladdin *(give)* ______________ his daughter, he *(allow)* ______________ the young man to marry her. Aladdin *(tell)* ______________ the genie to build him a palace, and the genie *(fulfil*)* ______________ Aladdin's wish. Now Aladdin, his new wife and his mother *(live)* ______________ in a wonderful new palace and they *(have)* ______________ everything they *(want)* ______________.

But the evil magician *(hear)* ______________ of Aladdin's good luck, and now he *(want)* ______________ the lamp for himself*. So he *(go)* ______________ to the palace with a cart* full of new lamps, and he *(shout)* ______________, "Old for new! Old for new!" Jasmine *(not know)* ______________ the value* of the old lamp, and so she *(exchange*)* ______________ it for a new one. At once, the magician *(order)* ______________ the genie to transport the palace and Jasmine to Africa.

When Aladdin *(hear)* ______________ of this, he *(sit)* ______________ down on his flying carpet and *(go)* ______________ to look for his wife and the magician. He soon *(find)* ______________ the old man and he *(punish*)* ______________ him – he *(put)* ______________ poison* in his drink, and so the evil man *(die)* ______________. But Aladdin, his mother and Jasmine *(live)* ______________ happily until the end of their days.

**impress* – beeindrucken **purposes* – Zwecke **flames* – Flammen **mumble* – murmeln
**the ground beneath them* – der Boden unter ihren Füßen **rub* – reiben
**genie* – Flaschengeist **appear* – erscheinen **at once* – sofort **fulfill* – erfüllen
**for himself* – für sich (selbst) **cart* – Karren **value* – Wert **exchange* – austauschen
**punish* – bestrafen **poison* – Gift

Quests
11.9
11.10
11.11

Üben

RELATIVE PRONOUNS – RELATIVPRONOMEN

A Was ist das?

- Mit dem ***relative pronoun*** kannst du **weitere Einzelheiten über eine Person oder eine Sache** angeben.

REGEL

The people ***who*** ***live next door*** *are very nice.*
Die Leute, **die** **nebenan wohnen**, sind sehr nett.
↓
zusätzliche Information zu *the people*

B Verwendung

- Bei **Personen** verwendest du ***who*** oder ***that***.
- Bei **Dingen** verwendest du ***which*** oder ***that***.
- Immer dann, wenn du auf Deutsch **„dessen" oder „deren"** sagst, verwendest du auf English ***whose*** – und zwar für Menschen und Dinge.

- *That's* ***the man who / that*** *repaired our car.*
  Is this ***the teacher who / that*** *gave you the homework?*
- ***The exercises which / that*** *we had to do for today were easy.*
  That's ***the dog which / that*** *tried to bite me!*
- *I know* ***the people whose photo*** *was on TV last night.*
  Eyafjallajökull is ***a mountain whose name*** *is difficult to remember.*

98 ✱✱✱ *Write who / that or which / that in the gaps in each sentence and tick what you think is the correct answer. Use the Internet or an encyclopaedia*.* – Schreibe *who / that* oder *which / that* in die Lücke bei jedem Satz und kreuze an, was du für die richtige Antwort hältst. Schau im Internet oder in einem Lexikon nach, wenn du die Antwort nicht weißt.

> What is the name of the famous tower which / that stands in Paris?
> A the Leaning Tower ~~B~~ the Eiffel Tower C the Trump Tower

1 What's the name of the little statue ______________ is awarded* as a prize for the best film every year?

A Oscar **B** Emmy **C** Golden Camera

2 What's the name of the man ______________ first climbed Mt. Everest without an oxygen mask?

A Edmund Hillary **B** Heinrich Harrer **C** Reinhold Messner

3 What's the name of the ship ______________ sank on its first voyage in 1912?

A Lusitania **B** Titanic **C** Andrea Doria

4 What's the name of the woman ______________ won two Nobel Prizes, one for Physics and one for Chemistry?

A Marie Curie **B** Jane Addams **C** Bertha von Suttner

5 What's the name of the rocket ______________ took the first men to the Moon?

A Saturn **B** Atlas **C** Aries

6 What's the name of the man ______________ founded* Amazon®?

A Steve Jobs **B** Bill Gates **C** Jeff Bezos

7 What was the name of the airplane ______________ Charles Lindbergh flew from New York to Paris in 1927?

A The Spirit of St. Louis **B** The Eagle **C** The Challenger

8 What's the name of the gymnast* ______________ won 25 world championship medals, 19 of them in gold?

A Olga Korbut **B** Simone Biles **C** Nadia Comaneci

**encyclopaedia* – Lexikon **is awarded* – wird verliehen **found* – gründen
**was destroyed* – wurde zerstört **gymnast* – Turner, Turnerin

Üben

Quest 12.1

99 **

Cross out the words that cannot be used in these sentences. – Streiche die nicht passenden Wörter in jedem Satz durch.

> *Sally was the one* **who** / ~~which~~ / **that** *answered all questions.*

1 Bicycles *who / which / that* have bad brakes are dangerous.
2 The blond woman *who / which / that* is talking to my mum is my English teacher.
3 The photos *who / which / that* hang on the wall of my room were taken by me.
4 The chef is the person *who / which / that* is in charge of* a restaurant kitchen.
5 The woman *who / which / that* let us into the house was very nice.
6 Joe works for a company *who / which / that* makes furniture*.
7 There are some boys in my class *who / which / that* don't like football.
8 The car *who / which / that* stands over there belongs to Ms Hill.
9 The old lady *who / which / that* lives upstairs is almost 90.
10 Mr Jenkins smokes only cigars *who / which / that* come from Cuba.

**is in charge of* – ist verantwortlich für **furniture* – Möbel

Üben

100 *

Combine two sentences to make one with the help of ***one*** *relative pronoun.* – Verbinde die zwei Sätze zu einem mit Hilfe **eines** *Relativpronomens.*

> *Where is* **the young man? He** *wants to speak with you.*
> *Where is* **the young man who / that** *wants to speak with you* ?

1 This is the bus. It stops at the bank.

____.

2 Where are the flowers? They were on the table.

____?

3 These are the people. They were making all that noise.

____.

4 What's the name of the man? He phoned you yesterday.

____?

5 Many young people get into trouble. They drink and take drugs.

____.

6 Have you met the guests? They arrived last night.

____?

7 The burglars took some jewels. They weren't really expensive.

____.

8 The tomatoes are excellent. They grow in Grandma's garden.

____.

101 *Complete the sentences with who, which or that.* – Setze *who, which* oder *that* ein.

✱✱✱

1 Vera watches only movies __________ have a happy end.
2 What was the name of the girl __________ invited you to her party?
3 The boy __________ broke his arm yesterday can't play volleyball now.
4 Can you remember the people __________ asked you for the way?
5 The shop __________ sells these jeans is closed today.
6 Are you the man __________ can help us?
7 Everybody __________ knows Jane likes her.
8 Ms Talbot is the architect __________ designed our house.
9 I don't know many young people __________ like folk music.
10 The fiddle is an instrument __________ looks and sounds like a violin.
11 The woman __________ sold me the stamps wasn't very helpful.
12 At the zoo you can see all the animals __________ live in the Alps.
13 'Star Trek' is one of the best TV series __________ have ever been written.
14 The people __________ live above us are from Russia.
15 I hate dogs __________ bark all night.
16 The pictures __________ were stolen from the museum have been found.
17 A baker is a person __________ makes bread and rolls and buns.
18 The postcard __________ came this morning is from Martin.

Quest 12.2

Üben

17

18

102 ✱✱✱ *Complete the text with who, which or that.* – Vervollständige den Text mit *who, which* oder *that.*

Amelia's grandmother is a woman ____________ doesn't act her age*. She's 80, but she knows everything about fashion and movies and politics, and she reads science books ____________ are much too complicated for Amelia.

Amelia's granny also loves the computer games ____________ she gets from Amelia and she plays as often as she can. She doesn't like the last one ____________ Amelia gave her. She says she hates games ____________ have guns and violence* in them.

Granny also loves cooking. She says people ____________ don't love good food don't know how to live. The food ____________ she loves best is always fresh and organic*. She buys her fruit and vegetables from farmers ____________ grow everything on their fields and in their gardens. She says the things ____________ people buy at supermarkets are not so good and healthy. She watches TV programmes ____________ deal with* food, and she listens to people ____________ know about these things. She is really a very unusual woman!

**doesn't act her age* – benimmt sich nicht ihrem Alter entsprechend **violence* – Gewalt
**organic* – Bio **deal with* – handeln von, sich befassen mit

Wissen

Üben

C *whose*

- ***whose?*** bedeutet nicht nur **„wessen?"** in Fragen wie z. B.
  Whose *shoes are these?* → **Wessen** Schuhe sind das?
- … sondern auch **„deren" oder „dessen"** in Aussagen wie z. B.

REGEL

*This is **the girl whose cat** ran away.*
→ … das Mädchen, **deren** Katze …

*That's **the man whose son** is in my class this year.*
→ … der Mann, **dessen** Sohn …

*Jenny is wearing **a dress whose buttons** are missing.*
→ … ein Kleid, **dessen** Knöpfe …

103 ✱ *Match the sentence halves.* – Welche Satzhälften passen zusammen?

David Hasselhoff is an actor	1
Can you show me the photos	2
The firefighters saved the people	3
Daniel Radcliffe is the actor	4
Beyoncé is an American singer	5
Mum buys only products	6
Mangos are tropical fruits	7
There's a nice café close-by	8

A	whose house was burning.
B	that grow on trees.
C	whose songs I like very much.
D	which are made in Austria.
E	who also sings.
F	who played Harry Potter.
G	which has the best cakes.
H	that you took in Thailand?

104 ✱✱ *Which is the correct relative pronoun? Draw a circle around it.* – Welches ist das richtige Relativpronomen? Kreise es ein.

1 Is this the driver ***who / whose / which*** caused* the accident?

2 These are the people ***who / whose / which*** parties are always great fun.

3 France is the country ***who / whose / which*** attracts the most tourists.

4 George Washington was a general ***who / whose / which*** became president.

5 The kiwi is a bird ***who / whose / which*** lives only in New Zealand.

6 That's the teacher ***who / whose / which*** name I cannot remember.

**cause* – verursachen

105 ✱ *In which of the sentences in exercise 104 can you also say that? Tick the boxes.* – Bei welchen Sätzen kannst du auch *that* verwenden? Kreuze die Kästchen an.

1 ☐ **2** ☐ **3** ☐ **4** ☐ **5** ☐ **6** ☐

106 ✱✱ *Put the words into the correct order to make sentences.* – Bringe die Wörter in die richtige Reihenfolge und schreibe die Sätze auf.

1 uncle ▪ an ▪ who ▪ in Dubai ▪ I've ▪ works ▪ got

____.

2 this ▪ goes ▪ the airport ▪ is ▪ that ▪ to ▪ the train ▪ ?

____?

3 doctor ▪ that's ▪ our ▪ is ▪ whose ▪ the man ▪ wife

____.

Üben

IT TAKES ME ... – ICH BRAUCHE ...

A Erklärung

REGEL

Wenn du sagen willst, wie lange etwas dauert oder wie viel Zeit jemand braucht, um etwas zu tun, verwendest du

It + (take) + person + time + (to do something)

It takes me half an hour to get to school. → *present*
It took Joe three weeks to finish the job. → *past*
It'll take you all day to find an answer. → *future*
It has taken us a year to understand the people. → *pres. perfect*

B Frage und Verneinung

present tense

*It **takes** me half an hour to get to school.*
Does it take you long to get to school?
It doesn't take me long to get to school.
How long does it take you to get to school?

past tense

*It **took** Joe three weeks to finish the job.*
Did it take him long to finish the job?
It didn't take him long to finish the job.
How long did it take him to finish the job?

future tense

*It **will take** you all day to find an answer.*
Will it take us / me / you long to find an answer?
It will not / won't take us / me / you long to find an answer.
How long will it take us / me / you to find an answer?

present perfect tense

*It **has taken** us a year to understand the people.*
Has it taken you long to understand the people?
It hasn't taken us long to understand the people.
How long has it taken you to understand the people?

107 ✱✱

Underline the correct word in the following sentences. Mind the tense. – Unterstreiche das richtige Wort in den folgenden Sätzen. Achte auf die Zeitstufe!

Quest 13.1

1 It always *takes / will take* George a long time to get ready for bed.
2 How long *does / did* it take you to do your homework yesterday?
3 It *takes / will take* them years to build their house, but by 2025 it will be finished.
4 It *took / has taken* me a month to finish my model plane, but now it's ready to fly.
5 How long *will it take / has it taken* you to pack your suitcase? – I don't know. I haven't started yet.
6 It never *has taken / takes* us more than ten minutes to tidy up our rooms.
7 When Grandpa was a boy, it *takes / took* him two hours to walk to school.
8 It *didn't / doesn't* take them long to clear the roads after last week's snowstorm.

108 ✱✱✱

Look at the pictures and write down how long it takes / took / will take / has taken the people to do these things? Mind the tense! – Schau dir die Bilder an und schreibe auf, wie lange die Leute für diese Dinge brauchen / brauchten / brauchen werden / gebraucht haben. Achte auf die Zeitstufe.

July 16–24, 1969

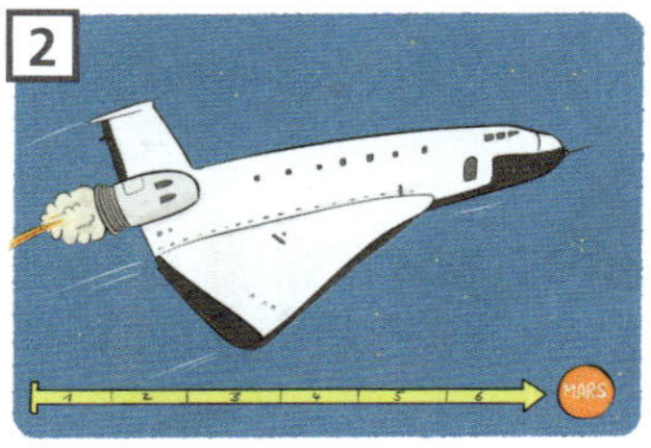
six months

two days

Paula

January 1887–March 1889

never?

1 It ______________________ Apollo 11 nine days to travel to the Moon and back.

2 It ______________________ astronauts six months or more to fly to Mars.

3 It usually ______________________ Julia two days to read a book.

4 It ______________________ Paula many years to learn playing the cello, but now she's very good.

5 How long ______________________ the French to build the Eiffel Tower? – Only 26 months, from January 1887 to March 1889.

6 How long ______________________ doctors to find a cure* for the common cold*?

**cure* – Heilung   **common cold* – gewöhnlicher Schnupfen

TIME LINKS – EINLEITUNG VON ZEITSÄTZEN

A Was ist das?

time links sind Wörter, die **Zeitsätze** einleiten.
Zeitsätze sagen uns, wann eine Handlung beginnt und endet, **wie lange sie andauert**, und ob sie **gleichzeitig**, **vor** oder **nach einer** anderen **Handlung** geschieht.

B *when – before – after*

REGEL

- ***when*** → ***als, wenn*** — *It was midnight **when** we came home.*
- ***after*** → ***nach(dem)*** — ***After** the guests were gone, we went to bed.*
- ***before*** → ***bevor*** — *We shut the windows **before** we went to bed.*

109 *Match the sentence halves.* – Welche Satzhälften gehören zusammen?

*

Mum always gives me a kiss	1		A	when he was in grammar school.
We all have dinner	2		B	after Mum switches off the light.
I was already in bed	3		C	before she goes to bed.
My dad played basketball	4		D	before I go to school in the morning.
Amy usually takes a shower	5		E	after he finishes work.
Little Joe falls asleep quickly	6		F	when I suddenly heard a loud bang.
We all stand up	7		G	after Dad comes home from work.
I do my homework	8		H	before I watch TV.
Dad often phones Mum	9		I	when a teacher comes into the room.

C during – while

REGEL

Beide Wörter bedeuten **„während"**.

Auf ***while*** folgt immer ein **Gliedsatz/ein Verb**.
Auf ***during*** folgt immer ein **Nomen**.

Everybody stayed in the house ***while the storm was blowing****.*
Everybody stayed in the house ***during the storm****.*

110 ✱ *During or while? Cross out the wrong word.* – *During* oder *while*? Streiche das falsche Wort durch.

Quest 14.1

1 My phone suddenly rang *during / while* the English lesson.
2 Grandma fell asleep *during / while* she was watching a film.
3 I talked to Marie *during / while* we were waiting for the bus.
4 Harold didn't feel well *during / while* the test.
5 *During / While* we were having dinner, somebody knocked on the door.
6 We don't speak very much *during / while* breakfast.
7 In my school, we can use our tablets *during / while* the breaks.
8 Cindy came into the bathroom *during / while* I was brushing my teeth.

111 ✱✱ *Complete the sentences with during or while so that a) and b) have the same meaning.* – Ergänze die Sätze mit *during* oder *while*, sodass a) und b) dasselbe bedeuten.

> Grandma fell asleep while she was watching a film. → during the film
> Joe broke his arm during the match. → while he was playing a match

1 I fell asleep during the conference. → ____________________
2 The lights went out while we were having dinner. → ____________________
3 The drummer* fell ill* while the band was on tour. → ____________________
4 We can't play tennis while it's raining. → ____________________
5 Joe met Sue during his holiday in Spain. → ____________________
6 Dad's phone rang three times during the concert. → ____________________

**drummer* – Schlagzeuger **fall ill* – erkranken, krank werden

Wissen
Üben

D until / till – by the time

REGEL

- ***until, till*** → bis
- ***by the time*** → bis / als (schließlich), wenn

I'll wait for you ***until / till you come back.***
Until tomorrow!
Till we meet again!

By the time we came back*, everybody was sleeping.*
It was getting dark ***by the time we reached the top of the hill****.*
By the time the ambulance arrived*, the man was dead.*

112 *Fill in by the time or till / until.* – Setze *by the time* oder *till / until* ein.

*

1 The shops are open ________________ 10 p.m.

2 Joe says he will finish his model ship ________________ we visit him again.

3 I waited for you ________________ 5 o'clock, but then I went home.

4 ________________ I got back home, dinner was ready.

5 The guests are going to stay ________________ the end of the week.

6 We won't go away ________________ you come back

7 Everybody was tired ________________ the match was over.

8 The food was cold ________________ it arrived at our table.

ACHTUNG

Für „**bis**" gibt es zwei Möglichkeiten:

until / till → *time* → ***until*** *dinner,* ***till*** *midnight,* ***until*** *Tuesday …*

as far as → *place* → ***as far as*** *the church,* ***as far as*** *here …*

We'll come with you ***as far as*** *the bus stop.*

We'll wait here ***till*** *your bus comes.*

113 *
until / till or as far as? Write the words from the box into the correct column. –
until / till oder *as far as*? Schreibe die Wörter in die richtige Spalte.

we meet again ▪ the next street ▪ the post office ▪ 5 a.m. ▪ next week
Christmas ▪ your house ▪ the bus stop ▪ tomorrow ▪ over there

until / till	as far as
____________	____________
____________	____________
____________	____________
____________	____________
____________	____________

114 * *
Complete the sentences with when, before, after, while, during, until / till or by the time so that a) and b) have the same meaning. – Ergänze die Sätze mit *when, before, after, while, during, until / till* oder *by the time*, sodass a) und b) dasselbe bedeuten.

> *a) Ryan played computer games for hours. Then he went to bed.*
> *b) Ryan played computer games for hours* ___before___ *he went to bed.*

1 **a)** I finished my homework. My eyes hurt.

b) ____________ I finished my homework, my eyes hurt.

2 **a)** Dad was listening to the radio. He was driving to work.

b) Dad was listening to the radio ____________ he was driving to work.

3 **a)** Mum shut all the windows and doors. She left the house.

b) Mum shut all the windows ____________ she left the house.

4 **a)** We were on holiday in Scotland. We met some very nice people.

b) We met some very nice people ____________ our holiday in Scotland.

5 **a)** We waited for you. At 6 o'clock we gave up.

b) We waited for you ____________ 6 o'clock.

6 **a)** Mum always checks her emails. She arrives at her office.

b) Mum always checks her emails ____________ she arrives at her office.

7 **a)** Bella was reading a book. She heard a strange noise.

b) Bella was reading a book ____________ she heard a strange noise.

Quest 14.2

Üben

115 ** *Read the story and choose the correct option: A, B or C.* – Lies die Geschichte und wähle das richtige Wort zum Einsetzen aus: A, B oder C.

By the time we got to the arena, lots of people were already there.

When the game was over, the home team were the happy winners.

Last weekend, Dad and I went to the sports arena in our town. We wanted to see my brother Alec play basketball with his team. *(1)* ______________ we arrived, there was still time to get drinks and hotdogs *(2)* ______________ the game began. Alec's Team was playing a team from a neighbouring* town, and many people were there to see their team win. *(3)* ______________ we were waiting for the game to begin, I took some photos with my new camera. *(4)* ______________ the players came onto the court* at last*, everybody in the auditorium was cheering, but *(5)* ______________ the game began, the people calmed down*. Both teams played well, and I took many photos *(6)* ______________ the match. Alec scored 21 points *(7)* ______________ the first two quarters, but then the coach* took him out of the game – Alec's arm hurt *(8)* ______________ a player from the other team hit him hard. Dad and I were very proud of him! *(9)* ______________ the game, we waited for Alec in the lobby, and *(10)* ______________ we were waiting, Dad looked at my photos. They were quite good! *(11)* ______________ Alec and his teammates came, we said well done and bravo and great game, and then we drove home. *(12)* ______________ we came back to our house, Alec's arm was hurting badly. So Dad drove him to the hospital, and that wasn't really a happy ending to a fine day!

**neighbouring* – benachbart **court* – Spielfeld **at last* – schließlich, endlich
**calmed down* – beruhigten sich **coach* – Trainer

1	**A**	After	**B**	During	**C**	When	7	**A**	during	**B**	before	**C**	after
2	**A**	after	**B**	before	**C**	during	8	**A**	before	**B**	by the time	**C**	after
3	**A**	While	**B**	During	**C**	By the time	9	**A**	After	**B**	During	**C**	Before
4	**A**	While	**B**	By the time	**C**	After	10	**A**	during	**B**	before	**C**	while
5	**A**	before	**B**	while	**C**	after	11	**A**	When	**B**	After	**C**	Before
6	**A**	after	**B**	during	**C**	before	12	**A**	While	**B**	By the time	**C**	After

Üben

116 ✱✱✱ *Look at the pictures and the sentences and cross out the wrong word.* – Schau dir die Bilder und Sätze an und streiche das falsche Wort durch.

1 *Till / While* we were walking up the hill, it was raining, but …

2 … *when / during* we reached the top, the sun was shining again.

3 I said good-bye to Laura *after / before* I got on the bus, and …

4 … *by the time / while* I came home, she had texted me twice*.

5 There was a terrible thunderstorm *during / until* the night, and …

6 … in the morning, *before / after* the storm, we saw many fallen* trees.

7 Some people left the cinema *during / while* the film.

8 Some people left the cinema *before / while* the film was over.

**had texted me twice* – hatte mir zwei SMS geschickt **fallen* – umgefallen, umgestürzt

LISTENING – HÖRVERSTÄNDNISÜBUNGEN

Die folgenden Übungen helfen dir dabei, dein **Hörverständnis** zu **trainieren**. **Spiele** den Hörtext **zweimal ab** und **mache** dir **beim Zuhören** eventuell **Notizen**! Dann löse die Aufgaben. Die richtigen Antworten kannst du im Lösungsheft nachschlagen und mit deinen vergleichen.

Du hast zwei Möglichkeiten, die Hörtexte abzuspielen:

In der MEDIATHEK (Die Erklärung zu dieser Handy-App findest du auf Seite 2.)

Auf der beiliegenden CD

Viel Spaß und Ohren spitzen!

Üben

117 **My favourite band**

*

Listen to Lisa talking about her favourite band and fill in the missing words.

1 Lisa's favourite band ______________ 'The Jonas Boys'.

2 They ______________ three handsome and talented boys from the USA.

3 Lisa ______________ it's cool that they are all songwriters.

4 'The Jonas Boys' ______________ about life and love and young people's problems.

5 The oldest brother is the lead singer and the ______________.

6 The youngest brother plays ______________.

7 The third band member is the 'sandwich child' and he plays the guitar ______________.

8 'The Jonas Boys' have many hits you can ______________.

9 ______________ is about the crazy things a boy does when he is in love.

10 ______________ because it is cool and funny.

11 ______________ everything about her favourite band.

12 ______________ a favourite band?

118 At a concert

✱✱

Listen to Paula talking about a concert and choose true or false.

		True	False
1	Last summer, Paula went to a concert with her family.	☐	☐
2	It was in Paris and it was wonderful.	☐	☐
3	They got there early and sat at the back.	☐	☐
4	The problem was that they could not see very well.	☐	☐
5	They also saw a cool laser show.	☐	☐
6	Everyone screamed when the concert started and Paula was scared.	☐	☐
7	The music at the concert was very loud.	☐	☐
8	Paula and her friends sang and danced to the music.	☐	☐
9	After the concert the girls bought ice cream.	☐	☐
10	It was a wonderful night for Paula.	☐	☐

119 Last night

✱

Listen to Dan talking about what was happening at his house last night and fill in past progressive.

1 Last night, many things ______________________ at Dan's house.

2 Dan ______________________ at his desk in his room.

3 He ______________________ his homework.

4 Dan's mum ______________________ a shower.

5 She ______________________ a love song.

6 Dan's dad ______________________ a football match on TV.

7 He ______________________ popcorn and chocolate.

8 And he ______________________ for his team.

9 Dan's brother ______________________ the bass guitar in his room.

10 Dan ______________________ problems with his homework.

Üben

120 Jim's holiday

Listen to Jim talking about his holiday and choose the correct words.

1 Jim was on *holiday / a class trip* in Paris.

2 He set off for the *airport / train station* on Monday morning.

3 He had to *get / get into* there by 7:30.

4 The plane *set off / took off* at 9:45.

5 Jim *got off / got on* the plane at about 9:30.

6 The flight *took / took off* about two hours.

7 The plane *landed / flew back* at around 11:45.

8 Then he waited for his bags and *get / got* a car.

9 Next, he *drove home / drove to the hotel*.

10 Travelling takes time but it is nice to get *out of / get into* the house.

121 Hannah's strange dream

Listen to the story about Hannah and fill in the missing words.

1 ______________ Hannah was a young girl, she wanted to be a princess.

2 ______________ she had a strange dream, and in her dream, she was swimming in a lake.

3 ______________ she was swimming it started to rain and she got out of the water.

4 ______________ she saw a big green frog that was smiling at her.

5 ______________ Hannah could touch the frog, it spoke to her and said: 'Hello, what is your name?'

6 ______________ the girl answered, 'My name is Hannah. And who are you?'

7 ______________ the frog said, 'I am Prince Louis of Burgundy and I am not a frog.'

8 ______________ Hannah listened to the frog, she knew it was a dream.

9 It ______________ her some time, but then she woke up.

10 ______________, Hannah was sad that it was just a dream and that she hadn´t kissed* the frog to see what happened.

**hadn´t kissed* – geküsst hatte

122 Life on Mars

Listen to the story about life on Mars and fill in the missing words.

Yesterday I watched a film called 'Life on Mars' and it was

____________________ film ever!

It was about a spaceship that landed on Mars and found ____________________ kangaroos there!

The spaceship that flies to Mars is not ____________________ the spaceships that fly to the Moon, and there is a problem.

The spaceship is ____________________ it should be and then starts to burn.

So it crashes on Mars where there are ____________________ mountains in the solar system.

Then the astronauts leave their spaceship and think they are on

____________________ part of the planet because it is very beautiful there.

Soon they see the kangaroos that are much ____________________ the ones at the zoo.

But they do not know that kangaroos on Mars are ____________________ animals there are.

The kangaroos can jump ____________________ half a football field.

Suddenly the strange kangaroos attack the astronauts but I don't want to tell you the end, just that it is ____________________ film ever.

Üben

123

Sights of London

Listen to the description of some famous sights of London and connect the sentence halves.

Big Ben is the name of the bell	1	A	which they raise when big ships come up the river.
The London Eye is a giant Ferris Wheel* by the River Thames	2	B	who are called Romeo and Juliet.
Tower Bridge is the bridge across the Thames	3	C	which you can find in the London Aquarium.
The Tower of London is a museum	4	D	who like to exercise or relax in the fresh air.
The Globe Theatre was financed by William Shakespeare,	5	E	who wrote about the Great Fire of London of 1666 in his diary.
His most famous play is about young lovers	6	F	which is in a huge clock tower.
Hyde Park is wonderful for people	7	G	who were very popular in their time.
Sharks and octopuses* are sea creatures	8	H	which used to be a castle and then a prison.
Samuel Pepys is the famous writer	9	I	who is known for writing many famous plays.
The Beatles were a band of four young British singers	10	J	which offers a great view over the city.

Example answer drawn on the page: 1 → F

**Ferris Wheel* – Riesenrad   **octopus* – Krake

124 Weekend plans

Listen to the dialogue and complete the if-sentences.

1 If the weather is nice, they ______________________________.

2 If they go to the park, they ______________________________.

3 Tim doesn't know if the weather ______________________________.

4 If it rains, they ______________________________.

5 Tina wonders what they will we do if ______________________________.

6 If it rains, they ______________________________.

7 If they go the cinema, Tina ______________________________.

8 Tim doesn't know if there ______________________________.

9 If they watch a scary film, Tina ______________________________.

10 Tim will sit close to Tina if she ______________________________.

125 Mia's new boyfriend

Listen to the girls talking about Mia's new boyfriend and choose true or false.

		True	False
1	The girls have not seen each other for a long time.	☐	☐
2	Anna has news about their friend Mia.	☐	☐
3	Jane has already heard the terrible news about Mia.	☐	☐
4	Anna says that Mia has fallen in love.	☐	☐
5	They met at a party and then went out for coffee together.	☐	☐
6	They have not been in close contact since the party.	☐	☐
7	Mia has had a boyfriend for seven months.	☐	☐
8	Anna has met Stan and she likes him.	☐	☐
9	Stan is nice and sweet to his girlfriend.	☐	☐
10	Jane is worried about Mia and mad at her.	☐	☐
11	Anna says that Mia is very happy now.	☐	☐

Üben

Üben

126 My favourite film

Listen to Iliana talking about her favourite film and do the tasks.

		True	False
1	Iliana's favourite film is about a woman who made a tour of Africa.	☐	☐
2	That summer, Donna fell in love with three different men.	☐	☐
3	Sophie owns a hotel on a Greek island.	☐	☐

4 Sophie is getting married and wants to know who her ______________________.

5 Sophie finds her mum's ______________________________________.

6 All three men show up at ____________________________________.

7 Sophie invites the men to her …
A birthday party **B** wedding **C** garden party

8 The girl decides that she does not want to know who her …
A husband is **B** grandfather is **C** father is

9 In the end, Sophie is glad to have …
A three men she can call 'Dad' **B** a wonderful husband **C** a Greek wedding

127 I am (not) allowed to …

Listen to the dialogue and complete the sentences.

1 Amy is allowed to ____________________________________.

2 George is not allowed to ______________________________.

3 George is allowed to __________________________________.

4 George is not allowed to ______________________________.

5 George is not allowed to ______________________________.

6 George is allowed to __________________________________.

7 Amy is not allowed to _________________________________.

128 Diane and Marco

Listen to the story about Diane and Marco and put the sentences into the correct order.

- [ ] They couldn't go a day without seeing each other.
- [ ] The two were together every day.
- [ ] They weren't able to spend an hour without thinking about the other person.
- [ ] The young lovers couldn't imagine life without each other.
- [ ] They weren't able to meet other friends without texting each other all the time.
- [1] Last year, Diane fell in love with a cute boy named Marco.
- [ ] They could tell each other everything.
- [ ] The two lovebirds sat on a bench in the park every afternoon.
- [ ] They couldn't sit side by side without touching each other.
- [ ] Diane and Marco talked on the phone for hours.
- [ ] They could look deep into each other's eyes for a very long time.

129 The future

Listen to Claudia and Thomas talking about the future and complete the sentences.

1 Thomas thinks in the future we will be able to have cars that ____________.

2 Claudia hopes that we will be able to ____________ with special wings.

3 Thomas also believes that we will be able to order food that drones*

____________.

4 Claudia says that we won't be able to ____________.

5 Thomas also thinks that we won't be able to ____________ because there won't be any parks anymore.

6 Claudia also believes that in the future we will be able to ____________.

7 Thomas asks if Claudia thinks we will be able to ____________ on the Moon.

8 Claudia thinks that we will be able to ____________ just for fun.

9 Thomas thinks in the future we won't be able to ____________.

10 Claudia says children will be able to ____________ from History books.

11 Thomas asks if Claudia thinks we will be able to ____________.

12 Claudia believes we will be able to ____________ in the future.

**drones* – Drohnen

Üben

130 What have you been up to?

Listen to the dialogue and fill in the missing words.

1 Lisa has been ________________ for a few weeks.
2 Lisa's aunt has been ________________ for a few weeks.
3 She has been ________________ with Lisa.
4 Lisa has been ________________ every day.
5 Lisa says it has been very nice ________________ with her aunt.
6 Merilyn has been ________________ music.
7 Merilyn has been ________________ every day.
8 Merilyn has ________________ songs.

131 Fire!

Listen to Julie talking about a fire and connect the sentence halves.

One day I was cooking	1	A	forgot about the pot on the stove.
They were happy because	2	B	'Fire! Fire!'
When they were finished,	3	C	I smelled smoke.
So I went upstairs and	4	D	they were enjoying the warm water.
I was looking at my phone when	5	E	they called me to come and help them.
Quickly I ran downstairs and	6	F	put out the fire.
I said to myself,	7	G	and my children were in the bathtub.
Next, I used the fire extinguisher	8	H	of the fire in my kitchen.
So I called the fire brigade and	9	I	but the fire didn't stop.
They came in five minutes and	10	J	said thank you to the brave firefighters.
We were safe now and the children and I	11	K	saw smoke in the kitchen.
That was the story	12	L	gave them my address.

132 Dilemmas

✱✱

Listen to the discussion about dilemmas and choose true or false.

		True	False
1	Zoey wants to talk to Marsha about dilemmas.	☐	☐
2	A dilemma is a situation where you always know just what to do.	☐	☐
3	Zoey tells Marsha a dilemma about a friend telling a secret.	☐	☐
4	Zoey gives examples of three different options.	☐	☐
5	Marsha thinks it is an easy situation and not really a dilemma.	☐	☐
6	Marsha would tell her friend that she must tell someone who can help her.	☐	☐
7	It would be a terrible problem for Marsha if her friend was angry at her.	☐	☐
8	Marsha has an idea for a possible dilemma situation for Zoey.	☐	☐
9	Marsha's dilemma situation is about lying for a friend.	☐	☐
10	Zoey would lie for her friend.	☐	☐
11	Zoey would tell her friend to talk to her mother, because that would help.	☐	☐

133 Into the wilderness

✱✱✱

Listen to the story about Alex and put the sentences into the correct order.

☐ Alex did not take a phone with him because nobody should know where he was.

☐ Many of them tried to help Alex, but he did not want their help.

[1] Alex had just finished school and he did not want to start working or have a 'normal' life.

☐ He bought books about how to survive in the wild and learned a lot about the wilderness.

☐ He was very thin because he hadn't eaten enough and he was very sick.

☐ The strange part is that Alex did not tell anyone about his plans.

☐ On the road, Alex met many different people.

☐ Soon he sold his car, packed a small bag with some clothes and food and left home.

☐ He was cold from sleeping on the ground and didn't know where he was or what day it was.

☐ So one day Alex decided that he wanted to go into the wilderness.

☐ He got on a train and then a bus and finally he walked north for a very long time.

☐ Soon his parents called the police because they did not know where their son was.

[14] That was the adventure of Alex in the wilderness.

☐ It took the police many months to finally find Alex deep in the wilderness.

Üben

READING – LESEÜBUNGEN

In diesem Kapitel kannst du das **Lesen** von englischen Texten üben. Am besten ist es, wenn du dir den **Text** immer **zweimal** durchliest, bevor du mit der dazugehörigen Übung beginnst. Mit Hilfe der Lösungen im Lösungsteil kannst du selbst überprüfen, ob du alles richtig gemacht hast.

Have fun!

How Kate became famous

134 ✱ *Read the text and tick true or false.* – Lies den Text und kreuze richtig oder falsch an.

Kate was always a great fan of Katy Perry. She loved her songs, her favourite one was "Never Really Over". Kate listened to it every day. The girl was so happy that her parents had named* her Kate.
Kate sang in the school choir and she hoped to become as good and famous as her role model one day.
One Monday morning, when Kate was on her way to school, she saw a big poster at the bus stop: "Are you good at singing? Prove your talent* and take part in our singing contest next Saturday. The winner will get a one-year contract with an international record label."
Of course, Kate was fascinated by* the advertisement and immediately* decided to take part. When she arrived at school, she said to her best friend Emily, "Guess what! There's going to be a singing contest next week. The winner will get a one-year contract with a record label." "Really? Are you going to take part?" her friend asked. "Of course! I am so excited!" "I'll keep my fingers crossed for you," Emily promised and smiled.

The following Saturday, Kate got up really early because she was so excited. She put on her coolest clothes and went to the local concert hall where the competition would take place*.
There were many people waiting outside. "Oh no, there are so many people. I hope they can't sing better than me," Kate thought. The stage was really big and there were many people in the auditorium*. Kate was nervous and her knees started shaking. Finally, it was her turn and she went on the stage. She wanted to sing her favourite song, "Never Really Over". The room fell silent and then the music started to play. When Kate heard the familiar tune*, she calmed down and started to sing. She was brilliant. Everyone was listening and some people even had tears in their eyes.
When Kate finished, there was complete silence for a moment ... then people started to clap their hands and cheer*. The applause lasted for at least five minutes. Kate felt so proud that tears were running down her cheeks.
At the end of the show, an elegant lady came onto the stage. She said, "I would like to thank all our young talents who gave their best today. But there can be only one winner, and the winner is ... KATE!!!" The audience started to cheer again. At first,

Kate could not believe it, but then her mum, who was sitting next to her, whispered, "Come on, darling! You must go up on stage, you are the winner."
For Kate, this was the beginning of an extraordinary* career.

**had named* – hatten ihr den Namen gegeben **prove your talent* – stelle dein Talent unter Beweis
**was fascinated by* – fasziniert von **immediately* – sofort **take place* – stattfinden
**auditorium* – Zuschauerraum **familiar tune* – bekannte Melodie **cheer* – jubeln
**extraordinary* – außergewöhnlich

		True	False
1	Kate always liked Katy Perry.	☒	☐
2	Kate was a member of the school band.	☐	☒
3	The winner of the singing contest gets 100,000 Pounds.	☐	☒
4	The concert took place at school.	☐	☒
5	Kate sang the song "Never Really Over".	☒	☐
6	People started to applaud after five minutes.	☐	☒

135 ✱✱ *Choose the correct answer.* – **Wähle die richtige Antwort aus.**

1 Kate sang in the school choir because …

A	she hoped to become as famous as her role model Katy Perry.	☒
B	she hoped to become as famous as her role model Adele.	☐
C	she wanted to practise for the contest.	☐

2 One Monday morning, when the girl was on her way to school, she saw …

A	a poster of her favourite band at the bus stop.	☐
B	a poster for a singing contest.	☒
C	a poster for a pop concert.	☐

3 On Saturday, Kate got up early because …

A	she was not tired.	☐
B	she was really excited.	☒
C	she did not want to miss the bus.	☐

4 When Kate heard the familiar tune, she …

A	started to cry.	☐
B	she calmed down and began to sing.	☒
C	she left the stage.	☐

Üben

136 ***

Answer the questions. – Beantworte die Fragen.

1 Who was Kate's favourite singer?

Katy Perry.

2 Why was Kate proud of her name?

it is imilar to Katy.

3 What did Kate decide to do when she saw the poster at the bus stop?

she decided to take part at the contest.

4 What did her best friend say to her?

I'll keep my fingers crossed.

5 Was Kate nervous when she started to sing?

no.

6 What did her mum say to her?

you are the winner, you have to go up the stage.

7 Who won the contest?

Kate.

A love story

137 **

Read the text and complete the sentences with no more than four words. – Vervollständige die Sätze! Verwende höchstens vier Wörter!

It was a beautiful summer day and Mary was sitting in her favourite café enjoying the sun and a cup of tea. Actually, the girl had to study for her next Maths test, but it was such a beautiful day and so she decided to study on the terrace by the river. Mary was really bad at Maths and she always had to study hard to get good marks.

Suddenly a young man stood in front of her and asked, "Excuse me, can I sit down next to you? I love the view of the river." Mary looked at him for a moment. She was not pleased* because she did not want to be disturbed*.

But the young man looked so friendly that she could not say no. They were sitting next to each other for a while, not talking at all. Suddenly the young man said, "Sorry to disturb you, but are you studying for your Maths test?" "Yes, I am," Mary answered and looked a bit surprised. "Indeed, there is going to be an important test tomorrow and I'm not really good at Maths," she said. "Oh, I see. I have the same problems with English. I just don't know how to write good essays. But I am very good at Maths, maybe I can help you. By the way, my name is Matthew." Mary smiled at him and answered," Oh, that's a good idea, and I can help you with English. I am the best essay writer in class. My name is Mary." They both shook hands and exchanged phone numbers.

The following month they met at the same café almost every day. After two months, they kissed for the first time and now they are very much in love.
By the way, Mary's Maths grades have improved* tremendously, and Matthew has even won a writing contest. How love can change things. …

**pleased* – erfreut   **did not want to be disturbed* – wollte nicht gestört werden
**improve* – verbessern

1 Mary ______________________________ her Maths test.

2 Mary did not ______________________________.

3 They were sitting next to each other, not ______________________________.

4 Mary and Matthew shook hands and ______________________________.

5 Matthew thought that he ______________________________ with Maths.

6 Mary said that she was ______________________________.

138 *

Tick true or false. – Kreuze richtig oder falsch an.

		True	False
1	Mary was sitting on a terrace by the sea.	☐	☐
2	Mary was bad at Maths.	☐	☐
3	An old man sat down next to her.	☐	☐
4	Matthew loved the view of the river.	☐	☐
5	Mary was not pleased at first.	☐	☐
6	The young man was called Mike.	☐	☐
7	He offered Kate to help her with Maths.	☐	☐
8	They exchanged email addresses.	☐	☐
9	Matthew's Maths grades have improved.	☐	☐
10	Now they are in love.	☐	☐

Üben

139 ✱✱✱ *Answer the questions in complete sentences.* – Beantworte die Fragen in ganzen Sätzen.

1 Why did Mary decide to study on the terrace of her favourite café?

______________________________.

2 What did the young man want from her?

______________________________.

3 Why was Mary not pleased at first?

______________________________.

4 What did Matthew suggest*?

______________________________.

5 What was Matthew not good at?

______________________________.

6 What did Mary suggest?

______________________________.

7 Where did they always meet?

______________________________.

8 When was their first kiss?

______________________________.

**suggest* – vorschlagen

A holiday adventure

140 ✱ *Read Julia's report and tick true or false.* – Lies Julias Bericht und kreuze richtig oder falsch an.

My most exciting trip ever was to Rome. My whole family went there by car. My younger brother Steven was really excited because it was the first time he had been to Italy. It took us about 14 hours to get there, but thanks to my parents it never got boring. We left late in the evening, so that we could sleep most of the time. The rest of the journey, we played games in the car.
When we arrived, we first went to our hotel to check in. It was a really nice building, not far from the famous Colosseum. Unfortunately, there was no lift*, so we had to carry all our luggage upstairs. But the rooms were really big, and the view of the city was spectacular.
On the first day, we did not do much, because we were really tired from the long drive.

On the second day, we got up quite early and had breakfast. When we left the hotel, my dad said that he just wanted to get his jacket from the car. The rest of us waited in front of the hotel. When my dad finally came back, he looked really angry. "What's wrong, darling?" my mum asked. "You won't believe it," he answered excitedly. "Our car is gone! We have to call the police!" "Oh no!" Mum shouted. She turned pale* and looked really worried. I was surprised because our car was old and I could not imagine that anyone would steal it. In the meantime, my parents had gone* to the receptionist and asked him to call the police. My brother started to cry because he thought that we would never get home without a car, so I tried to comfort* him.
After about an hour, two police cars stopped in front of our hotel and a man and a woman with sunglasses got out. They looked really cool, like actors in a Hollywood movie. "Can you tell us where you parked your car?" the policeman asked. "Yes, of course, in Via dei Serpenti," Dad answered. "It's a blue Ford." "Okay," the police officers said, "We'll try to find your car."
After five minutes they returned. We were a bit surprised because we had not expected* them to come back so quickly. The policeman smiled at us and said, "We have found your car, sir, but not in Via dei Serpenti. It was in Via dei Clementi. But don't worry, a lot of tourists confuse these two streets."
At first, we could not say anything, but then we started laughing and did not stop for at least ten minutes.
The rest of the holidays were great … although my dad got lost from time to time. He just could not remember the street names!

**lift* – Lift **turned pale* – wurde blass **had gone* – waren gegangen
**comfort* – trösten **had not expected* – hatten nicht erwartet

		True	False
1	The whole family went to Rome by car.	☐	☐
2	It was the second time Steven went to Italy.	☐	☐
3	The journey was boring.	☐	☐
4	The hotel was close to the Colosseum.	☐	☐
5	On the first day, they did a lot of sightseeing.	☐	☐
6	Their dad wanted to get his jacket from the car.	☐	☐
7	Their car was a new SEAT.	☐	☐
8	Julia's brother was sad because he thought he would never get home.	☐	☐
9	The police did not find their car.	☐	☐
10	Their dad never got lost.	☐	☐

Üben

141 Complete the sentences. – Vervollständige die Sätze.

✱✱

1 Steven was really excited because ______________________________.

2 The journey was not boring because ______________________________.

3 They liked the rooms because ______________________________.

4 Dad went to the car because ______________________________.

5 Dad looked really angry because ______________________________.

6 The receptionist ______________________________.

7 The police officers looked ______________________________.

8 They thought that their car was parked ______________________________.

9 The family were surprised because the police officers ______________________________.

10 The policeman smiled because ______________________________.

142 Answer the questions in complete sentences. – Beantworte die Fragen in ganzen Sätzen.

✱✱✱

1 How many hours did it take them to get to Rome?

______________________________.

2 What did the children do during the journey?

______________________________.

3 Why did they have to carry their luggage?

______________________________.

4 What happened to their car?

______________________________.

5 What did the parents do then?

______________________________.

6 What did the two police officers want to know?

______________________________.

7 What did the policeman say when he came back?

______________________________.

8 Why did their dad not find the car?

______________________________.

Dangerous animals in the desert

143 ** *Tick the correct sentences.* – Kreuze die richtigen Sätze an.

It was early in the morning when Paul decided to go for a walk. He was spending his holidays with his parents in Morocco. Their hotel was very nice, surrounded by a beautiful garden with lots of exotic plants and flowers. Paul already felt a little bored and so he decided to explore the surrounding area. His parents said he should not leave the area because there were a lot of dangerous animals in the desert. So the boy pretended* to have a headache and waited until they were at the beach. He ran along the corridors of the hotel, and when he reached the garden, he first looked left, then right, to check if his parents were really gone. He waited until the coast was clear* and left the garden through the big gate.

As far as he could see, there was only desert in front of him. The sun was shining brightly from the sky and the sand was glittering. "Let's find out where all the dangerous animals are," Paul thought excitedly and started to follow the small path from the hotel into the desert. After a while, the boy felt thirsty, but his water bottle was in the hotel room. At first, he thought that he should go back to the hotel, but then he saw some palm trees in the distance. "This must be an oasis* and there must be water, too," the boy thought happily and decided to go on. After about ten minutes, he had not got any closer to the palm trees and he felt really weak and thirsty. Suddenly he stepped on something, and then he felt terrible pain. When he looked down, he saw that it was a scorpion. "Oh my God!" Paul screamed. He started to panic and immediately* felt dizzy*. Before he fainted*, he thought, "My parents were right. There are dangerous animals in the desert."

When he came to*, he saw two men looking down at him. "Are you okay, boy?" one of them asked. He had a long, dark beard and was wearing a turban. "I'm not sure, I think a scorpion bit me," Paul answered. "Let me see," the second man said and looked at the wound on Paul's leg. The two men said something to each other in a strange language Paul did not understand, and then the first man turned to him and said, "Don't worry, young man! You'll be fine soon. This kind of scorpion is not really dangerous. Its poison cannot kill you, it just makes you feel sick for a while. Drink some water first and then we will take you home." He gave him a bottle of water. "Thank you!" Paul answered and quickly gulped down* the water. Immediately he felt better. Luckily, the two men had a car and drove him back to the hotel. "Be careful next time you go into the desert!" his rescuers* warned him when they left.

When Paul was in his room again, he thought, "Thank God, my parents haven't noticed anything. Next time I will listen to them." Then he fell asleep.

**pretended* – vortäuschen   **until the coast was clear* – bis die Luft rein war   **oasis* – Oase
**immediately* – sofort   **dizzy* – schwindelig   **faint* – in Ohnmacht fallen
**come to* – wieder zu sich kommen   **gulp down* – hinunterschlucken
**rescuer* – Retter

Bitte umblättern! ↺

Üben

Üben

1 Paul wanted to explore the desert because …

A	he felt bored.	☐
B	he wanted to find his parents.	☐
C	he wanted to see exotic plants.	☐

2 When Paul noticed that he had no water with him …

A	he went back to the hotel.	☐
B	he phoned his parents.	☐
C	he decided to go on.	☐

3 When Paul stepped on something, he noticed that …

A	it was a piece of wood.	☐
B	it was a snake.	☐
C	it was a scorpion.	☐

4 Before Paul fainted, he thought …

A	that his parents were right.	☐
B	that he would not survive.	☐
C	that he would never get back to the hotel.	☐

5 The man said to him that …

A	this kind of scorpion was very dangerous.	☐
B	this kind of scorpion was not really dangerous.	☐
C	it was really a snake.	☐

144 *Tick true or false.* – Kreuze richtig oder falsch an.

*

		True	False
1	Paul spent his holidays at a campsite in Morocco.	☐	☐
2	Paul did not tell his parents that he wanted to explore the desert.	☐	☐
3	When Paul left the hotel, he met his parents.	☐	☐
4	In the distance, he suddenly saw an oasis.	☐	☐
5	When the scorpion bit him, he felt terrible pain.	☐	☐
6	When Paul woke up, he saw a man and a woman.	☐	☐
7	The men promised to take him back to the hotel.	☐	☐
8	Paul's parents were already waiting for him when he came back.	☐	☐
9	Paul thought that next time he would listen to his parents.	☐	☐

145 ✱✱✱ *Complete the sentences. Do not use more than four words.* – Vervollständige die Sätze. Verwende nicht mehr als vier Wörter.

1 Paul's hotel was surrounded ______________________.

2 His parents thought that there were ______________________ desert.

3 Paul pretended to ______________________.

4 Paul did not go back to the hotel because he saw ______________________ in the distance.

5 One of the men who found him said that the ______________________.

6 When Paul was back in his room, he was ______________________.

Save our school library!

146 *Tick true or false.* – Kreuze richtig oder falsch an.

✱

In the classroom:

Caro: Hi Barbara! Have you heard about our school library?
Barbara: No! What's the matter?
Caro: The headmaster wants to close it because he needs more classrooms.
Barbara: Really? I can't believe it. But where can we spend our breaks and where can we borrow all the books?
Caro: The headmaster says that most students prefer e-books today and that we do not need a library at school anymore.
Barbara: I can't believe it! Does Mrs Simmons already know about this?
Caro: I think so, but I'm afraid she can't do anything about it.
Barbara: All my friends go to the library … we must do something!
Caro: But what?
Barbara: Let's go and organise a meeting and inform the other students.

At the meeting:

Caro: Thanks for coming! I don't know if you've already heard that the headmaster wants to close the school library.
Boy 1: What? This is terrible! How can he do that, we need the library!
Girl 1: What cheek!* We have to do something!
Boy 2: Yes, let's organise a protest march!
Girl 2: We could also start a petition on Instagram.
Boy 3: And I could write an article for the school magazine.
Barbara: That sounds great! I think we've got many brilliant ideas now. Maybe we should get into groups. One group organises the protest march, one prepares the petition and the third group writes the article for the school magazine.
Caro: Good idea! Let's start! We don't have much time.

A few days later in front of the school:

Pupils: Save our school library! We need it! Save our library!
Barbara: Wow! I did not expect so many people!
Caro: And the petition on Instagram has already got a 1,000 likes. That's a real success.
Barbara: Let's hope the headmaster will change his mind.
Caro: Oh look! The headmaster is coming!
Headmaster: Dear students! I am really impressed by your commitment* and I've got good news for you. I don't have to close the school library because we'll get an additional* building with enough space for new classrooms.

All the pupils are applauding.

Barbara: That's so cool!
Caro: I can't believe it. We did it!
Mrs Simmons: Thank you so much for your help!

**cheek* – Frechheit   **commitment* – Einsatz   **additional* – zusätzlich

Üben

		True	False
1	The headmaster wants to close the library because it is too expensive.	☐	☐
2	Barbara doesn't know that the library might be closed.	☐	☐
3	Barbara wants to organise a meeting to inform the teachers.	☐	☐
4	Girl 2 wants to start a petition.	☐	☐
5	Boy 3 wants to organise a protest march.	☐	☐
6	Barbara says they should get into groups.	☐	☐
7	Only a few people come to the protest march.	☐	☐
8	The headmaster doesn't have to close the library.	☐	☐

147 ✱✱✱ *Answer the questions in complete sentences.* – Beantworte die Fragen in ganzen Sätzen.

1 Why is Barbara so upset?

______________________________.

2 Why does the headmaster want to close the library?

______________________________.

3 Does Mrs Simmons know about the headmaster's plans?

______________________________.

4 What do Barbara and Caro decide to do?

______________________________.

5 What does the first group do?

______________________________.

6 What does the second group do?

______________________________.

7 What does the third group do?

______________________________.

8 Why is the library not closed in the end?

______________________________.

9 Do you think that a school library is still important?

______________________________.

10 Is there anything at your school you would protest against?

______________________________.

Üben

WRITING – SCHREIBÜBUNGEN

In diesem Kapitel kannst du ausprobieren, welche **Texte** du bereits **schreiben** kannst. Im **Lösungsteil** findest du zu jeder Aufgabe einen **Mustertext**, mit dem du deinen eigenen vergleichen kannst.

Viel Spaß beim Verfassen deiner englischen Texte!

148 **Dialogue about a pop concert**

* *

Write a dialogue between you and a friend about a pop concert you once visited. Write about 150 words. – Schreibe einen Dialog zwischen dir und einer Freundin/einem Freund, in dem du von einem Popkonzert erzählst, das du einmal besucht hast. Schreibe ca. 150 Wörter.

Write about:

- *which concert you went to*
- *what was good/what was not so good about the concert*
- *who you went with*

TIPP

Falls du schon einmal bei einem Popkonzert warst, kannst du natürlich darüber berichten. Ansonsten überlege dir, welchen Popstar du gerne einmal live sehen würdest.
Vergiss nicht darauf, deine Freundin/deinen Freund am Anfang zu begrüßen und am Schluss zu verabschieden.

149 ✱✱ **Email about my worst school trip**

Imagine that you are on a school trip with your class and it was the worst trip you ever took part in. Now you write an email to your parents. Write about 100 words. – Stelle dir vor, du bist mit deiner Klasse auf einem mehrtägigen Ausflug, welcher der schlimmste ist, den du jemals erlebt hast. Schreibe ein E-Mail an deine Eltern. Schreibe ca. 100 Wörter.

Write about:

- *where you are*
- *what the problems are*
- *what you don't like*

TIPP

Vergiss nicht darauf, generell im **Präsens** (in der Gegenwart) zu schreiben, da du dich ja noch auf diesem Ausflug befindest.

Üben

150 ✱✱✱ **Article about London**

You have recently been to London, so your English teacher asks you to write a short article about your favourite sights for your school magazine. Find a catchy title! Write about 150–180 words. – Da du vor kurzem in London warst, fragt dich deine Englischlehrerin/dein Englischlehrer, ob du einen Text über deine Lieblingssehenswürdigkeiten schreiben kannst. Finde einen interessanten Titel! Schreibe etwa 150–180 Wörter.

Write about:

- *the sights you saw*
- *the sights you liked best*
- *what you liked about them*
- *what you would recommend* doing there*

**what you would recommend* – was du empfehlen würdest

TIPP

Wähle **zwei bis drei Sehenswürdigkeiten** aus, die dir besonders gut gefallen. Versuche deinen Text interessant zu gestalten, indem du deine **Leserinnen und Leser direkt ansprichst** und möglichst viele **Adjektive** (Eigenschaftswörter) verwendest!

151 Dialogue about superstitions

**

Write a dialogue between a boy and a girl about superstitions. Write about 110 words. – Schreibe einen Dialog, in dem ein Bub und ein Mädchen über Aberglauben sprechen. Schreibe ca. 110 Wörter.

You can start like this:

Girl: *Hi, Jacob! How are you?*
Boy: *Hi, Julie! I'm fine. What's this? A new book?*
Girl: *Yes, it's really interesting. It's about superstitions from all over the world …*

TIPP

Besonders interessant wird dein Dialog, wenn du verschiedene abergläubische Gebräuche im Internet recherchierst! Verwende ***if-sentences*** *(if you see …, then you'll …)*

152 *

Text on rules

Write a short text about rules at your home. Write what you are (not) allowed to do. Write between 60 and 100 words. – Schreibe einen kurzen Text über die Regeln bei dir zu Hause. Schreibe, was du (nicht) tun darfst. Schreibe zwischen 60 und 100 Wörter.

Write about:

- *two things you are allowed to do*
- *two things you are not allowed to do*
- *which rules you think are good or bad*
- *which rules you would change*

TIPP

In jeder Familie gibt es Regeln, die eingehalten werden müssen – bestimmt auch in deiner! Beschreibe sie kurz!

153 ✱ ✱ **Designing a leaflet**

Remember the dialogue on page 112 about closing the school library. Design a leaflet with arguments against it. – Erinnere dich an den Dialog von Seite 112, in dem es um die Schließung der Schulbibliothek geht. Entwirf ein Flugblatt, in dem du Argumente gegen die Schließung anführst.

You should:

- *find an interesting slogan*
- *inform about the problem*
- *find good arguments for leaving the library open*
- *say what you are going to do to change the situation*

TIPP

Verwende **kurze Sätze**, vor allem **Aufforderungssätze**! Überlege dir ein passendes **Layout**! Du kannst dein Flugblatt auch am Computer schreiben und **interessante Bilder** einfügen. Wichtig ist, dass du die **Aufmerksamkeit** der Leserinnen und Leser gewinnst.

154 ✱✱✱ **Email from California**

Imagine you are spending your holidays in California. Write an email to a friend. Write about 120–160 words. – Stelle dir vor, du verbringst deine Ferien in Kalifornien. Schreibe ein E-Mail an deine Freundin/deinen Freund. Schreibe 120–160 Wörter.

In your email you should say …

- *where you are*
- *who is with you*
- *how long you are staying*
- *what you have already done / seen*
- *what you are going to do / see*
- *what you like / don't like about California*

TIPP

Erzähle, welche Plätze du bereits gesehen hast und welche dich besonders beeindruckt haben.

Üben

155 ***

Description of an accident

Imagine you had a bike accident. Write a story about it. Use past tense! Write about 280 words. – Stelle dir vor, du hattest einen Radunfall. Schreibe eine Geschichte darüber. Erzähle im Präteritum (Mitvergangenheit). Schreibe etwa 280 Wörter.

You should say:

- *where you were*
- *why the accident happened*
- *if you were hurt*
- *who helped you*

TIPP

Versuche eine **interessante** und **dramatische Geschichte** zu erzählen. Baue **direkte Reden** ein und beschreibe deine **Gefühle**. Gliedere deine Geschichte in **Einleitung**, **Hauptteil** und **Schluss**. Mache dazwischen jeweils einen **Absatz**.

156 Invitation

*

You have been invited by a friend who lives in London to stay with her / him. You send her / him an email to ask for information. Write about 60–80 words. – Eine Freundin / ein Freund von dir, die / der in London lebt, hat dich eingeladen, bei ihr / ihm zu bleiben. Du schreibst ihr / ihm ein E-Mail, um mehr Informationen zu bekommen. Schreibe etwa 60–80 Wörter.

You should ask:

- *where she / he lives*
- *what type of house it is*
- *what you should pack*

TIPP

Am **Beginn** deines E-Mails **bedanke** dich für die Einladung und **verabschiede** dich am **Schluss**.

157 ✱ **Dialogue on asking for help**

Write a dialogue in which a friend asks you to help her / him with her / his English homework. Write about 60–90 words. – Du schreibst einen Dialog, in welchem eine Freundin / ein Freund dich darum bittet, ihr / ihm bei der Englisch-Hausübung zu helfen. Schreibe etwa 60–90 Wörter.

You can start like this:

A: *Hi, Andy! How are you?*
B: *Not very good, to be honest.*
A: *Oh no! What's the matter?*
B: *I have to write this really difficult English essay …*

TIPP

Versetze dich in die Lage deiner Freundin / deines Freundes und überlege, wie du sie / ihn **aufmuntern** und ihr / ihm **helfen** könntest.

158 ✱✱ **A recommendation**

You have just been to a new restaurant you really liked. Now you write an email to a friend recommending the restaurant. Write about 80–100 words. – Du hast vor kurzem ein Restaurant besucht, das dir sehr gut gefallen hat. Nun schreibst du ein E-Mail an eine Freundin/einen Freund und empfiehlst ihr/ihm dieses Restaurant. Schreibe ca. 80–100 Wörter.

You should mention:

- *what kind of restaurant it is*
- *what was great about it*
- *what you ate*
- *who went with you*

TIPP

Am besten schreibst du über ein Restaurant, das du wirklich gerne magst.

TESTS – SCHULARBEITEN

Nun kannst du zeigen, was du schon alles gelernt hast. Nimm dir für jeden Test ca. **30 bis 50 Minuten Zeit** und versuche, konzentriert und ohne Hilfe zu arbeiten. Wenn du fertig bist, kannst du deine Antworten mit den Lösungen im Lösungsteil vergleichen!

Good luck!

A *Test 1* – Schularbeit 1

Teststoff	
Listening	Morning madness in the classroom
Reading	The 'Donauinselfest'
Grammar	Present simple or past simple, what the people do and don't do, past continuous, after/before/when/during/while/until/by the time, as … as or not as … as
Writing	Text about a favourite pop star

Listening Comprehension – Morning madness in the classroom

159 Listen to Joelle talking about what was happening when she came into the classroom and fill in the past progressive forms.

/ 10 Punkte

1 Tom ______________ a piece of paper into the trash.

2 Gina ______________ on her phone.

3 Mel ______________ at Lucy.

4 Lucy ______________.

5 My best friend ______________ at me.

6 Jim ______________ out my name.

7 A girl in the front ______________ a book.

8 Tom ______________ a song.

9 Two boys ______________ to music on their phones.

10 I ______________ about leaving the classroom and going home.

Reading Comprehension – The "Donauinselfest"

Read the text.

The 'Donauinselfest' is a free open-air music festival taking place every June at the Donauinsel in Vienna. It is hosted by the Social Democratic Party. With over three million visitors in three days, it's the biggest open-air music festival in the world.
Performances take place on eleven different open-air stages and in 16 tents around the island. Local bands and DJs as well as many world-famous artists have performed there since 1984.
There are areas which are usually sponsored by radio stations, newspapers and other companies. Musicians of various genres perform there.
The festival first took place in 1983 and was organised by Harry Kopletz, an SPÖ politician, in order to make the Donauinsel more popular. The organizers expected about 15,000 visitors, but around 160,000 turned up. Since then, the 'Donauinselfest' has taken place every year at the end of June.

160 Tick true or false. / 4 Punkte

		True	False
1	The 'Donauinselfest' takes place every July.	☐	☐
2	There a performances on eleven open-air stages.	☐	☐
3	It first took place in 1982.	☐	☐
4	You can listen to various genres of music there.	☐	☐

161 Answer the questions in complete sentences. / 4 Punkte

1 How many people visit the 'Donauinselfest' every year?

______________________________.

2 When did the festival first take place?

______________________________.

3 How many stages are there?

______________________________.

4 How long does the festival last?

______________________________.

Grammar

162 Present simple or past simple? Complete the sentences with the verbs from the box.

/ 6 Punkte

be ▪ cannot ▪ check ▪ help ▪ keep ▪ look
need ▪ not be ▪ not find ▪ put
remember ▪ tell

This morning I _______________ for my bus pass everywhere, but I _______________ find it. I usually _______________ it in my school bag because I _______________ it every day on my way to and from school. But when I _______________ the bag this morning, the bus pass _______________ there. I _______________ my mum, and she _______________ me to look for it, but we _______________ it. But then I _______________ – I sometimes _______________ it in my jeans pocket after I've shown it to the driver. So I looked there, and there it _______________!

163 Say what the people do *(+)* and don't do *(–)*.

/ 8 Punkte

Felix ▪ play ▪ with cars (+) ▪ with dolls (–)
Felix plays with cars. He doesn't play with dolls.

1 Max ▪ like ▪ ice cream *(+)* ▪ chocolate cake *(–)*

____

2 all my friends ▪ listen ▪ to rock music *(+)* ▪ to folk music *(–)*

____

3 for breakfast ▪ we ▪ have ▪ tea and toast *(+)* ▪ ham and eggs *(–)*

____

4 in the morning, ▪ Dad ▪ drive to work *(+)* ▪ take the bus *(–)*

____

164 Complete the sentences with the past continuous form of the verbs in brackets.

/ 7 Punkte

1 When I came home from school today, my mum *(prepare)* ______________ lunch.
2 When we left the house this morning, the sun *(shine)* ______________.
3 When I took a photo of Emily and Sophie, they *(smile)* ______________.
4 While the boys *(wait)* ______________ for the bus, it started raining.
5 Ben and I *(watch)* ______________ TV when Ben's phone suddenly rang.
6 At the concert last night, Susan and Tom *(sing)* ______________ and Brian *(play)* ______________ the piano.

165 Complete the sentences with after/before/when/during/while/until/by the time so that *(a)* and *(b)* mean the same.

/ 7 Punkte

1 *(a)* Dad comes home from work. He watches the news on TV.
(b) __________ Dad comes home from work, he watches the news on TV.
2 *(a)* At weekends, my brother and I play games. We stop at midnight.
(b) At weekends, my brother and I play games __________ midnight.
3 *(a)* We got to the train station. Our train was gone.
(b) __________ we got to the train station, our train was gone.
4 *(a)* They showed two or three trailers. Then the real movie began.
(b) They showed two or three trailers __________ the real movie began.
5 *(a)* Julia and James were dancing. Then the lights went out.
(b) Julia and James were dancing __________ the lights went out.
6 *(a)* Somebody ate my sandwich. I was talking to a friend.
(b) Somebody ate my sandwich __________ I was talking to a friend.
7 *(a)* My parents stayed at a castle in Scotland. They saw a ghost
(b) My parents saw a ghost __________ their stay at a castle in Scotland.

166 Compare the people and things with as … as or not as … as. / 4 Punkte

1 our flat, 4 rooms ▪ Brenda's flat, 2 rooms ▪ big

Brenda's flat ______________________________.

2 Barbara, 1.35 m ▪ Jimmy, 1.35 m ▪ tall

Barbara ______________________________.

3 air ▪ wood ▪ heavy

Air ______________________________.

4 Patrick, only 'A's ▪ Michael, only 'A's ▪ clever

Patrick ______________________________.

Writing

167 Write a text about your favourite pop star. Write about 120–140 words. / 7 Punkte

Write about:

- *who your favourite pop star is*
- *what your favourite songs are*
- *if you have ever been to one of his / her concerts*
- *what you like about him / her*

____

____

____

____

____

____

____

____

____

Bewertung	
52 bis 57 Punkte	Sehr gut
46 bis 51 Punkte	Gut
40 bis 45 Punkte	Befriedigend
unter 40 Punkte	Wiederhole die Stoffgebiete noch einmal, bei denen du die wenigsten Punkte erreicht hast.

/ 57 Punkte
GESAMT

Üben

B *Test 2* – Schularbeit 2

Teststoff	
Listening	New neighbour
Reading	Nora, the crazy inventor
Grammar	who or which, 1st conditional, present perfect and for or since, present perfect or past simple
Writing	A text about your best friend

Listening Comprehension – New neighbour

168 Listen to Lorna describing the neighbours to the new neighbour and fill in the present perfect forms.

/ 10 Punkte

Hello, Susie. Welcome to the neighbourhood. I know you

______________________ here very long but I hope you'll feel

at home very soon. We ______________________ here for about ten years, so I can tell you everything about our neighbours.

Mrs Jason ______________________ on this street for ever. She is a very sweet old lady. She always gives me candy when I visit her and I'm sure you will quickly learn to like her. She is nice

to everybody and ______________________ a very friendly person.

Mr James, who lives just down the street,

______________________ to have a beautiful garden since I've known him. Make sure you do not step on his lawn or trample his flowers or else he will get very mad.

I ______________________ a ball into his garden before and I don't want to or else he won't give it back.

Mr Johnson, who lives at the end of the street, is always in a bad

mood. I ______________________ him smile! I don't think he even knows how to smile. I always try to walk on the other side of the street to avoid his house.

Ms Jakelyn is a very active person. She ______________________ jogging in the morning for as long as I can remember. I often go

jogging with her at weekends. She ______________________

for as long as I ______________________ her.

Reading Comprehension – Nora, the crazy inventor

Read the story.

Nora was a very clever woman and she had an unusual hobby. She always invented new things and earned a lot of money. This time she invented a camera which did not only make you 20 years younger, but also prettier and slimmer*.

When she was done, she invited all her friends to show them her brilliant new invention. She decorated her house, prepared snacks and drinks and was really excited. "Thank you for coming, my dear friends! Today I'm going to present you my new camera which automatically turns you into the most beautiful woman in the world," she announced proudly when they were all assembled* in the living room. "Wow, that sounds great!" Anne, one of her friends, said and applauded loudly. "I can't wait to try it out," another woman shouted. "Who wants to be first?" Nora asked. Corina, her boss, put her hand up. Nora got a little nervous because she knew that her boss was a very critical woman and could easily get angry. Corina was wearing an elegant dress and she looked really pretty. Nora took the camera and pressed the green button. Then she had to wait a minute. There was complete silence, then she hesitantly looked at the display of her camera. Nora turned pale, she looked really horrified. "What's up?" Corina wanted to know. "Show me the picture!" She grabbed the camera and blushed*. "Oh no! I look like a monster!" she screamed. "You are fired!"

**slimmer* – schlanker   **assembled* – versammelt   **blush* – rot werden

Üben

169 Tick true or false.

/ 5 Punkte

		True	False
1	Nora was a clever woman.	☐	☐
2	One day she invented a new mobile phone.	☐	☐
3	Nora invited her whole family to show them her new invention.	☐	☐
4	Nora took a photo of Corina, her boss.	☐	☐
5	Nora's invention was a real success.	☐	☐

170 Answer the questions in complete sentences.

/ 4 Punkte

1 What did Nora invent one day?

____.

2 Why did Nora get nervous?

____.

3 Why did Nora turn pale when she looked at the camera?

____.

4 How did her boss react when she saw the picture?

____.

Grammar

171 'who' or 'which'? Match the sentence halves. / 8 Punkte

There's only one boy in my class	1		A	who are polite and helpful.
Where are the oranges	2		B	which comes from Spain.
Mum likes people	3		C	who can run faster than me.
This is the shop	4		D	who want to visit the castle.
These are the tourists	5		E	which we bought yesterday?
Mr Black drinks only wine	6		F	who makes bread and buns.
That's the book	7		G	which sells the coolest clothes.
A baker is a person	8		H	which we must read for school.

172 1st Conditional: Fill in the correct form of the verbs in brackets. / 8 Punkte

1 If you *(be)* ______________ nice to others, they *(be)* ____________________ nice to you.

2 Nothing *(happen)* _________________________ if you *(do)* ______________ what I say.

3 If we *(not go)* ______________ now, we *(miss)* ______________ our bus.

4 If I *(tell)* ______________ you the whole story, you *(not like)* _________________________ it.

5 You *(catch)* ______________ cold unless you *(put on)* ______________ a sweater.

6 Unless you *(try on)* ______________ these jeans, you *(not know)* _________________________ if they fit you.

7 Nobody *(leave)* ____________________ the room if it *(not stop)* _________________________ raining.

8 This smell *(not go)* ____________________ away unless you *(open)* ______________ the windows.

173 Complete the sentences in present perfect and circle for or since. / 6 Punkte

1 This picture *(be)* ______________ in our family *for / since* many years.

2 Martin and Ellie *(know)* ______________ each other *for / since* they were children.

3 Dad *(have)* ______________ his computer *for / since* before I was born.

4 I *(not speak)* ______________ with Cathrine *for / since* two months.

5 My team *(not win)* ______________ a game *for / since* the beginning of the season.

6 Alex and I *(build)* ______________ two model planes *for / since* his birthday.

174 Present perfect or past simple? Fill in the correct form of the verbs in brackets. / 8 Punkte

1 Look, I *(buy)* ________________ new sunglasses. I *(lose)* ________________ my old ones during the summer holidays.

2 Dora *(go)* ________________ shopping an hour ago, but she *(not return)* ________________ yet.

3 Grandma *(give)* ________________ me three DVDs for Christmas, and I *(already, watch)* ________________ two.

4 Gina *(send)* ________________ me five emails yesterday, but I *(not answer)* ________________ them yet.

Üben

Writing

175 Write a text about your best friend. Write about 120–140 words. / 8 Punkte

Include the following:

- *tell your friend's name*
- *mention for how long you have known each other*
- *what you do together*
- *what makes him / her special*

TIPP

Du kannst auch den Tag eurer ersten Begegnung beschreiben.

Bewertung	
52 bis 57 Punkte	Sehr gut
46 bis 51 Punkte	Gut
40 bis 45 Punkte	Befriedigend
unter 40 Punkte	Wiederhole die Stoffgebiete noch einmal, bei denen du die wenigsten Punkte erreicht hast.

/ 57 Punkte
GESAMT

C Test 3 – Schularbeit 3

Teststoff	
Listening	The Mennonites
Reading	Text on Tobias
Grammar	(not) allowed to/can/can't, let, (not) be able to, present perfect continuous
Writing	Dialogue about a holiday in California

Listening Comprehension – The Mennonites

176 Listen to the facts on the Mennonites and connect the sentence halves.

/ 9 Punkte

The Mennonites are a religious group	1	A	electricity, machines or telephones.
He claimed* it is important to	2	B	choose to become a part of the group for ever.
Mennonites live without	3	C	and talking with friends and family.
They live in houses which they build themselves*	4	D	they make their final decision.
They spend much time praying	5	E	and the men work in the fields or build houses.
In a Mennonite family, the women cook and clean	6	F	into the world to do anything they want to do.
The system is old-fashioned but	7	G	that was founded by Menno Simons.
When the children are old enough, they can	8	H	and eat food which they make themselves*.
But first they leave for a while and go out	9	I	many young people decide to stay with the group.
This is called 'rumspringa' and when they come back,	10	J	concentrate on family, faith and friends.

**claim* – behaupten **themselves* – (sie) selbst

Reading Comprehension

Read the text.

Hi! I'm Tobias and I live in Wiener Neustadt, which is a town in Lower Austria*. The population of Wiener Neustadt is about 50,000, which is a lot for Austria.
I live in an old house with a small garden together with my mum, my sister Linda and my dog Maya. My parents are divorced, and my dad lives with his girlfriend not far from us.
I like Wiener Neustadt, because it is a wonderful town and you can do a lot of things there. There is a cinema, a bowling centre and many shops and good restaurants. The only thing I miss is a public swimming pool.
My mum is not very strict, and I am allowed to do many things. For example, I can go out and meet friends whenever I want to. I only have to tell her where I am going and who I am spending time with. Since I have a big room, I usually invite many friends to my place. Then we watch TV together, play computer games or just talk. As long as we are not too loud, I am also allowed to play music. In the summer, I often have a barbecue in our garden. I love steaks and sausages! The only thing that is important to my mum is that I walk our dog every second day and that I unload the dishwasher twice a week. But I think that's fair!
My school, which is a grammar school*, is also in Wiener Neustadt.
I like my school because the teachers are very relaxed and there are not many rules we have to follow. We are allowed to drink during the lessons and the teachers do not mind if we are sometimes late in the morning. There are only two things we should never do: cheat and talk back to the teachers!

**Lower Austria* – Niederösterreich   **grammar school* – Gymnasium

177 Tick true or false. / 3 Punkte

		True	False
1	Tobias lives in Wiener Neustadt.	☐	☐
2	This is a very small town in Lower Austria.	☐	☐
3	The only thing Tobias misses about Wiener Neustadt is a cinema.	☐	☐

178 Choose the correct answer. / 3 Punkte

1 The population of Wiener Neustadt is about
☐ 50,000 ☐ 30,000 ☐ 25,000

2 In Wiener Neustadt there is
☐ a theatre. ☐ a cinema. ☐ a university.

3 Tobias is allowed to
☐ smoke. ☐ watch horror movies. ☐ go out and meet friends.

179 Answer the questions in complete sentences. / 3 Punkte

1 Why does Tobias like Wiener Neustadt?

____.

2 What is important to Tobias' mum?

____.

3 What are the two rules in Tobias' school?

____.

Grammar

180 Use allowed to or not allowed to instead of can or cannot/can't. / 4 Punkte

1 You cannot smoke in a restaurant.

____.

2 Children can bring their toys to school.

____.

3 Nobody can leave the room during a test.

____.

4 You can't park your car here.

____.

181 Use let and the correct form of the verbs in brackets to complete the sentences. / 6 Punkte

> Dad sometimes **(me, drive) lets me drive** his car.

1 My sister never *(me, wear)* ____________________ her T-shirts.

2 They *(us, not see)* ____________________ the photos because they were terrible.

3 In the holidays my parents *(me, stay up)* ____________________ late.

4 The police *(the men, not go)* ____________________ after the fight.

5 I always *(my friends, use)* ____________________ my school things.

6 Mr Jones *(us, not play)* ____________________ in his garden.

182 Complete the sentences with the correct form of *(not)* be able to.

/ 6 Punkte

1 If we switch off all the lights, we ______________________ see the stars in the sky.

2 Last night, I ______________________ fall asleep because I was too tired.

3 What's wrong with Richard? We ______________________ speak with him for days.

4 The burglars tried to get into the house, but they ______________________ open the window.

5 You ______________________ answer my questions if you don't listen!

6 Mike has wanted a camera for a long time, but he ______________________ buy one yet. They're all too expensive.

183 Complete the sentences with the present perfect continuous form of the verbs in brackets.

/ 6 Punkte

1 Mum *(work)* ______________________ for Smith & Company for six years.

2 You *(learn)* ______________________ English for three years now.

3 It *(snow)* ______________________ heavily since Monday.

4 The neighbours' dog *(bark)* ______________________ for half an hour!

5 The girls *(practise)* ______________________ their dance for weeks.

6 I *(dream)* ______________________ about going out with Julia since I met her.

Writing

184 You have recently been to California and talk with your best friend about your holiday. Write a dialogue of about 130–160 words.

/ 10 Punkte

Talk about:

- *which places you visited*
- *where you stayed*
- *what you liked / did not like about your trip*

TIPP

Frage deinen Freund / deine Freundin auch, wie es ihm / ihr geht und verabschiede dich am Schluss des Gesprächs.

Bewertung	
45 bis 50 Punkte	Sehr gut
40 bis 44 Punkte	Gut
34 bis 39 Punkte	Befriedigend
unter 34 Punkte	Wiederhole die Stoffgebiete noch einmal, bei denen du die wenigsten Punkte erreicht hast.

/ 50 Punkte
GESAMT

D *Test 4* – Schularbeit 4

Teststoff	
Listening	Tsunami
Reading	The big earthquake
Grammar	passive, 1st or 2nd conditional, 2nd conditional, going to
Writing	Give advice to a friend

Listening Comprehension – Tsunami

185 Listen to the description of a tsunami and put the sentences into the correct order.

/ 11 Punkte

- ☐ Suddenly there is a huge wave coming towards them.
- 1 Yesterday I watched a film about a tsunami that suddenly hit an island.
- ☐ Before it does, the air is extremely quiet, and everyone looks up into the sky.
- ☐ She calls for help and crawls a long way to find her family again.
- ☐ Her body circles around and it takes a while for her to get out of the water.
- ☐ When the wave hits, the mother is swept away.
- ☐ In the film, a family is on holiday on this island.
- ☐ When she looks around, she sees a car stuck in a tree.
- ☐ They are relaxing by the pool when the tsunami hits the island.
- ☐ She is pushed under water and cannot get up.
- ☐ It takes a while for her to understand what is going on.
- ☐ Many birds start flying away and making terrible noises.

Üben

Reading Comprehension

Read the text.

When Joanna suddenly woke up, it was still dark outside. At first, she did not know what was happening. Why was she awake? But then she heard it again. There was this strange noise and it felt as it the whole house was shaking. "Oh my God!" she thought, "It is an earthquake! I have to get out of here!" Earthquakes were nothing unusual in her area but this time it seemed to be stronger. Joanna jumped out of bed and quickly ran into her parents' bedroom. "Mum, Dad! Get up! There is an earthquake!" she shouted. At first, her parents were a bit confused but then they realised that they were in real danger. Parts of the ceiling came down and the whole house seemed to collapse any minute. "Come on! Let's get out of here!" Joanna's dad shouted and grabbed her arm. But it was too late. The door was blocked. Joanna started to panic but then her mum quickly opened the kitchen window and they all crawled outside. They were really lucky because five minutes later the whole house collapsed.

186 Complete the sentences not using more than four words. / 4 Punkte

1 When Joanna woke up, she did ______________________.

2 In her area, earthquakes ______________________.

3 Joanna's parents soon realised that ______________________.

4 The whole house ______________________.

187 Answer the questions in complete sentences. / 4 Punkte

1 Why did Joanna wake up?

______________________.

2 Why could they not open the door?

______________________.

3 How did they manage to get outside?

______________________.

4 Why were they lucky?

______________________.

Grammar

188 Complete the sentences with the correct passive form *(present or past)*. Use the verbs from the box.

/ 8 Punkte

destroy ▪ direct* ▪ make ▪ play ▪ organise
register* ▪ speak ▪ visit

1 340,000 cars ________________ in Austria in 2018.

2 German ________________ in almost 10 countries in Europe.

3 Today, most computers ________________ in Asia.

4 In 2005, New Orleans ________________ by hurricane Katrina.

5 The 'Indiana Jones' films ________________ by Steven Spielberg, …

6 … and Indian Jones ________________ by Harrison Ford.

7 The London Dungeon ________________ by thousands of people every year.

8 Olympic Games ________________ in different cities every four years.

**direct* – Regie führen   **register* – anmelden

189 2nd conditional: Fill in the correct form of the verbs in brackets.

/ 8 Punkte

1 If Simon was here, we *(listen)* ________________ to some music.

2 Grandma would visit us more often if she *(live)* ________________ closer.

3 If Joe *(have)* ________________ enough money, he would buy a bigger TV.

4 You *(get)* ________________ better grades in your tests if you studied more.

5 If Dan *(not be)* ________________ my best friend, I would be angry with him.

6 We *(not go)* ________________ to bed if the film wasn't so boring.

7 If you lost your keys here, you *(not find)* ________________ them again.

8 Bill would have more friends if he *(not bully)* ________________ everybody.

190 1st or 2nd conditional? Cross out the wrong words. / 5 Punkte

1 You *will be / would be* fitter if you did more sport.
2 If the sun *doesn't shine / didn't shine* tomorrow, we'll stay indoors all day.
3 Dad would not like it if we *are / were* late again.
4 If they see us, they *will catch / would catch* us.
5 Joey *won't tell / wouldn't tell* the teacher if I copied his homework.

191 Write sentences with going to. / 5 Punkte

1 we ▪ meet ▪ a famous musician ▪ after the concert

____.

2 who ▪ clean ▪ the blackboard ▪ ?

____?

3 I ▪ visit ▪ some art museums ▪ in Paris

____.

4 you ▪ tell ▪ your parents ▪ about the school trip ▪ ?

____?

5 Sally ▪ not like ▪ this book

____.

Writing

192 A friend of yours is bullied by some older pupils at school. They want to have money from him/her. If he/she does not give them any, they will punch him. Your friend has hardly got any pocket money left, now he/she does not know what to do. You write your friend an email and try to give him/her some advice. Write about 110–130 words in your exercise book. / 9 Punkte

You can start like this:
- *Dear xxx,*
- *I was really shocked when you told me about your problem.*

Bewertung	
50 bis 54 Punkte	Sehr gut
45 bis 49 Punkte	Gut
40 bis 44 Punkte	Befriedigend
unter 40 Punkte	Wiederhole die Stoffgebiete noch einmal, bei denen du die wenigsten Punkte erreicht hast.

/ 54 Punkte
GESAMT

Üben

IRREGULAR VERBS – UNREGELMÄßIGE ZEITWÖRTER

base form	*past form*	*past participle*	Deutsch
be	*was, were*	*been*	sein
beat	*beat*	*beaten*	schlagen
become	*became*	*become*	werden
begin	*began*	*begun*	beginnen, anfangen
bite	*bit*	*bitten*	beißen
blow	*blew*	*blown*	blasen, wehen
break	*broke*	*broken*	brechen
bring	*brought*	*brought*	(her)bringen
build	*built*	*built*	bauen
burn	*burnt*[1]	*burnt*[1]	(ver)brennen
buy	*bought*	*bought*	kaufen
catch	*caught*	*caught*	fangen
choose	*chose*	*chosen*	(aus)wählen
come	*came*	*come*	kommen
cut	*cut*	*cut*	schneiden
dig	*dug*	*dug*	graben
do	*did*	*done*	tun, machen
draw	*drew*	*drawn*	ziehen, zeichnen
dream	*dreamt*[2]	*dreamt*[2]	träumen
drink	*drank*	*drunk*	trinken
drive	*drove*	*driven*	(Auto) fahren
eat	*ate*	*eaten*	essen, fressen
fall	*fell*	*fallen*	fallen
feel	*felt*	*felt*	fühlen
fight	*fought*	*fought*	kämpfen, streiten
find	*found*	*found*	finden
fly	*flew*	*flown*	fliegen
forget	*forgot*	*forgotten*	vergessen
freeze	*froze*	*frozen*	(er)frieren
get	*got*	*got*	werden, bekommen
get up	*got up*	*got up*	aufstehen
give	*gave*	*given*	geben
go	*went*	*gone*	fahren, gehen
grow	*grew*	*grown*	wachsen, anbauen, züchten
hang	*hung*	*hung*	hängen
have	*had*	*had*	haben
hear	*heard*	*heard*	hören
hide	*hid*	*hidden*	verstecken
hit	*hit*	*hit*	schlagen, treffen
hold	*held*	*held*	(fest)halten

[1] *auch möglich: burned – burned* [2] auch möglich: *dreamed – dreamed*

Wissen

base form	*past form*	*past participle*	**Deutsch**
hurt	*hurt*	*hurt*	verletzen, schmerzen
keep	*kept*	*kept*	(be)halten
know	*knew*	*known*	wissen, kennen
lay	*laid*	*laid*	legen
learn	*learnt*[3]	*learnt*[3]	lernen
leave	*left*	*left*	zurücklassen, verlassen
let	*let*	*let*	zulassen, erlauben
lie	*lay*	*lain*	liegen, sich hinlegen
lose	*lost*	*lost*	verlieren
make	*made*	*made*	machen, es schaffen
mean	*meant*	*meant*	meinen, bedeuten
meet	*met*	*met*	treffen, kennenlernen
pay	*paid*	*paid*	(be)zahlen
put	*put*	*put*	stellen, geben, legen
read [ri:d]	*read* [red]	*read* [red]	lesen
ride	*rode*	*ridden*	(Rad) fahren, reiten
ring	*rang*	*rung*	(an)läuten
run	*ran*	*run*	laufen, rennen
say	*said*	*said*	sagen
see	*saw*	*seen*	sehen
sell	*sold*	*sold*	verkaufen
send	*sent*	*sent*	senden, schicken
set	*set*	*set*	setzen
shoot	*shot*	*shot*	schießen
show	*showed*	*shown*	zeigen
sing	*sang*	*sung*	singen
sink	*sank*	*sunk*	sinken, versenken
sit	*sat*	*sat*	sitzen, sich setzen
sleep	*slept*	*slept*	schlafen
smell	*smelt*[4]	*smelt*[4]	riechen
speak	*spoke*	*spoken*	sprechen
spend	*spent*	*spent*	ausgeben, verbringen
stand	*stood*	*stood*	stehen
steal	*stole*	*stolen*	stehlen
swim	*swam*	*swum*	schwimmen
take	*took*	*taken*	nehmen, (hin)bringen
take off	*took off*	*taken off*	ausziehen, abheben
teach	*taught*	*taught*	lehren, unterrichten
tell	*told*	*told*	sagen, erzählen
think	*thought*	*thought*	denken
throw	*threw*	*thrown*	werfen
understand	*understood*	*understood*	verstehen
wake (up)	*woke (up)*	*woken (up)*	(auf)wachen
win	*won*	*won*	siegen, gewinnen
write	*wrote*	*written*	schreiben

[3] *auch möglich: learned – learned* [4] auch möglich: *smelled – smelled*

Wissen

eSquirrel

Die Quiz-App - jetzt kostenlos zu Durchstarten Englisch

Tausend zusätzliche Übungsbeispiele

Der eSquirrel-Kurs zu diesem Buch enthält tausend zusätzliche Übungsbeispiele und Erklärungen, die genau auf dieses Buch abgestimmt sind.

Spielerisch zu langfristigen Lernerfolgen

Indem du Quizfragen beantwortet sammelst du Nüsse.
Je öfters du Fragen wiederholst, desto wertvollere Nüsse erhältst du.
Schaffst du es dich im Leaderboard ins beste Drittel deiner Klasse oder Freunde zu spielen?

Offline verfügbar

Nach einmaligem Download des Kurses sind alle Inhalte offline verfügbar.
Kein WLAN oder Datenvolumen notwendig!

Durchstarten mit eSquirrel!

Scanne den QR-Code, um die App „eSquirrel“ zu laden und suche in der App dieses Buch. Um den Kurs dazu kostenlos zu erhalten, gib dort in der App den Code ein, den du ganz vorne in diesem Buch findest.

Überall, wo du dieses Eichkätzchen-Symbol siehst, findest du eine Quest mit wichtigen Übungsbeispielen zu dieser Einheit. Öffne einfach die App und suche im Kurs nach der Quest (z.B. Quest 9.3).

Auf Smartphone, Tablet und Web!

JETZT BEI Google Play | Laden im App Store | Im Web auf www.eSquirrel.at

Sie sind LehrerIn?

eSquirrel ist ein hervorragendes Tool für den Unterricht und ermöglicht klasseninterne Ranglisten, Einsicht in die Lernfortschritte, Erstellung von Hausaufgaben, Tests und vieles mehr!

Alle Infos unter www.eSquirrel.at/veritas.

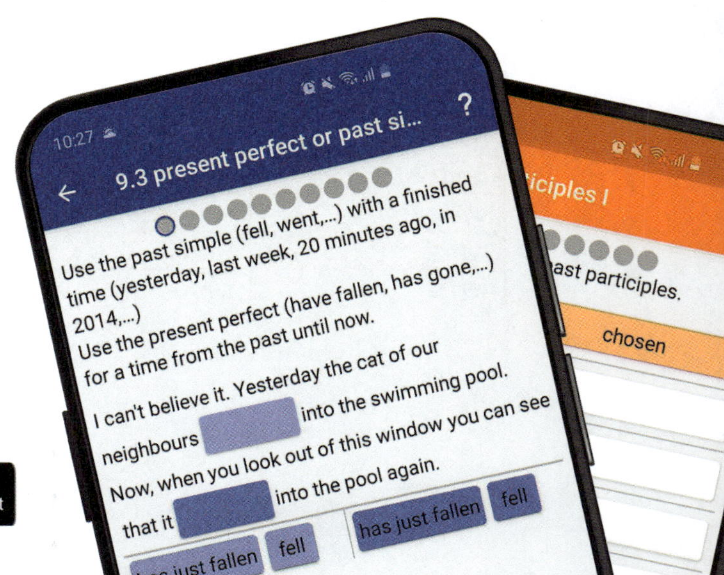

DURCH STARTEN

ENGLISCH

LERNHILFE

Lösungen

3

VERITAS

Gemeinsam besser lernen

Liebe Eltern!

Dieses Lernhilfebuch umfasst **alle wichtigen Lerninhalte der 3. Klasse in Englisch**. Damit ist Durchstarten **der ideale Lernbegleiter durch das gesamte Schuljahr**. Egal, welches Thema in der Schule gerade besprochen wird, Durchstarten bietet dazu **verständliche Erklärungen** und **umfangreiche Übungen** in drei Schwierigkeitsgraden. Sie müssen sich nicht mehr überlegen, wo Sie passende Übungen für Ihr Kind herbekommen oder wie Sie das Thema Ihrem Kind noch einmal verständlich erklären können – Durchstarten erledigt das für Sie!

Damit entlastet Sie Durchstarten und verhilft Ihnen zu einem entspannten Familienleben ohne Schul- und Notenstress.

Wie das Üben mit dem Buch **funktioniert**, lesen Sie bitte auf der **inneren Umschlagseite** 2 nach.

Wo Sie das jeweils passende **Übungsthema** finden, steht vorne im **Inhaltsverzeichnis**.

Wenn Ihr Kind die **Mittelschule** besucht, wird es in Englisch im **Leistungsniveau „Standard"** oder **„Standard AHS"** unterrichtet. Die Übungen mit einem ✱ oder zwei ✱✱ entsprechen dem Leistungsniveau „Standard", die Übungen mit drei ✱✱✱ dem Leistungsniveau „Standard AHS". So kann Ihr Kind **je nach** seinem **Leistungsniveau optimal trainieren und** sich **verbessern**.

Unsere Leitlinien

- Diese Durchstarten-Lernhilfe wurde **von erfahrenen PädagogInnen / LehrerInnen entwickelt**.
- Wir orientieren uns an den **aktuellen Anforderungen des österreichischen Lehrplans**.
- Diese Lernhilfe kann **unabhängig vom jeweils verwendeten Schulbuch** eingesetzt werden.
- Bei der Produktentwicklung haben wir den Fokus auf die Anforderungen und **Wünsche von Ihnen und Ihrem Kind** gelegt.
- Digitale Inhalte und Funktionen werden nur dort eingesetzt, wo sie das **Lernen sinnvoll unterstützen**.

Immer am neuesten Stand

Auf www.durchstarten.at/aktuell informieren wir Sie gratis über inhaltliche Neuerungen/Ergänzungen zum Buch.

Wir wünschen Ihnen und Ihrem Kind ein erfolgreiches Schuljahr in der 3. Klasse!

Ihr Durchstartenteam

1

1 If I lose my bus pass, I**'ll get (will get)** into trouble.
2 If Lydia invites me to her party, I**'ll come (will come)**.
3 If we ask Dad to help us, he**'ll do (will do)** it.
4 If you break a mirror, you**'ll have (will have)** bad luck for seven years.
5 If an asteroid hits the Earth, many people and animals **will die**.
6 I**'ll tell (will tell)** you a funny story if you want to hear it.
7 Lenny **will come** with us if we wait a minute.
8 My parents **will be** disappointed if I don't pass the test.
9 We**'ll stay (will stay)** in the house if it rains or snows.
10 Aunt Natalie **will earn** a lot of money if she gets the new job.

2

1 If you **read** in the dark, you'll ruin your eyes.
2 If Hannah **makes** another mistake, she'll lose the match.
3 If Adrian **isn't (is not)** at home, we'll leave him a message.
4 If the weather **doesn't (does not) change**, we'll go sailing tomorrow.
5 If I **don't (do not) feel** better soon, I won't go to school.
6 You'll miss your bus if you **don't (do not) leave** now.
7 Our neighbours won't like it if we **play** loud music.
8 It'll get very cold in here if you **don't (do not) shut** the window.
9 Everything will be fine if you **do** what I say.
10 Nobody will know that we're here if we **don't (do not) make** a noise.
11 If Sophia **doesn't (does not) get** Lenny a birthday present, he'll be very sad.

3

(1H), 2C, 3E, 4J, 5I, 6B, 7D, 8A, 9F, 10G

4

1 If you **visit**/~~will visit~~ us next time, we ~~go~~/**will go** skiing with you.
2 We ~~take~~/**will take** a taxi if it **rains**/~~will rain~~.
3 If I **don't see**/~~won't see~~ you tomorrow, I ~~phone~~/**will phone** you.
4 Nothing ~~happens~~/**will happen** to you if you **tell**/~~will tell~~ the truth.
5 If you **read**/~~will read~~ these stories, you ~~know~~/**will know** more about superstitions.
6 If Grandpa **wins**/~~will win~~ the lottery, he ~~buys~~/**will buy** a new and bigger car.
7 We ~~visit~~/**will visit** Ground Zero if we ever **go**/~~will go~~ to New York City.
8 You ~~don't see~~/**won't see** who is in the room if you **don't**/~~won't~~ switch on the light.
9 Veronica ~~gets~~/**will get** a headache if she **doesn't**/~~won't~~ wear a hat.
10 You ~~don't~~/**won't** lose weight if you **sit**/~~will sit~~ in front of the computer all day.
11 Penny ~~comes~~/**will come** to my party if she **isn't**/~~won't be~~ busy.
12 The vase ~~breaks~~/**will break** if you **drop**/~~will drop~~ it.
13 If you **don't**/~~won't~~ behave, you ~~don't~~/**won't** get any presents.
14 Antonia ~~is~~/**will be** sad if we **don't**/~~won't~~ invite her.
15 If the sun ~~will shine~~/**shines** tomorrow, we **will go**/~~go~~ for a walk.

5

1 If you **find** a penny and pick it up, you**'ll (will) have** good luck all day.
2 If a black cat **crosses** your way, something bad **will happen**.
3 If you **walk** under a ladder, you**'ll (will) get** bad news.
4 If you **carry** a rabbit's foot with you, everything **will be** fine.

Bitte umblättern! ↺

5 If you **see** a shooting star and make a wish, your wish **will come** true.
6 Bad things **won't (will not) come** your way if you **knock** on wood.
7 Things **will go** well if you **cross** your fingers.
8 You**'ll (will) succeed** with your plans if you **spit** on a coin.
9 You**'ll (will) be** lucky all year if you **see** a chimney sweep on New Year's Day.
10 Things **will turn out** badly if you **do** them on Friday, the 13th.

6

1 If somebody **sees** us here, we**'ll (will) get** into trouble.
2 If you ever **go** back to Canada, we**'ll (will) be** very sorry.
3 If Charlie **doesn't (does not) get** up now, he **won't (will not) get** breakfast.
4 If you **don't (do not) learn** English, you **won't (will not) understand** the people in England.
5 If you **study**, you **won't (will not) fail** the test.
6 If Gina **comes** to my birthday party, I**'ll (will) be** the happiest boy on Earth.
7 You**'ll (will) feel** hungry if you **don't (do not) finish** your breakfast.
8 Everybody **will laugh** at us if we **wear** these silly costumes.
9 The bus driver **won't (will not) wait** for us if we **are** late again.
10 You**'ll (will) catch** cold if you **don't (do not) put on** a warm coat today.
11 We**'ll (will) go** to the cinema tonight if Maria **comes** with us.
12 You**'ll (will) know** where I am if you **read** my emails.
13 If you **wear** a mask, people **won't (will not) recognise** you.
14 If we **meet** Elsie in town, **we'll (will) say** hello.
15 Joe **will buy** these sneakers if they **aren't** too expensive.
16 Chloe **won't (will not) keep** the dress if she **doesn't (does not) like** it.

7

1 **Unless you do** your homework first, Mum won't let you watch TV.
Mum won't let you watch TV **unless you do** your homework first.
2 Please don't call me today **unless it is** really important.
3 **Unless Liam leaves** right now, he will miss his train.
Liam will miss his train **unless he leaves** right now.
4 Dad will work in the garden all week **unless it rains**.
5 **Unless Mum's bus is** late, she'll be back in an hour.
Mum will be back in an hour **unless her bus is late**.
6 Your friends won't know about your concert **unless you tell** them.
Unless you tell your friends, they won't know about your concert.
7 **Unless you wear** a mask, people will recognise you.
People will recognise you **unless you wear** a mask.
8 I will pass the exam **unless I am** too nervous.
9 **Unless the firefighters come** soon, the house will burn down.
The house will burn down **unless the firefighters come** soon.
10 Miranda will be very disappointed **unless you dance** with her.
11 **Unless Dad finds** a petrol station soon, we'll be in deep trouble.
We'll be in deep trouble **unless Dad finds** a petrol station soon.

8

1 I**'d (would) give** you Jenny's phone number if I knew it.
2 Alex **would come** with us if he had more time.
3 Grandma **would be** disappointed if I forgot her birthday.

4 We'**d (would) play** outdoors if it stopped raining.
5 Brian **would earn** more money if he had a better job.
6 If I missed the train, Dad **would drive** me to school.
7 If Camilla spoke Chinese, she'**d (would) understand** the tourists.
8 If we asked Dad to help us, he'**d (would) do** it.
9 If I found a wallet, I'**d (would) take** it to the nearest police station.
10 If electric cars were cheaper, my dad **would buy** one.

9

1 If you **did** your homework, everything would be fine.
2 If Jeremy **made** another mistake, he would lose the match.
3 If Adrian **wasn't (was not)** at school, we would notice it.
4 If they **didn't (did not) speak** so fast, we would understand them.
5 I would go to the party if I **didn't (did not) study** for the Maths test.
6 You would miss your bus if I **didn't (did not) drive** you to the bus stop.
7 Felix wouldn't like it if we **played** with his game console.
8 Mum **wouldn't (would not) worry** so much if we phoned her.

10

1 If you **asked**/~~would ask~~ me nicely, I ~~lent~~/**would lend** you my bicycle.
2 We ~~took~~/**would take** a taxi if it **rained**/~~would rain~~.
3 If you **wrote**/~~would write~~ your homework on the computer, it ~~was~~/**would be** easier to read.
4 Nobody ~~believed~~/**would believe** you if you **told**/~~would tell~~ them this story.
5 Daniel ~~didn't~~/**wouldn't** play today if he **didn't**/~~wouldn't~~ feel well.
6 If pigs **had**/~~would have~~ wings, they ~~flew~~/**would fly**.
7 This soup ~~tasted~~/**would taste** better if it **had**/~~would have~~ more salt in it.
8 I ~~called~~/**would call** Evelyn today if I **knew**/~~would know~~ her phone number.
9 We ~~went~~/**would go** swimming if it **wasn't**/~~wouldn't be~~ so cold.
10 You ~~found~~/**would find** your things if you **tidied up**/~~would tidy up~~ your room.
11 Vivian ~~wasn't~~/**wouldn't be** so nervous if she **didn't**/~~wouldn't~~ drink so much coffee.
12 You ~~didn't~~/**wouldn't** make so many mistakes if you **listened**/~~would listen~~ to me.

11

(1E), 2I, 3A, 4F, 5C, 6G, 7H, 8B, 9D

12

1 Fred ~~will~~/**would** sell his stamp collection if he needed the money.
2 If you **break**/~~broke~~ my glasses, you will have to buy me new ones.
3 If Tony ~~invites~~/**invited** me to his party, I would go.
4 I ~~won't~~/**wouldn't** open the door if I were you.
5 Charlie wouldn't help us if he ~~doesn't~~/**didn't** want to.
6 If you go out with Sandra, I **won't**/~~wouldn't~~ be your friend anymore.
7 What **will**/~~would~~ you do if you don't find your keys?
8 If Connor **doesn't**/~~didn't~~ answer the phone, we'll have to text him.

13

1 Who **can** translate this sentence into German?
Who **is able** to translate this sentence into German?
2 I **can**not come to the gym with you.
I **am** not **able** to come to the gym with you.

Bitte umblättern!

3 We **can** beat the other team.
We**'re able** to beat the other team.
4 **Can** Justin answer these questions?
Is Justin **able** to answer these questions?
5 Sarah **can**'t come to my birthday party.
Sarah **is** not **able** to come to my birthday party.
6 What **can** the police do about the traffic jams?
What **is / are** the police **able** to do about the trafic jams?
7 Nobody **can** look into the future.
Nobody **is able** to look into the future.
8 Mum is the only person who **can** help us now.
Mum is the only person who **is able** to help us now.

14
1 It rained last night, but we ~~could~~/**were able to** finish the tennis match.
2 Carol played well, but I ~~could~~/**was able to** beat her in two sets.
3 In the Middle Ages, more people **could**/~~were able to~~ ride horses than today.
4 Every evening I **could**/~~was able to~~ watch lions come to drink water.
5 **Could you**/~~Were you able to~~ ride a bike when you were six?
6 In 1911, Amundsen ~~could~~/**was able to** reach the South Pole before Scott.
7 When Dad was in school, he **could**/~~was able to~~ choose between Latin and French.
8 Our neighbours' cat ran away, but they ~~could~~/**were able to** catch it again.
9 Last week was so hot that we **could**/~~were able to~~ go swimming every day.
10 From my room in the old house, I **could**/~~was able to~~ see a big park.

15
1 I **was able to** answer all the questions in yesterday's test.
2 Doris wasn't at home, but I **was able to** talk to her on the phone.
3 After two days on the slopes, Anthony **was able to** ski.
4 Dad had nothing to do all day, so he **was able to** play with us.
5 My little brother **could** walk when he was 11 months old.
6 I spoke very slowly, but they **could** not understand me.
(auch möglich: weren't able to understand)
7 After her accident, Lucy **wasn't able to** walk for two weeks.
(auch möglich: couldn't walk)
8 It was terribly hot in the room, but we **could** not open the windows.
(auch möglich: weren't able to open)

16
1 We **couldn't** play outside. (auch möglich: We **weren't able to** play outside.)
2 Max **was able to** finish his model ship.
3 Amy's parents **were able to** buy a new car.
4 Sue **couldn't** ride her bike. (auch möglich: Sue **wasn't able to** ride her bike.)

17
1 Little Tommy **will be able to** ride a bike when he's older.
2 You**'ll be able to** speak with my parents tomorrow.
3 I hope they **will be able to** repair our car soon!
4 The doctors say Nick **will be able to** leave the hospital soon.

5 If it gets really warm, you **won't be able to** see our snow castle.
6 Callie **will be able to** finish first, I think.
7 The girls **won't be able to** remember what you said.
8 If you don't read the book, you **won't be able to** talk about it.
9 I'm sure you **will be able to** find your tickets again!
10 **Will** we **be able to** visit Central Park in New York City?

18
1 Jake **has been able to** fix his broken kite.
2 I'm sorry, I **haven't been able to** come sooner.
3 Grandma **hasn't been able to** find her glasses yet.
4 The bank robbers **have been able to** escape the police.

19
1 *A:* Have you done your homework, Julie?
B: Yes, and I**'ve been able to** answer every question!
2 *A:* Where's Violet?
B: No idea. We **haven't been able to** phone her.
3 *A:* Has your father sold his car yet?
B: Oh yes, and he**'s been able to** get a good price for it.
4 *A:* Are we going to the concert next week?
B: Yes! I**'ve been able to** buy some tickets.
5 *A:* Is Uncle Joe's car running again?
B: No, he **hasn't been able to** find a mechanic who can fix it.
6 *A:* Has your suitcase arrived?
B: No, they **haven't been able to** deliver it yet.

20
1 Joe Smith ~~was~~/**has been** able to speak Spanish since his visit to Spain.
2 Grace **will be**/~~was~~ able to visit us again next month.
3 The Coopers ~~weren't~~/**haven't been** able to sell their house yet.
4 We **were**/~~have been~~ able to catch the last bus yesterday.
5 You **won't be**/~~haven't been~~ able to see anything. It's too dark outside.
6 Hailey **hasn't been**/~~won't be~~ able to get an A in English since last year.
7 I ~~have been~~/**will be** able to help you if you ask me.
8 Nobody **was**/~~has been~~ able to find their shoes after the party.
9 Helen had a broken finger, so she **wasn't**/~~hasn't been~~ able to play the violin.
10 Jason ~~wasn't~~/**hasn't been** able to run and jump since his accident.

21
1 Theo **will be able to buy a camera**.
2 Lilly is ill. She **won't be able to go to the dance**.
3 In the holidays, we**'ll be able to see different sights**.
4 Richard **won't be able to play basketball**.
5 Mum **will be able to cook dinner**.
6 My grandparents **won't be able to visit us this year**.

22
1 We**'ve been able to win the football cup**.
2 Nora **has been able to sell her painting**.
3 Mr Frederick **has been able to grow a huge pumpkin**.

23

1 Reading English is easy, but I ~~couldn't~~/**am not able** to speak it very well.
2 Hundreds of people ~~can~~/**were able** to watch the concert live last night.
3 Are you still looking for your glasses, Hannah? – Yes, I am.
I **haven't been**/~~won't be~~ able to find them yet.
4 I've hidden the Easter eggs so well you ~~aren't~~/**won't be** able to find them.
5 Why **couldn't**/~~won't~~ you answer the phone when I called you?
6 We were so tired that we ~~won't~~/**weren't** able to stay awake during the film.
7 Max is very clever. He **can**/~~could~~ play the guitar and the saxophone.
8 ~~Were~~/**Are** you able to hear me or is it too loud here?
9 Nobody ~~will be~~/**is** able to contact Mrs Jones. Where can she be?
10 Last week we **could**/~~can~~ play outdoors, this week we ~~couldn't~~/**can't**.

24

erste Reihe: 5 – 3 – 6; zweite Reihe: 1 – 4 – 2

25

1 **People mustn't feed the ducks.**
2 **We mustn't ride our bikes here.**
3 **The man mustn't cross the street.**
4 **You mustn't fish here.**
5 **I mustn't drive Dad's car.**
6 **A child mustn't drink beer.**

26

1 *Alice:* Why **am I not allowed to go** to Gina's party, Mum? Betty **is allowed to** go!
2 *Mother:* Yes, but …
3 *Alice:* All my friends **are allowed to do** what they want!
4 *Mother:* That's not true. Betty **isn't allowed to go out** during the week and she**'s allowed to bring** friends home only at the weekend. So she **isn't allowed to do** what she wants.
5 *Alice:* Maybe, but she**'s allowed to watch** TV in her room. I**'m not even allowed to have** my own TV set!
6 *Mother:* That's because …
7 *Alice:* Why? Why **am I not allowed to do** what Betty does?
8 *Mother:* Because 12-year-old girls **aren't allowed to do** the things 18-year-olds do! And that's the end of the discussion!

27

1C, 2F, 3H, 4A, (5D), 6B, 7E, 8G

28

1 Every year, Martin **is**/was allowed to choose a place for the summer holiday.
2 I won't be/**haven't been** allowed to hold my sister's new baby yet.
3 The girls were/**are** allowed to have earrings and piercings in our school.
4 We aren't/**won't be** allowed to make so much noise next time.
5 Afro-Americans aren't/**weren't** allowed to ride at the front of the bus.
6 Ms Miller says we **will be**/have been allowed to go on a school trip next year.
7 In our English lessons we won't be/**aren't** allowed to speak German.
8 **Are**/Were you allowed to use your brother's mountain bike? – Yes, sometimes.

29

1 You mustn't **feed the animals**.
2 You're not allowed **to tease the animals**.
3 You mustn't **litter**.
4 **You're not allowed to play music**.
5 **You mustn't climb (on / up) trees**.
6 **You're not allowed to have picnics**.
7 **You mustn't smoke**.
8 **You're not allowed to bring a dog**.
9 **You mustn't climb over the fence**.

30

1 My parents sometimes **let me sleep** in their bed.
2 I always **let Sylvia use my pen**.
3 **Do** your parents **let you dye your hair purple**?
4 They didn't **let us listen to loud music**.
5 They **will let you go home soon**.
6 My parents **didn't let me watch the late night movie**.

31

adjective	comparative	superlative
mad	madder	the maddest
young	younger	the youngest
narrow	narrower	the narrowest
wonderful	more wonderful	the most wonderful
pretty	prettier	the prettiest
useful	more useful	the most useful
thirsty	thirstier	the thirstiest
rude	ruder	the rudest
successful	more successful	the most successful
quiet	quieter	the quietest

32

1F, 2G, 3D, 4A, 5H, (6B), 7C, 8E

33

1 Monday was **colder than** Tuesday.
2 Pineapples are **as cheap as** papayas.
3 The necklace is **more expensive than** ring.
4 A helicopter is **not as fast as** a jet plane.
5 Elephants are **more exotic than** sheep.
6 A supermarket is **not as impressive as** a castle.

34

1 Golf is an expensive sport, but polo is **more expensive**.
2 Cookies are good, but donuts are **better**.
3 A headache is painful, but a toothache is even **more painful**.
4 This is an incredible story, but my story is **more incredible**.
5 'Dracula' was frightening, but 'Frankenstein' was **more frightening**.
6 You're early, but we were even **earlier**.

35

1 Table tennis is faster than tennis, but squash is **the fastest**.
2 Dad is older than me, and Grandpa is **the oldest**.
3 San Marino is smaller than Liechtenstein, and Monaco is **the smallest**.
4 Simon's sisters are really pretty, but my sister is **the prettiest**.
5 Peaches and cherries are sweet, but grapes are **the sweetest**.

Bitte umblättern! ↺

6 Rick and Tony are talented players, but I am **the most talented**.
7 Zoe's and Nora's hats are elegant, but Emma's is **the most elegant**.
8 Purple and orange are popular colours, but pink is **the most popular**.
9 I get angry sometimes, but Mr Black is **the angriest** person I know.
10 Biology and History are cool subjects, but Physics is **the coolest**.
11 The Browns and the Nelsons have new cars, but ours is **the newest**.
12 'Buddy' and 'Molly' are cute dogs, but 'Coco" is **the cutest**.

36 Hi, I'm Ethan – Ethan Cole. I'm 13, and I live in San Francisco, the **loveliest** city on Earth. No other city is as **beautiful as** San Francisco! And here's my family. I'll start with Tracy, my **younger** sister. She's only 3, and she's really the **cutest** little girl. Then there's Mia. She's one year **older than** me. We are **good (best)** friends, but sometimes she can be quite **touchy**. Then it's **good (best)** to get out of her way as **fast as** you can! My dad's name is Owen. He's forty. He's a policeman. My mum, Esther, is forty, too, so she's **as old as** my dad. She's an IT expert. My parents are really **nice**. Mum is **more patient** than Dad, but I think this has to do with his job. We've also got a cat named Tiger. He's the **laziest** cat in the world! He sleeps most of the day and only gets up to eat. So he's also **the fattest** cat in the world!

37
1 The ~~taller~~/**tallest** building of the world is in Dubai.
2 Last Friday was the **worst**/~~baddest~~ day of my life.
3 A foot (30.3 cm) is not ~~long~~/**as long as** a yard (91 cm).
4 The **richest**/~~richer~~ person of the world lives in the USA.
5 Jeff is ~~nicer as~~/**as nice as** his twin brother David.
6 Your hands are **as cold as**/~~the coldest~~ ice.
7 Melissa is ~~as intelligent~~/**more intelligent** than all the other girls.
8 Wood is **not as heavy as**/~~heavier as~~ gold.
9 Our dog isn't **as cute**/~~cuter~~ as our cat, but he's ~~the cleverest~~/**cleverer**.
10 Winter holidays are usually ~~expensiver~~/**more expensive** than summer holidays.

38

1 Buckingham Palace is older than Schönbrunn Castle.	**T**	F
2 Schönbrunn Castle is bigger than Buckingham Palace.	**T**	F
3 The White House is the youngest building.	**T**	F
4 The White House is bigger than Buckingham Palace.	T	**F**
5 Buckingham Palace is the oldest building.	**T**	F
6 The White House is the biggest building.	T	**F**

39 obere Reihe: 4 – 5 – 2; untere Reihe: 3 – 6 – 1

40
1 **Is** Allison **going to** sing and dance tonight?
2 **Are** you **going to** tell me about your plans?
3 **Am** I **going to** get an answer to my question?
4 What **are** you **going to** say to your parents?
5 **Is** Michael **going to** fix his bike or not?
6 When **are** you **going to** tidy up your rooms?
7 **Is** it **going to** rain today? – I think so. Look at the clouds!
8 **Are** they **going to** visit Salzburg or Innsbruck first?
9 Who **is going to** take the dog for a walk today?

41

1 **Is Mr. Hicks going to sell his car?**
2 **You're going to hear a funny story.**
3 **I'm not going to invite Joe again.**
4 **Are you going to help me?**
5 **When are we going to visit Granny?**
6 **Liz is going to move to another town.**
7 **Jackie isn't going to like this.**
8 **Aren't you going to open the box?**
9 **Is Linda going to study in Vienna?**
10 **We're going to England next week.**

42

1 What **are you going to** do this afternoon? – I'm going to watch TV.
2 Who **is going to** clean the bird cage today? – No me!
3 When **are you going to** finish your model ship? – Next week, perhaps.
4 Why **aren't** you **going to** come to my party? – Mum says I can't.
5 **Is** your father **going to** help us? – He is if we ask him.
6 How **are you/we going to** get to Joe's house? – We're going to take a taxi.
7 Where **are we going to** meet next time? – Let's meet at the gym.
8 **Am** I **going to** see you again? – Of course! I'll be back soon.

43

Emilia: Hi, Felix! What are you doing this weekend?
Felix: Hi! I**'m going to see** the new play tomorrow. [für die nahe Zukunft geplante Handlung]
Emilia: Have you got the tickets yet?
Felix: I**'m going to get** them later today. Would you like to come? [für die nahe Zukunft geplante Handlung]
Emilia: Oh, thanks! That would be wonderful.
Felix: I**'ll get** you a ticket, too. [plötzliche Entscheidung]
Emilia: Great! What time does it start?
Felix: Seven thirty, but we**'re all going to meet** at the 'Burger Bar' at 6 o'clock. [für die nahe Zukunft geplante Handlung]
Emilia: Okay, I**'ll meet** you there, but I**'m going to be** there a little later. [zuerst plötzliche Entscheidung, dann für die nahe Zukunft geplante Handlung]
Felix: No problem! I**'ll phone** the others and tell them that you**'re going to come** with us. [zuerst plötzliche Entscheidung, dann für die nahe Zukunft geplante Handlung]
Emilia: Thanks a lot, Felix! This **will be / is going to be** great fun! [beide Formen möglich: entweder Vorhersage/Hoffnung oder feste Absicht]

44

1 passive
2 active
3 passive
4 active
5 passive
6 active
7 active
8 passive

45

1 Wood and coal ~~use~~/**are used** for making fire.
2 Many of my friends **love**/~~are loved~~ football.
3 The USA **celebrates**/~~is celebrated~~ Independence Day on July 4th.
4 A lot of wine ~~produce~~/**is produced** in Italy.
5 St. Paul's Cathedral ~~build~~/**was built** in the 17th century.
6 The Vikings **discovered**/~~were discovered~~ America long before Columbus.
7 A volcano **destroyed**/~~was destroyed~~ the city of Pompeii in 79 AD.
8 Pompeii ~~buried~~/**was buried** under 4 m of ash.

46
1 Opel cars **are made** in Germany.
2 At the airport, every passenger **is asked** for an ID.
3 A lot of fish **is caught** in the North Atlantic.
4 Chopsticks **are used** for eating in China and Japan.
5 Excellent food **is served** in this restaurant.
6 Fresh vegetables **are sold** at the market all day.

47
1 Many important things **were invented** in the 19th century.
2 The New Testament **was written** in Latin.
3 Gold **was found** in California in 1849.
4 The boys **were paid** some money for mowing the lawn.
5 The bank robbers **were arrested** very quickly.
6 In 1066, a big battle **was fought** near Hastings in England.

48
1 **The explosion was heard by everybody.**
2 **I was hit by a tennis ball.**
3 **English is poken by many people.**
4 **The bill was paid by my parents.**
5 **These pictures were painted by my mother.**

49
1 **Our car was stopped by the police.**
2 **The / A treasure was buried by (the) pirates.**
3 **The houses were damaged by the / a storm.**
4 **The UFO was seen by many people.**
5 **The ruins were discovered by (the) explorers.**
6 **These photos were taken by Mrs Clark.**

50
First, the kettle **is filled** with water. Then the kettle **is put** on the heater and the heat **is turned** on. In the meantime, the teapot **is rinsed** with hot water and the water **is poured** out again. Then some spoonfuls of tea **are put** into the pot, one for each cup and one for the pot. When the water boils, it **is poured** on the tea in the pot. After 3 to 5 minutes, the tea is ready. It **is drunk** with or without milk and sugar. Tea **is enjoyed** by many people in England.

51
1 Basketball **was played for the first time in 1891**.
2 Iceland **was settled by Vikings in the 10th century**.
3 The dinosaurs **were killed by a meteor 60 million years ago**.
4 The Great Wall of China **was begun over 2,500 years ago**.
5 The 'Mona Lisa' **was painted by Leonardo da Vinci**.
6 The Winnetou stories **were written by Karl May**.
7 Penicillin **was discovered by Alexander Fleming**.
8 The Eurovision Song Contest **was won by Conchita Wurst in 2014**.
9 Rabbits **were brought to Australia by European settlers**.
10 The United Nations **were founded in 1945**.
11 More than 150 songs **were composed by Lennon and McCartney**.
12 Steven Spielberg **was nominated for the 'Oscar' 15 times**.

52 The Statue of Liberty **was given** to the United States by France. It **was** a present on the 100th 'birthday' of the USA. The statue **was designed** by a French artist named Frederic Bartholdi. It **was completed** in France in 1884. Then it **was transported** to America in 350 pieces. They **arrived** in New York in 1885. There the pieces **were put** together and the statue **was opened** in October 1886.

53
1 No, the first satellite **was sent into space by the Russians**.
2 No, **Pompeii was destroyed by a volcano**.
3 No, **Australia was discovered by James Cook**.
4 No, **'Indiana Jones' was created by George Lucas**.
5 No, **the World Wide Web was invented by Tim Berners-Lee in 1989**.
6 No, **'Don Giovanni' and 'The Magic Flute' were written by Mozart**.

54
1 When we left the restaurant, it **was snowing**.
2 We **were sitting** in the garden when the phone rang.
3 When I woke up this morning, the sun **was shining**.
4 Bill **was walking** home from school when he found a wallet.
5 When Joe met Marylin, he **was living** in London.
6 Jason and Jill **were reading** a book when the lights went out.

55
1 Dad **was making** breakfast for the family.
2 My sisters **were helping** him.
3 Mum **was reading** the newspaper.
4 Our dog **was running** around in the garden.
5 The cats **were sleeping** in their baskets.
6 I **was brushing** my teeth.
7 My little brother **was playing** with his toys.
8 Outside, the birds **were singing** …
9 … and the sun **was shining**.
10 We all **were having** a good time.

56
1 The ice cream man **was coming** along the street.
2 Joe and Mia **were running** to the ice cream man.
3 Adam **was riding** his skateboard down the sidewalk.
4 Lilly **was looking** for her bicycle in the garage.
5 Simon **was climbing** onto the roof of the garage.
6 Little Annie **was sitting** in the pool.
7 Archie **was jumping** into the pool.
8 The cat **was chasing** the butterflies across the lawn.
9 Some birds **were flying** through the air.
10 Mrs Smith **was watching** the kids from the upstairs window.

57
1 I fell asleep while I was watching TV.
2 Brian **fell while he was climbing up the ladder**.
3 Sandra **was reading a book when the phone rang**.
4 The girls **met some friends while they were going to the bus stop**.
5 The boys **were playing in the park when it started raining**.
6 Dad **was working in the garden when he cut his finger**.

58

S	L	E	P	T	F	G
A	E	A	U	D	I	D
S	A	T	T	O	O	L
W	R	I	T	I	N	G
E	N	N	I	N	E	H
N	E	G	N	G	O	T
T	D	B	G	C	D	I

past forms

1 **slept**
2 **did**
3 **sat**
4 **got**
5 **went**
6 **learned**

ing-forms

1 **writing**
2 **eating**
3 **putting**
4 **doing**

59

1 When I **walked** into the classrooms, all my friends **were standing** by the windows, looking out.
2 Eric **was watching** a horror movie when he **heard** a strange noise from the next room.
3 We **were playing squash** when I **slipped** and **hurt** my elbow.
4 Dad **was driving** home in the evening when a rabbit **jumped** across the road in front of him.
5 My mother **was living** in Vienna when she **met** my father.
6 While we **were playing** games with our parents, our cat **was sleeping** on my lap.
7 I **was playing** tennis when a ball **hit** me.
8 We **were drinking** tea in the warm living room while outside a terrible storm **was howling**.
9 The Coopers **were having** dinner when somebody **knocked** on their door.
10 I **was packing** my bags while Dad **was getting** the car ready.

60

I **heard** a terrible explosion while I **was walking** into my office on the 24th floor of the north tower, so I **looked** out the window. Lots of paper **was falling** from the sky. A voice on the loudspeaker **said** we should leave the building, so we **started** walking down the stairs. As we **were going** down, we saw some firefighters. They **were running** up the stairs. When we **got** to the ground floor, we **ran** away from the building as fast as we could, and after about ten minutes we **stopped** in a small park. That's where we **were standing** when the second tower **fell**.

61

Rick and his friends **were playing** basketball in the gym when Rick's friend Tony **stumbled** and **hurt** his wrist. While one of the boys from the team **was looking** for help, Rick **phoned** Tony's parents and **told** them about the accident.

Last evening, I **was reading** a book while my parents **were watching** a show on TV. My little sisters **were playing** with their toys and Tiger, our dog, **was sitting** by the door. I think he **wanted** to go for his walk!

62

1 Sarah was snoring in her sleep. → **Sarah wasn't snoring in her sleep**.
2 We were waiting for you. → **We weren't waiting for you**.
3 I was daydreaming. → **I wasn't daydreaming**.
4 You were listening. → **You weren't listening**.
5 The boys were playing games. → **The boys weren't playing games**.
6 Dad was listening to Queen. → **Dad wasn't listening to Queen**.

63

1 **Dad wasn't listening to Queen.** He doesn't like rock music.
2 **Sarah wasn't snoring in her sleep.** She was having a bad dream.
3 **The boys weren't playing games.** They were working on their PCs.
4 **I wasn't daydreaming.** I was thinking about what you said.
5 **We weren't waiting for you.** We were just standing there.
6 We told you the whole story, but **you weren't listening**.

64

1 The farmers were milking the cows.
(a) Were **the farmers milking the cows**?
(b) Who **was milking the cows**?
(c) What **were the farmers doing**?
(d) What **were the farmers milking**?

2 James was living in Manchester.
(a) Was **James living in Manchester**?
(b) Who **was living in Manchester**?
(c) What **was James doing**?
(d) Where **was James living**?

3 The girls were laughing because they were happy.
(a) Were **the girls laughing because …**?
(b) Who **was laughing**?
(c) What **were the girls doing**?
(d) Why **were the girls laughing**?

4 Dad was driving to work at 8 a.m.
(a) Was **Dad driving to work at 8 a.m.**?
(b) Who **was driving to work at 8 a.m.**?
(c) What **was Dad doing at 8 a.m.**?
(d) When **was Dad driving to work**?

65

A	J	C	L	O	T	S	R
B	F	O	R	G	E	T	E
D	G	M	A	M	G	E	T
B	R	E	A	K	I	A	V
Y	E	B	U	A	V	L	H
C	A	T	C	H	E	K	O
U	D	L	F	I	N	D	L
T	O	V	S	T	A	N	D

across →
forget/forgotten
get /got
break/broken
catch/caught
find/found
stand/stood

down ↓
cut/cut
read/read
come/come
hit/hit
give/given
steal/stolen
hold/held

66

1 **I've lost** my keys! I can't get in!
2 Melanie **has won** the tennis tournament.
3 Ryan **has had** a skiing accident.
4 Grandma **has baked** our favourite cake.
5 Oh no, **I've spent** all my money!
6 Dad looks tired. He**'s slept** only four hours.
7 Look, the guests **have arrived**!
8 The children **have gone** to bed.
9 Mum **has bought** new shoes for me.

67

1 The baby has woken up.
(a) **Has the baby woken up?**
(b) **Who has woken up?**
(c) **The baby hasn't woken up.**

2 They have built a snowman.
(a) **Have they built a snowman?**
(b) **Who has built a snowman?**
(c) **They haven't built a snowman.**

Bitte umblättern! ↺

3 You have tidied up your room.
(a) **Have you tidied up your room?** *(b)* **Who has tidied up your room?**
(c) **You haven't tidied up your room.**

4 Our dog has eaten the sausages.
(a) **Has our dog eaten the sausages?** *(b)* **Who has eaten our sausages?**
(c) **Our dog hasn't eaten the sausages.**

68

1 Dad ~~will fix~~/**has fixed** my bike.
2 **Have you ever touched**/~~Did you ever touch~~ a snake?
3 I **have never thought**/~~never think~~ about this problem.
4 Who ~~ate~~/**has eaten** my snack?
5 You **haven't thanked**/~~didn't thank~~ Uncle Harry for the present yet!
6 We **have stayed**/~~will stay~~ long enough.
7 What ~~did you bring~~/**have you brought** with you?
8 **Has Joe answered**/~~Did Joe answer~~ your email yet?
9 Who ~~painted~~/**has painted** this beautiful picture?
10 **Have you heard**/~~Will your hear~~ from Julia yet?
11 Andy ~~drops~~/**has dropped** the vase.
12 Tina **has fed**/~~fed~~ the hamster.

69

for		since	
ten days	**half an hour**	**midnight**	**2011**
many months	**a short time**	**January**	**Christmas**
hours	**more than a year**	**May 1st**	**we arrived**
a little while	**for a few seconds**	**7 o'clock**	**I met you**

70

1 Gina hasn't read a book **since** she left school a year ago.
2 Mum hasn't slept **for** three nights in a row. She looks really tired.
3 I haven't been shopping with my friends **since** Ellie's birthday.
4 Grandma hasn't watched a movie **since** 1989.
5 Harry hasn't spoken with me **since** our silly fight last week.
6 My computer hasn't properly worked **for** a week.
7 Mum hasn't made pizza **for** a long time.
8 I haven't heard from Melissa **for** over a year.
9 We haven't had ham and eggs for breakfast **since** our trip to England.
10 Dad hasn't played hockey **for** many years.

71

(1D), 2F, 3B, 4H, 5A, 6C, 7E, 8G

72

1 **I have known Jim since kindergarten.**
2 **Mila hasn't eaten for two days.**
3 **The apples have fallen from the tree.**
4 **Diego has learned with Durchstarten for three years.**

73

1	It has rained. The streets are wet.	**yes**	can't say
	It rained. The streets are wet.	yes	**can't say**
2	Ben hurt his elbow. He can't move his arm.	yes	**can't say**
	Ben has hurt his elbow. He can't move his arm.	**yes**	can't say
3	We have lived here for two years. We still live here.	**yes**	can't say
	We lived here for two years. We still live here.	yes	**can't say**
4	The bell rang. Somebody is at the door.	yes	**can't say**
	The bell has rung. Somebody is at the door.	**yes**	can't say
5	Somebody opened the window. It's cold in here.	yes	**can't say**
	Somebody has opened the window. It's cold in here.	**yes**	can't say

74

1 I've had (PS) (PPF) a terrible headache all day. – Oh no! When did it start? (PS) (PPF)
2 I had (PS) (PPF) a phone call from Larissa last night. – How is she?
I haven't heard (PS) (PPF) from her for weeks.
3 When Mum was (PS) (PPF) 17, she spent (PS) (PPF) a year at an American high school.
She has been (PS) (PPF) back to the USA many times since then.
4 Look at this mess! What have you done? (PS) (PPF) – I'm sorry.
When I opened (PS) (PPF) the drawer, everything fell (PS) (PPF) to the floor.

75

1B, 2C, 3F, 4E, 5G, 6A, 7D

76

1 *A:* I**'ve had** this camera since 2017.
B: **Did you buy** it or (be) **was** it a present?
A: I **bught** it with my birthday money.

2 *A:* I **texted** Sue some days ago, but so far she **hasn't answered**. I hope she's alright.
B: I **spoke** to her yesterday. She**'s had** a fever since Tuesday, but she's getting better.

3 *A:* Do you know Andy Miller?
B: Of course. I**'ve known** him since kindergarten. Why?
A: Well, I **met** him at a party last weekend and I **liked** him.

4 *A:* Ah, you're here at last. Where **have you been**?
B: I'm sorry I'm late, but the bus **didn't come** on time and I **had** to wait for twenty minutes.

77

1 **Have you ever heard** of a man called Tenzing Norgay? –
I have. He **reached** the summit of Mt. Everest in 1953.
2 **Have you ever been** to Japan? – No, I haven't, but my father **went** there on business last year.
3 What's wrong with Sophie? I **haven't seen** her for a week. –
Don't you know? She **had** an accident last Monday.
4 **Did you like** the movie last night? – It **was** alright, but I**'ve seen** better films.

78

1 When **did you meet Alice**?
2 **Uncle Herbert bought his car 20 years ago.**
3 **Rupert has just arrived.**
4 **We've lived in this town for a year.**

Bitte umblättern!

5 **Diana's plane landed a moment ago.**
6 **How long have you been the number one player of your club?**
7 **Daniel fell in love with Grace in high school.**

79 I think I **have had** a very interesting life. I'm 75 now and I **haven't worked** for six years. I **made** my last movie at 69. I **started** acting at the age of 18. **I've played** in more than 60 films and **I've had** some success. **I've been (was)** nominated for the 'Oscar' three times, but I **won** it only once, in 2001. While I was working, I **visited** many beautiful places, like Canada, New Zealand and Hawaii, but I never **went** to Austria and Switzerland. I **liked** New Zealand best.
I've never played a role in a TV series because nobody **has ever asked** me, but **I've recorded** a few audio books, so you can hear my voice without seeing me.
I've met many fascinating people and **I've worked** with many great actors and actresses and directors. As I **said** at the beginning, my life **has been** very interesting!

80 1 Mum **bought** a beautiful vase in Rome last summer.
Tiger **has just knocked over** Mum's beautiful vase.
2 I **got** an awfully old-fashioned blouse for my birthday.
I **haven't worn** it yet. It still hangs in my closet.

81 1 My father has been working for the same company **for** 12 years.
2 Isabel and Oscar have been dancing **since** the beginning of the party.
3 Mr Zacharias has been teaching at our school **since** 2002.
4 That tree has been standing there **for** a very long time.
5 Dad has been trying to fix the old radio **for** days.
6 My grandparents have been driving their car **since** before I was born.

82 obere Bilderreihe: 3 – 2 – 5; untere Bilderreihe: 6 – 1 – 4

1 Oliver **has been waiting** for Kate for half an hour.
2 The children **have been playing** in the garden all afternoon.
3 Nigel **has been listening** to his favourite music since lunch.
4 Mum and I **have been shopping** all morning.
5 It **has been snowing** since yesterday.
6 Olivia **has been painting** her fingernails for ten minutes.

83 1E, 2G, 3A, 4F, 5B, 6C, 7H, (8D)

84 1 Grandpa **has had** his driving licence for 50 years, and he **has been driving** the same old car since I can remember.
2 These trees **have been standing** next to our school for years and years. I'm glad they **haven't cut** them down yet.
3 It**'s been raining** for a week, so we **haven't been** able to play football.
4 The children **have been playing** on the beach for hours, and they **have already built** three lovely sandcastles.

5 **Have you finished** tidying up your room yet? – No, not yet, but I**'ve been working** since this morning.
6 Our neighbours **have been painting** their house all week, and they **have already finished** four rooms.

85

Amanda: This is unbelievable! We**'ve been sitting** here for half an hour and nobody **has asked** us what we want to order. I think the waiter **has forgotten** us.
Melanie: I'm sure he has. He **has walked** past us ten times! Perhaps he thinks we**'ve already ordered**.
Amanda: Look at these people over there! They **have been** here for only ten or twelve minutes and they are already eating!
Melanie: The waiter must see that we **haven't ordered** yet. After all, we**'ve been** here for half an hour!
Amanda: Well, he**'s been running** around and taking orders and serving food, but he **hasn't bothered** to ask us yet. Let's call him. … Here, waiter!
Waiter: Just a minute, ladies, I'll be with you in a moment …

86

1 *A:* How long **has Joe been sleeping**?
B: Well, he **went** to bed at around 8, so that makes it more than twelve hours.
2 *A:* How long **have you been playing** football?
B: Not very long.
A: When **did you begin**?
B: Only ten minutes ago.
3 *A:* How long **has Tina been watching** TV?
B: Since she **came** home from school.
A: That's four hours! That's too long!

87

1 **Dad has been driving for six hours.** 2
2 **Cousin Melody has been looking for a flat since May.** 4
3 **Simon has been studying for his exams for a week.** 3
4 **Mum and Dad have been decorating the Christmas tree all evening.** 5
5 **The band has been practising for months.** 6
6 **Those men have been watching our house since last week.** 1

88

1 That's why we've called the police.	(kommt nach Satz 6)
2 That's why he needs a break.	(kommt nach Satz 1)
3 That's why it's been so quiet in the house.	(kommt nach Satz 3)
4 That's why she always checks the newspapers.	(kommt nach Satz 2)
5 That's why they've locked the door into the living room.	(kommt nach Satz 4)
6 That's why they play much better now.	(kommt nach Satz 5)

89

1 The sun **doesn't shine** at night.
2 Ali never **drinks** beer or wine.
3 My parents **don't work** in an office in town.
4 We usually **have** pancakes for breakfast on Sunday.
5 Many tourists **arrive** by plane.
6 The Amazon **empties** into the Atlantic Ocean.
7 Oranges **don't grow** in Austria.
8 Gorillas **live** in the jungle.
9 Trevor **goes** to school in Sheffield

90

1 Gina always **does** her homework at school.
2 Harry and I **play** squash every Saturday.
3 The school bus **stops** across the street from my house.
4 My friends and I usually **walk** to school together.
5 Ellie often **listens** to her favourite songs.
6 Young children **ask** lots of questions.
7 I **don't believe** in vampires and ghosts.
8 Mum sometimes **takes** the bus to work in the morning.

91

1 Dad **walks** to work. He **doesn't drive**.
2 We **spend** our holidays on the beach, but we **don't go** skiing in winter.
3 The students **don't wear** uniforms. They **wear** jeans and T-shirts.
4 Britney **lives** in a large flat. She **doesn't live** in a house with a garden.
5 I **have** two sisters, but I **don't have** a brother.
6 Margaret **doesn't like** dogs, but she **loves** cats.

92

Angela and her family **live** in the country. She **likes** the country because they **are** far away from the noise and pollution of the city. Angela usually **gets** up early because she **loves** going for a short walk in the morning. Her father and her brother Freddie often **go** with her. Her mother **stays** at home and **prepares** breakfast. After the walk, they all **have** breakfast together. Then Angela and Freddie **take** the bus to school, and their father **drives** to work. He **is** a dentist and he **works** in the small town near their village. Angela's mother and a neighbour **walk** to the village kindergarten where they **work** until 2 p.m. At the end of the school day, the children usually **do not return** to their house together. Angela **takes** the bus back but Freddie **stays** at school longer because he **plays** rugby for the school team. Angela's father **doesn't finish** working before 5 p.m. Then he **picks up** Freddie and they **drive** back home in time for dinner.

93

							7							
				5	6		T	8					13	
1			4	W	B		A	A	9				T	
C	2		B	E	U		U	R	H	10		12	R	14
A	G	3	E	R	I		G	R	U	A	11	T	I	D
M	**A**	**R**	**C**	**E**	**L**	■	**H**	**I**	**R**	**S**	**C**	**H**	**E**	**R**
E	V	O	A		T		T	V	T	K	U	R	D	O
	E	D	M					E		E	T	E		V
		E	E					D		D		W		E

And the 'mysterious person' is **MARCEL HIRSCHER**.

94
1 We went (**I**) to Italy last summer, and we visited (**R**) many beautiful cities.
2 Joe's father liked (**R**) his car, but then he bought (**I**) a bigger one.
3 When I was (**I**) new at this school, I sometimes felt (**I**) lonely.
4 The men got (**I**) into the car and drove (**I**) away quickly.
5 I found (**I**) a mobile phone in the locker room and gave it (**I**) to the teacher.
6 The Wright brothers flew (**I**) the first aeroplane in 1903. It stayed (**R**) in the air for only twelve seconds.

95
1 **go**
2 **buy**
3 **be** ▪ **feel**
4 **get** ▪ **drive**
5 **find** ▪ **give**
6 **fly**

96
1 In London, we **visited** Madame Tussauds, but we **didn't ride** the London Eye.
2 Rosie **didn't finish** her breakfast, but she **drank** all the milk.
3 You **played** computer games all afternoon, but you **didn't tidy up** your room.
4 Lisa **took** 'Alfie' for a walk, but she **didn't feed** him.
5 Linus **didn't watch** the movie, but he **read** the book.
6 I **didn't see** Ruthie today, but I **talked** to her on the phone.

97
A long, long time ago, in Bagdad, there **lived** a boy named Aladdin. One day, an old man **came** to his house and **said** that he **was** his uncle. Aladdin's father **died** many years before, so Aladdin's mother **was** very happy and **invited** the old man into her house.
The next day, the uncle **gave** Aladdin nice clothes to wear and **took** him on a tour through the city gardens. All this **impressed** the boy very much, and so he **said** yes when the old man **asked** him to work for him. But this old man **wasn't really** Aladdin's uncle. He **was** an evil magician, and he **wanted** to use the boy for his purposes. Of course, Aladdin and his mother **had** no idea.
So he **went** on long walks with the old man, and on one of these walks they **came** to the foot of a mountain. They **sat** down to rest, and the old man **lit** a fire. He **threw** something into the flames and mumbled some words. Aladdin **didn't understand** what his 'uncle' was saying, but suddenly the ground beneath them **opened** and they **could** see a tunnel. Aladdin **didn't like** this, and he **was** afraid, but the old man **said**, "Don't be afraid. Nothing will happen to you. But you must do what I say. Walk through this tunnel until you come to a beautiful garden. In the middle of this garden there is a shining lamp. Bring me this lamp, but do not touch anything!"
Aladdin **walked** through the tunnel, he **found** the lamp and he **took** it with him. When he **reached** the end of the tunnel, the magician **wanted** to grab the lamp from Aladdin's hands, but Aladdin **didn't let** it go. The evil old man **was** so angry that he **closed** the tunnel before the boy **could** get out. Aladdin **didn't know** what to do, and in his panic he **rubbed** the lamp. Suddenly a genie **appeared** and **said**, "You are my master now and I will do everything you say!" "Take me home," Aladdin **answered**. "I want to be with my mother!"
Aladdin's mother **was** happy. Now they **had** everything – enough to eat, nice clothes and a beautiful new house. Every wish **came** true, and for some years everything **went** well. One day, Aladdin **saw** Jasmine, the king's daughter, and he **fell** in love with her at once. When the king **saw** the expensive gifts Aladdin **gave** his daughter, he **allowed** the young man to marry her. Aladdin **told** the genie to build him a palace, and the genie **fulfilled** Aladdin's wish. Now Aladdin, his new wife and his mother **lived** in a wonderful new palace and they **had** everything they **wanted**.
But the evil magician **heard** of Aladdin's good luck, and now he **wanted** the lamp for himself. So he **went** to the palace with a cart full of new lamps, and he **shouted**, "Old for new! Old for new!" Jasmine **didn't know** the value of the old lamp, and so she **exchanged** it for a new one. At once, the magician **ordered** the genie to transport the palace and Jasmine to Africa.

Bitte umblättern! ↺

When Aladdin **heard** of this, he **sat** down on his flying carpet and **went** to look for his wife and the magician. He soon **found** the old man and he **punished** him – he **put** poison in his drink, and so the evil man **died**. But Aladdin, his mother and Jasmine **lived** happily until the end of their days.

98

1 What's the name of the little statue **which / that** is awarded as a prize for the best film every year?
A Oscar | **B** Emmy | **C** Golden Camera

2 What's the name of the man **who / that** first climbed Mt. Everest without an oxygen mask?
A Edmund Hillary | **B** Heinrich Harrer | **C Reinhold Messner**

3 What's the name of the ship **which / that** sank on its first voyage in 1912?
A Lusitania | **B Titanic** | **C** Andrea Doria

4 What's the name of the woman **who / that** won two Nobel Prizes, one for Physics and one for Chemistry?
A Marie Curie | **B** Jane Addams | **C** Bertha von Suttner

5 What's the name of the rocket **which / that** took the first men to the Moon?
A Saturn | **B** Atlas | **C** Aries

6 What's the name of the man **who / that** founded Amazon®?
A Steve Jobs | **B** Bill Gates | **C Jeff Bezos**

7 What was the name of the airplane **which / that** Charles Lindbergh flew from New York to Paris in 1927?
A The Spirit of St. Louis | **B** The Eagle | **C** The Challenger

8 What's the name of the gymnast **who / that** won 25 world championship medals, 19 of them in gold?
A Olga Korbut | **B Simone Biles** | **C** Nadia Comaneci

99

1 Bicycles ~~who~~/**which/that** have bad brakes are dangerous.
2 The blond woman **who/**~~which~~**/that** is talking to my mum is my English teacher.
3 The photos ~~who~~/**which/that** hang on the wall of my room were taken by me.
4 The chef is the person **who/**~~which~~**/that** is in charge of a restaurant kitchen.
5 The woman **who/**~~which~~**/that** let us into the house was very nice.
6 Joe works for a company ~~who~~/**which/that** makes furniture.
7 There are some boys in my class **who/**~~which~~**/that** don't like football.
8 The car ~~who~~/**which/that** stands over there belongs to Ms Hill.
9 The old lady **who/**~~which~~**/that** lives upstairs is almost 90.
10 Mr Jenkins smokes only cigars ~~who~~/**which/that** come from Cuba.

100

1 This is the bus. It stops at the bank.
This is the bus that stops at the bank. / This is the bus which stops at the bank.

2 Where are the flowers? They were on the table.
Where are the flowers that were on the table?
Where are the flowers which were on the table?

3 These are the people. They were making all that noise.
These are the people who were making all that noise.
These are the people that were making all that noise.

4 What's the name of the man? He phoned you yesterday.
What's the name of the man who phoned you yesterday?
What's the neme of the man that phoned you yesterday?

5 Many young people get into trouble. They drink and take drugs.
Many young people who drink and take drugs get into trouble.
Many young people that drink and take drugs get into trouble.

6 Have you met the guests? They arrived last night.
Have you met the guests who arrived last night?
Have you met the guests that arrived last night?

7 The burglars took some jewels. They weren't really expensive.
The burglars took some jewels that weren't really expensive.
The burglars took some jewels which weren't really expensive.

8 The tomatoes are excellent. They grow in Grandma's garden.
The tomatoes that grow in Grandma's garden are excellent.
The tomatoes which grow in Grandma's garden are excellent.

101

1 Vera watches only movies **that / which** have a happy end.
2 What was the name of the girl **who / that** invited you to her party?
3 The boy **who / that** broke his arm yesterday can't play volleyball now.
4 Can you remember the people **who / that** asked you for the way?
5 The shop **that / which** sells these jeans is closed today.
6 Are you the man **who / that** can help us?
7 Everybody **who / that** knows Jane likes her.
8 Ms Talbot is the architect **who / that** designed our house.
9 I don't know many young people **who / that** like folk music.
10 The fiddle is an instrument **that / which** looks and sounds like a violin.
11 The woman **who / that** sold me the stamps wasn't very helpful.
12 At the zoo you can see all the animals **that / which** live in the Alps.
13 'Star Trek' is one of the best TV series **that / which** have ever been written.
14 The people **who / that** live above us are from Russia.
15 I hate dogs **that / which** bark all night.
16 The pictures **which / that** were stolen from the museum have been found.
17 A baker is a person **who / that** makes bread and rolls and buns.
18 The postcard **that / which** came this morning is from Martin.

102 Amelia's grandmother is a woman **who / that** doesn't act her age. She's 80, but she knows everything about fashion and movies and politics, and she reads science books **that / which** are much too complicated for Amelia.

Amelia's granny also loves the computer games **that / which** she gets from Amelia and she plays as often as she can. She doesn't like the last one **that** Amelia gave her. She says she hates games **that / which** have guns and violence in them. Granny also loves cooking. She says people **who / that**

Bitte umblättern!

don't love good food don't know how to live. The food **that / which** she loves best is always fresh and organic. She buys her fruit and vegetables from farmers **who / that** grow everything on their fields and in their gardens. She says the things **that / which** people buy at supermarkets are not so good and healthy. She watches TV programmes **that / which** deal with food, and she listens to people **who / that** know about these things. She is really a very unusual woman!

103 1E, 2H, 3A, 4F, 5C, 6D, 7B, 8G

104
1 Is this the driver **(who)**/whose/which caused the accident?
2 These are the people who/**(whose)**/which parties are always great fun.
3 France is the country who/whose/**(which)** attracts the most tourists.
4 George Washington was a general **(who)**/whose/which became president.
5 The kiwi is a bird who/whose/**(which)** lives only in New Zealand.
6 That's the teacher who/**(whose)**/which name I cannot remember.

105 1 ☒ 2 ☐ 3 ☒ 4 ☒ 5 ☒ 6 ☐

106
1 **I've got an uncle who works in Dubai.**
2 **Is this the train that goes to the airport?**
3 **That's the man whose wife is our doctor.**

107
1 It always **takes** George a long time to get ready for bed.
2 How long **did** it take you to do your homework yesterday?
3 It **will take** them years to build their house, but by 2025 it will be finished.
4 It **has taken** me a month to finish my model plane, but now it's ready to fly.
5 How long **will it take** you to pack your suitcase? – I don't know. I haven't started yet.
6 It never **takes** us more than ten minutes to tidy up our rooms.
7 When Grandpa was a boy, it **took** him two hours to walk to school.
8 It **didn't** take them long to clear the roads after last week's snowstorm.

108
1 It **took** Apollo 11 nine days to travel to the Moon and back.
2 It **will take** astronauts six months or more to fly to Mars.
3 It usually **takes** Julia two days to read a book.
4 It **has taken** Paula many years to learn playing the cello, but now she's very good.
5 How long **did it take** the French to build the Eiffel Tower? – Only 26 months, from January 1887 to March 1889.
6 How long **will it take** doctors to find a cure for the common cold?

109 (1D), 2G, 3F, 4A, 5C, 6B, 7I, 8H, 9E

110
1 My phone suddenly rang **during** the English lesson.
2 Grandma fell asleep **while** she was watching a film.
3 I talked to Marie **while** we were waiting for the bus.

4 Harold didn't feel well **during** the test.
5 **While** we were having dinner, somebody knocked on the door.
6 We don't speak very much **during** breakfast.
7 In my school, we can use our tablets **during** the breaks.
8 Cindy came into the bathroom **while** I was brushing my teeth.

111
1 I fell asleep during the conference. → **while I was at the conference**
2 The lights went out while we were having dinner. → **during dinner**
3 The drummer fell ill while the band was on tour. → **during the tour**
4 We can't play tennis while it's raining. → **during the rain**
5 Joe met Sue during his holiday in Spain. → **while he was on holiday in Spain**
6 Dad's phone rang three times during concert. → **while he was at the concert**

112
1 The shops are open **until** 10 p.m.
2 Joe says he will finish his model ship **by the time** we visit him again.
3 I waited for you **till** 5 o'clock, but then I went home.
4 **By the time** I got back home, dinner was ready.
5 The guests are going to stay **until** the end of the week.
6 We won't go away **till** you come back
7 Everybody was tired **by the time** the match was over.
8 The food was cold **by the time** it arrived at our table.

113

until / till	as far as
we meet again	**the next street**
5 a.m.	**the post office**
next week	**your house**
Christmas	**the bus stop**
tomorrow	**over there**

114
1 **a)** I finished my homework. My eyes hurt.
b) **By the time** I finished my homework, my eyes hurt.
2 **a)** Dad was listening to the radio. He was driving to work.
b) Dad was listening to the radio **while** he was driving to work.
3 **a)** Mum shut all the windows and doors. She left the house.
b) Mum shut all the windows **before** she left the house.
4 **a)** We were on holiday in Scotland. We met some very nice people.
b) We met some very nice people **during** our holiday in Scotland.
5 **a)** We waited for you. At 6 o'clock we gave up.
b) We waited for you **until** 6 o'clock.
6 **a)** Mum always checks her emails. She arrives at her office.
b) Mum always checks her emails **after** she arrives at her office.
7 **a)** Bella was reading a book. She heard a strange noise.
b) Bella was reading a book **when** she heard a strange noise.

115

1	**A** After	**B** During	**C When**	7	**A during**	**B** before	**C** after
2	**A** after	**B before**	**C** during	8	**A** before	**B** by the time	**C after**
3	**A While**	**B** During	**C** By the time	9	**A After**	**B** During	**C** Before
4	**A** While	**B By the time**	**C** After	10	**A** during	**B** before	**C while**
5	**A** before	**B** while	**C after**	11	**A When**	**B** After	**C** Before
6	**A** after	**B during**	**C** before	12	**A** While	**B By the time**	**C** After

Last weekend, Dad and I went to the sports arena in our town. We wanted to see my brother Alec play basketball with his team. *(1)* **When** we arrived, there was still time to get drinks and hotdogs *(2)* **before** the game began. Alec's Team was playing a team from a neighbouring town, and many people were there to see their team win. *(3)* **While** we were waiting for the game to begin, I took some photos with my new camera. *(4)* **By the time** the players came onto the court at last, everybody in the auditorium was cheering, but *(5)* **after** the game began, the people calmed down. Both teams played well, and I took many photos *(6)* **during** the match. Alec scored 21 points *(7)* **during** the first two quarters, but then the coach took him out of the game – Alec's arm hurt *(8)* **after** a player from the other team hit him hard. Dad and I were very proud of him! *(9)* **After** the game, we waited for Alec in the lobby, and *(10)* **while** we were waiting, Dad looked at my photos. They were quite good! *(11)* **When** Alec and his teammates came, we said well done and bravo and great game, and then we drove home. *(12)* **By the time** we came back to our house, Alec's arm was hurting badly. So Dad drove him to the hospital, and that was not really a happy ending to a fine day!

116

1 **While** we were walking up the hill, it was raining, but …
2 … **when** we reached the top, the sun was shining again.
3 I said good-bye to Laura **before** I got on the bus, and …
4 … **by the time** I came home, she had texted me twice.
5 There was a terrible thunderstorm **during** the night, and …
6 … in the morning, **after** the storm, we saw many fallen trees.
7 Some people left the cinema **during** the film.
8 Some people left the cinema **before** the film was over.

117

1 Lisa's favourite band **is (called)** 'The Jonas Boys'.
2 They **are** three handsome and talented boys from the USA.
3 Lisa **thinks** it's cool that they are all songwriters.
4 'The Jonas Boys' **sing (songs)** about life and love and young people's problems.
5 The oldest brother is the lead singer and the **leader of the band**.
6 The youngest brother plays **the piano (and sings)**.
7 The third band member is the 'sandwich child', and he plays the guitar **and bass (and he also sings)**.
8 'The Jonas Boys' have many hits you can **listen to on the radio**.
9 **Lisa's favourite song** is about the crazy things a boy does when he is in love.
10 **She really likes it** because it is cool and funny.
11 **Now you know** everything about her favourite band.
12 **Do you have** a favourite band?

Transcript mit Lösungshinweisen
Hi, my name is Lisa and today I want to tell you about my favourite band. They are called 'The Jonas Boys' and they are three boys from the USA. They are all very handsome and talented and they are also actors.

'The Jonas Boys' sing songs about life and love and about young people's problems. All of them are songwriters, which I think is very cool. The oldest brother is the lead singer, and he's also the leader of the band. The youngest brother plays the piano and sings. The third band member is the 'sandwich child'. He plays the guitar and bass and he also sings. Their voices sound great together and they have many hits that you can listen to on the radio. My favourite song is about the crazy things a boy does when he is in love. I really like it because it is cool and funny. So now you know everything about my favourite band. Do you have a favourite band?

118

1	Last summer, Paula went to a concert with her family.	**False**	(friends)
2	It was in Paris and it was wonderful.	**False**	(Vienna)
3	They got there early and sat at the back.	**True**	
4	The problem was that they could not see very well.	**False**	(could see everything very well)
5	They also saw a cool laser show.	**True**	
6	Everyone screamed when the concert started and Paula was scared.	**False**	(really happy)
7	The music at the concert was very loud.	**True**	
8	Paula and her friends sang and danced to the music.	**True**	
9	After the concert the girls bought ice cream.	**False**	(T-shirts)
10	It was a wonderful night for Paula.	**True**	

Transcript mit Lösungshinweisen

Last summer, I was at a concert with my friends. It was in Vienna and it was wonderful. We got there an hour before it started and we had seats at the back. We could see everything very well because there were huge screens everywhere. Before the concert began, there was a great laser show with many lights and cool effects and when the band began to play, everyone suddenly screamed very loudly. I was really happy to be at the concert and not just watching it on TV. The music was very loud but great. My friends and I knew all the songs, so we sang along. We also danced to the music and it was wonderful! When the concert was over, we bought T-shirts. It was a very magical night which I will never forget.

119

1 Last night, many things **were happening** at Dan's house.
2 Dan **was sitting** at his desk in his room.
3 He **was doing** his homework.
4 Dan's mum **was taking** a shower.
5 She **was singing** a love song.
6 Dan's dad **was watching** a football match on TV.
7 He **was eating** popcorn and chocolate.
8 And he **was shouting** for his team.
9 Dan's brother **was playing** the bass guitar in his room.
10 Dan **was having** problems with his homework.

Transcript mit Lösungshinweisen

Last night was very stressful. Many things were happening at our house. I was sitting at my desk in my room. I was doing my homework. I had to write a text about my favourite band. But it was hard because it was very loud in our house.

Mum was in the bathroom. She was taking a shower and she was singing a love song! It didn't sound bad but it was not helpful because I had to concentrate.

Dad was watching a football match on TV. He was eating popcorn and chocolate. And he was shouting for his team. It was hard for me to do my homework because I wanted to watch the match with him.

Bitte umblättern!

My brother was playing the bass guitar in his room. His room is next to mine and so I found it even harder to concentrate.
Now you know why I had problems doing my homework last night. What was happening at your house last night?

120

1 Jim was on **holiday** in Paris.
2 He set off for the **airport** on Monday morning.
3 He had to **get** there by 7:30.
4 The plane **took off** at 9:45.
5 Jim **got on** the plane at about 9:30.
6 The flight **took** about two hours.
7 The plane **landed** at around 11:45.
8 Then he waited for his bags and **got** a car.
9 Next, he **drove to** the hotel.
10 Travelling takes time but it is nice to **get out of** the house.

Transcript mit Lösungshinweisen

Tina: Hello, Jim!
Jim: Hi, Tina. How are you?
Tina: I'm doing great, thanks. And how are you?
Jim: I'm doing great, too. I just got back from my holiday in Paris and it was wonderful.
Tina: Oh yeah … I forgot. How was it? Tell me everything.
Jim: Okay … I set off for the airport last Monday at 6:30 in the morning.
Tina: Wow, that's early.
Jim: Well, I had to get to the airport by 7:30 because the plane took off at 9:45.
Tina: I see. And when did you get on the plane?
Jim: Let me think… it was at about 9:30.
Tina: And how long was your flight then?
Jim: It took about two hours. The plane landed at around 11:45.
Tina: And then you had to wait for your bags and get the car and drive to the hotel.
Jim: Yes, travelling takes time, but it's nice to get out of the house.

121

1 **When** Hannah was a young girl, she wanted to be a princess.
2 **One night** she had a strange dream, and in her dream, she was swimming in a lake.
3 **While** she was swimming, it started to rain and she got out of the water.
4 **Suddenly** she saw a big green frog that was smiling at her.
5 **Before** Hannah could touch the frog, it spoke to her and said, 'Hello, what is your name?'
6 **Then** the girl answered, 'My name is Hannah. And who are you?'
7 **Next** the frog said, 'I am Prince Louis of Burgundy and I am not a frog.'
8 **After** Hannah listened to the frog, she knew it was a dream.
9 It **took** her some time, but then she woke up.
10 **In the end**, Hannah was sad that it was just a dream and that she hadn't kissed the frog to see what happened.

122

Yesterday I watched a film called 'Life on Mars' and it was **the craziest** film ever!
It was about a spaceship that landed on Mars and found **the strangest** kangaroos there!
The spaceship that flies to Mars is not **as new as** the spaceships that fly to the Moon and there is a problem.

The spaceship is **faster than** it should be and then starts to burn.
So it crashes on Mars where there are **the biggest** mountains in the solar system.
Then the astronauts get out of the spaceship and think they are on **the best** part of the planet because it is very beautiful there.
Soon they see the kangaroos that are much **bigger than** the ones at the zoo.
But they do not know that kangaroos on Mars are **the most dangerous** animals there are.
The kangaroos can jump **as far as** half a football field.
Suddenly the strange kangaroos attack the astronauts but I don't want to tell you the end, just that it is **the best** film ever.

123 (1F), 2J, 3A, 4H, 5I, 6B, 7D, 8C, 9E, 10G

Transcript mit Lösungshinweisen
Big Ben is the name of the bell which is in a huge clock tower.
The London Eye is a giant Ferris Wheel by the River Thames which offers a great view over the city.
Tower Bridge is the bridge across the Thames which they raise when big ships come up the river.
The Tower of London is a museum which used to be a castle and then a prison.
The Globe Theatre was financed by William Shakespeare, who is known for writing many famous plays.
His most famous play is about young lovers who are called Romeo and Juliet.
Hyde Park is wonderful for people who like to exercise or relax in the fresh air.
Sharks and octopuses are sea creatures which you can find in the London Aquarium.
Samuel Pepys is the famous writer who wrote about the Great Fire of London of 1666 in his diary.
The Beatles were a band of four young British singers who were very popular in their time.

124

1. If the weather is nice, they **will go to the park**.
2. If they go to the park, they **will have a picnic (together)**.
3. Tim doesn't know if the weather **will be nice (at the weekend)**.
4. If it rains, they **will do something else**.
5. Tina wonders what they will do if **it rains**.
6. If it rains, they **will go to the cinema**.
7. If they go the cinema, Tina **will buy popcorn**.
8. Tim doesn't know if there **will be a good film on (at the cinema)**.
9. If they watch a scary film, Tina **will hold Tim's hand**.
10. Tim will sit close to Tina if she **needs him**.

Transcript mit Lösungshinweisen
Tim: What will we do at the weekend?
Tina: Well, if the weather is nice, we'll go to the park.
Tim: Great idea. If we go to the park, we'll have a picnic together.
Tina: That sounds fun, but I don't know if the weather will be nice at the weekend.
Tim: Well, if it rains, we will do something else.
Tina: Alright, what will we do if it rains?
Tim: Let me think … I know! If it rains, we'll go to the cinema.
Tina: Okay, that's also a good idea. If we go the cinema, I'll buy some popcorn because I love popcorn with butter on it.
Tim: So do I. But I don't know if there will be a good film on at the cinema.
Tina: That doesn't matter. If we watch a scary film, I will hold your hand.
Tim: That's okay, and I will sit close to you if you need me.

125

1	The girls have not seen each other for a long time.	**True**	
2	Anna has news about their friend Mia.	**True**	
3	Jane has already heard the terrible news about Mia.	**False**	(she has not heard the good news)
4	Anna says that Mia has fallen in love.	**True**	
5	They met at a party and then went out for coffee together.	**False**	(they met at a wedding and then they had ice cream together)
6	They have not been in close contact since the party.	**False**	(they have been in close contact since the wedding)
7	Mia has had a boyfriend for seven months.	**False**	(five/almost six months)
8	Anna has met Stan and she likes him.	**True**	
9	Stan is nice and sweet to his girlfriend.	**True**	
10	Jane is worried about Mia and mad at her.	**False**	(she is happy for her)
11	Anna says that Mia is very happy now.	**True**	

Transcript mit Lösungshinweisen

Anna: Hey Jane, nice to see you.
Jane: Hi Anna, I haven't seen you for a long time.
Anna: That's true. Have you heard about Mia?
Jane: No, I haven't heard any news lately. How is she?
Anna: Well, Mia is doing wonderfully because she has fallen in love.
Jane: What? When did that happen?
Anna: Uhm … Last May she met a nice guy at the wedding of a friend and then they had ice cream together. Later that day he texted her and they have been in close contact ever since.
Jane: So, what you are saying is that Mia has had a boyfriend for five months already?
Anna: Yes, and they have been a couple for almost half a year. Time flies when you're having fun.
Jane: And have you met him?
Anna: Yes, I have. His name is Stan and he is very nice and so sweet to Mia.
Jane: That's great. I'm very happy for Mia. I know it has been a long time since she was in love.
Anna: You're right, but now Mia has found her Prince Charming and she is the happiest girl I know.
Jane: How wonderful. So, how about you? What has happened in your life lately?

126

1	Iliana's favourite film is about a woman who made a tour of Africa.	**False**	(Europe)
2	That summer, Donna fell in love with three different men.	**True**	
3	Sophie owns a hotel on a Greek island.	**False**	(Donna)

4 Sophie is getting married and wants to know who her **real father is**.
5 Sophie finds her mum's **old diary**.
6 All three men show up at **Donna's hotel**.

7 Sophie invites the men to her **wedding**.
8 The girl decides that she does not want to know who her **father is**.
9 In the end, Sophie is glad to have **three men she can call 'Dad'**.

Transcript mit Lösungshinweisen

My favourite film is about a woman called Donna who went on a tour of Europe when she was young. There she met three different men and had romantic affairs with them. Now, twenty years later, Donna owns a hotel on a small Greek island and has a daughter named Sophie. The girl is getting married soon and she wants to know who her real father is. Sophie finds her mum's old diary about her trip through Europe and her love affairs. So she invites the three men to her wedding because she wants her real father to be with her. Soon all three of them come to stay at Donna's hotel. But when Sophie gets to know them, she likes all of them so much that she decides that she doesn't want to know anymore who her real father is. In the end, Sophie is happy to have three men she can call 'Dad'.

127

1 Amy is allowed to **go to Tom's party (on Friday)**.
2 George is not allowed to **go out at weekends**.
3 George is allowed **to hang out with friends**.
4 George is not allowed to **come home after ten**.
5 George is not allowed to **go to a disco**.
6 George is allowed to **have a party at home**.
7 Amy is not allowed to **go to two parties at the weekend**.

Transcript mit Lösungshinweisen

Amy: Hey George, I have just talked to my mum and I am allowed to go to Tom's party on Friday. Can you come, too?
George: Hi Amy. I don't think so because I'm not allowed to go out at weekends.
Amy: Really? But you are allowed to hang out with friends, aren't you?
George: Well, yes, I am but I am not allowed to come home after ten.
Amy: I see. So you are not allowed to go to a disco?
George: No, I'm not. But I am allowed to have a party at home.
Amy: So, if you cannot come to Tom's party on Friday, you can have a party at your house on Saturday.
George: That's a wonderful idea. Then you can come to my house party on Saturday.
Amy: Oh, well, I am not allowed to go to two parties at the weekend.

128

[3] They couldn't go a day without seeing each other.
[2] The two were together every day.
[6] They weren't able to spend an hour without thinking about the other person.
[11] The young lovers couldn't imagine life without each other.
[7] They weren't able to meet other friends without texting each other all the time.
[1] Last year, Diane fell in love with a cute boy named Marco.
[5] They could tell each other everything.
[8] The two lovebirds sat on a bench in the park every afternoon.
[9] They couldn't sit side by side without touching each other.
[4] Diane and Marco talked on the phone for hours.
[10] They could look into each other's eyes for a very long time.

Transcript mit Lösungshinweisen

1 Last year, Diane fell in love with a cute boy named Marco.
2 The two were together every day.
3 They couldn't go a day without seeing each other.
4 Diane and Marco talked on the phone for hours.

Bitte umblättern!

5 They could tell each other everything.
6 They weren't able to spend an hour without thinking about the other person.
7 They weren't able to meet other friends without texting each other all the time.
8 The two lovebirds sat on a bench in the park every afternoon.
9 They couldn't sit side by side without touching each other.
10 They could look deep into each other's eyes for a very long time.
11 The young lovers couldn't imagine life without each other.

129

1 Thomas thinks in the future we will be able to have cars that **fly through the air**.
2 Claudia hopes that we will be able to **fly to school** with special wings.
3 Thomas also believes that we will be able to order food that drones **bring to our houses**.
4 Claudia says that we won't be able to **live normal lives**.
5 Thomas also thinks that we won't be able to **play ball games** in parks because there won't be any parks anymore.
6 Claudia also believes that in the future we will be able to **travel to any planet (on holiday)**.
7 Thomas asks if Claudia thinks we will be able to **enjoy the summer holidays** on the Moon.
8 Claudia thinks that we will be able to **travel into space** just for fun.
9 Thomas thinks in the future we won't be able to **imagine what life was like now**.
10 Claudia says children will be able to **learn about our way of life** from History books.
11 Thomas asks if Claudia thinks we will be able to **enjoy the future**.
12 Claudia believes we will be able to **have a great time** in the future.

Transcript mit Lösungshinweisen

Claudia: Hey Thomas! Can I ask you something?
Thomas: Hi Claudia! Of course, you can ask me anything.
Claudia: Great! What do you think we will be able to do in the future?
Thomas: That's a good question. Well, I think we will be able to have cars that fly through the air.
Claudia: Really? That's interesting. I hope that we'll be able to fly to school with special wings.
Thomas: That would be great. I also believe that we will be able to order food that drones bring to our houses.
Claudia: So we won't be able to live a normal life, that's for sure.
Thomas: I also think that we won't be able to play ball games in parks because there won't be any parks anymore.
Claudia: I believe that in the future we will be able to travel to other planets on holiday.
Thomas: Really? You think we'll be able to enjoy the summer holidays on the Moon?
Claudia: Yes, I think that we'll be able to travel into space just for fun.
Thomas: In the future we won't be able to imagine what life was like in our days.
Claudia: You're right, children will be able to learn about our way of life from History books.
Thomas: So, do you think we'll be able to enjoy our future?
Claudia: Oh yes, we'll be able to have a great time in the future.
Thomas: Wow, that was interesting! Nice talking to you, Claudia!

130

1 Lisa has been **learning French** for a few weeks.
2 Lisa's aunt has been **staying with them** for a few weeks.
3 She has been **speaking French** with Lisa.
4 Lisa has been **practising French** every day.
5 Lisa says it has been very nice **spending time** with her aunt.
6 Marilyn has been **practising her** music.
7 Marilyn has been **playing the guitar** every day.
8 Marilyn has **written some new** songs.

Transcript mit Lösungshinweisen

Lisa: Hi Marilyn, nice to see you!
Marilyn: Nice to see you, too, Lisa. What have you been doing lately?
Lisa: Well, I have been learning French for a few weeks now and I love it!
Marilyn: Really? How interesting.
Lisa: My aunt has been staying with us for a few weeks and she speaks French with me.
Marilyn: Wow, that's cool. Has it been difficult?
Lisa: Uhm … I have been practising every day, so that makes it easier but French is a difficult language to learn.
Marilyn: Have you had problems with your aunt living at your house?
Lisa: No, it has been very nice spending time with her.
Marilyn: What have you been doing, besides speaking French?
Lisa: Let me think, we have gone for long walks in the park with her dog, Fipsi.
Marilyn: That sounds fun. I love dogs!
Lisa: And what have you been doing lately, Marilyn?
Marilyn: I haven't learnt any new languages like you, Lisa.
Lisa: That's too bad. Have you been practising your music?
Marilyn: Yes, I have been playing the guitar every day and now I am quite good.
Lisa: That's wonderful. Maybe you can play for me sometime.
Marilyn: Of course, I would love to. I also have written some new songs.
Lisa: Wonderful! I would really like to hear them sometime.
Marilyn: Sure, no problem! You can come over now if you want to.

131

(1G), 2D, 3E, 4A, 5C, 6K, 7B, 8I, 9L, 10F, 11J, 12H

Transcript mit Lösungshinweisen

One day I was cooking and my children were in the bathtub. They were happy because they were enjoying the warm water. When they were finished, they called me to come and help them. So I went upstairs and forgot about the pot on the stove. I was looking at my phone when I smelled smoke. Quickly I ran downstairs and saw smoke in the kitchen. I said to myself, 'Fire! Fire!' Next, I used the fire extinguisher but the fire didn't stop. So I called the fire brigade and gave them my address. They came in five minutes and put out the fire. We were safe now and the children and I said thank you to the brave firefighters. That was the story of the fire in my kitchen.

132

1	Zoey wants to talk to Marsha about dilemmas.	**True**	
2	A dilemma is a situation where you always know just what to do.	**False**	(do not know what to do)
3	Zoey tells Marsha a dilemma about a friend telling a secret.	**True**	
4	Zoey gives examples of three different options.	**True**	
5	Marsha thinks it is an easy situation and not really a dilemma.	**False**	(it's really hard)
6	Marsha would tell her friend that she must tell someone who can help her.	**True**	
7	It would be a terrible problem for Marsha if her friend was angry at her.	**False**	(it is more important that she gets help, even if she is angry later)
8	Marsha has an idea for a possible dilemma situation for Zoey.	**True**	
9	Marsha's dilemma situation is about lying for a friend.	**True**	
10	Zoey would lie for her friend.	**False**	(she would not lie)
11	Zoey would tell her friend to talk to her mother, because that would help.	**False**	(she would not tell her, because that is her friend's decision)

Transcript mit Lösungshinweisen

Zoey: Hey Marsha, do you have a minute?

Marsha: Hi Zoey, of course. What's up?

Zoey: Well, at school we talked about dilemmas and I have a question for you.

Marsha: All right, what is it?

Zoey: Well, a dilemma is a situation where you do not know what to do because there are different options.

Marsha: Okay, what dilemma would you like to talk about?

Zoey: Imagine your best friend told you a secret that was harmful for your friend. You are afraid that your friend might be in trouble or need help, but you have promised not to tell anyone. What would you do?

Marsha: That's a good question. What are the options?

Zoey: Would you tell someone you trust so that your friend does not know but you can help her? Would you tell your friend that you must tell someone else that can help her? Or would you keep your promise to tell your friend and not tell anyone?

Marsha: Hmm … That's very difficult. I think I would tell my friend that I must tell someone who can help her because it's important that my friend gets help, even if she is angry with me later.

Zoey: Alright, thank you. Do you have a dilemma situation for me?

Marsha: Uhm … let me think. Okay, I have an idea. Your friend wants to go out, but her mum said that she can't. Your friend asks you to tell her mother that she is at your house, but she is really out with friends. What would you do?

Zoey: That's an interesting dilemma, too.

Marsha: Would you lie for your friend? Would you tell your friend to ask her mother again if she could go out? Would you tell your friend that you will not lie to her mother for her?

Zoey: Wow, that's not easy. I wouldn't lie for my friend, but I wouldn't tell her to talk to her mother, because that is her decision.

Marsha: I see.

Zoey: Nice talking to you and thanks a lot for your help, Marsha.

Marsha: No problem, Zoey.

133

7	Alex did not take a phone with him because nobody should know where he was.
9	Many of them tried to help Alex, but he did not want their help.
1	Alex had just finished school and he did not want to start working or have a 'normal' life.
3	He bought books about how to survive in the wild and learned a lot about the wilderness.
12	He was very thin because he hadn't eaten enough and he was very sick.
5	The strange part is that Alex did not tell anyone about his plans.
8	On the road, Alex met many different people.
4	Soon he sold his car, packed a small bag with some clothes and food and left home.
13	He was cold from sleeping on the ground and didn't know where he was or what day it was.
2	So one day Alex decided that he wanted to go into the wilderness.
6	He got on a train and then a bus and finally he walked north for a very long time.
10	Soon his parents called the police because they did not know where their son was.
14	That was the adventure of Alex in the wilderness.
11	It took the police many months to finally find Alex deep in the wilderness.

Transcript

1 Alex had just finished school and he did not want to start working or have a 'normal' life.
2 So one day Alex decided that he wanted to go into the wilderness.
3 He bought books about how to survive in the wild and learned a lot about the wilderness.
4 Soon he sold his car, packed a small bag with some clothes and food and left home.
5 The strange part is that Alex did not tell anyone about his plans.
6 He got on a train and then a bus and finally he walked north for a very long time.
7 Alex did not take a phone with him because nobody should know where he was.
8 On the road, Alex met many different people.
9 Many of them tried to help Alex, but he did not want their help.
10 Soon his parents called the police because they did not know where their son was.
11 It took the police many months to finally find Alex deep in the wilderness.
12 He was very thin because he hadn't eaten enough and he was very sick.
13 He was cold from sleeping on the ground and didn't know where he was or what day it was.
14 That was the adventure of Alex in the wilderness.

134

1	Kate always liked Katy Perry.	**True**
2	Kate was a member of the school band.	**False**
3	The winner of the singing contest gets 100,000 Pounds.	**False**
4	The concert took place at school.	**False**
5	Kate sang the song "Never Really Over".	**True**
6	People started to applaud after five minutes.	**False**

135 **1 A** **2 B** **3 B** **4 B**

136
1. Her favourite singer was Katy Perry.
2. Because she had the same name as her role model.
3. She decided to take part ın the singing contest.
4. She said she would keep her fingers crossed.
5. Yes, she was.
6. She said she should come on stage.
7. Kate won the contest.

137
1. Mary **had to study for** her Maths test.
2. Mary did not **want to be disturbed**.
3. They were sitting next to each other, not **talking at all**.
4. Mary and Matthew shook hands and **exchanged their phone numbers**.
5. Matthew thought that he **could help her** with Maths.
6. Mary said that she was **the best essay writer**.

138

1	Mary was sitting on a terrace by the sea.	**False**
2	Mary was bad at Maths.	**True**
3	An old man sat down next to her.	**False**
4	He loved the view of the river.	**True**
5	Mary was not pleased at first.	**True**
6	The young man was called Mike.	**False**
7	He offered Kate to help her with Maths.	**True**
8	They exchanged email addresses.	**False**
9	Matthew's Maths grades have improved.	**False**
10	Now they are in love.	**True**

139
1. She wanted to enjoy the nice weather.
2. He wanted to sit down at her table.
3. She didn't want to be disturbed.
4. He suggested that he could help her with Maths.
5. He was not good at English.
6. She suggested that she could help him because she was very good at English.
7. They always met at the same café.
8. After two months they kissed each other for the first time.

140

1	The whole family went to Rome by car.	**True**
2	It was the second time Steven went to Italy.	**False**
3	The journey was boring.	**False**
4	The hotel was close to the Colosseum.	**True**
5	On the first day, they did a lot of sightseeing.	**False**
6	Their dad wanted to get his jacket from the car.	**True**
7	Their car was a new SEAT.	**False**
8	Julia's brother was sad because he thought he would never get home.	**True**
9	The police did not find their car.	**False**
10	Their dad never got lost.	**False**

141
1 Steven was really excited because **it was the first time he went to Italy**.
2 The journey was not boring because **they slept most of the time or played games**.
3 They liked the rooms because **they were very big and the view was fantastic**.
4 Dad went to the car because **he wanted to get his jacket**.
5 Dad looked really angry because **he couldn't find his car**.
6 The receptionist **phoned the police**.
7 The police officers looked **for the car**.
8 They thought that their car was parked **in Via dei Serpenti**.
9 The family were surprised because the police officers **returned so quickly**.
10 The policeman smiled because **he had found the car in Via dei Clementi**.

142
1 It took them 14 hours.
2 They slept or played games.
3 There was no elevator (and so they had to carry their luggage).
4 It was gone.
5 They asked the receptionist to phone the police.
6 They wanted to know where they had parked their car.
7 They told them where their car was.
8 He looked in the wrong street.

143 1 **A** 2 **C** 3 **C** 4 **A** 5 **B**

144

1	Paul spent his holidays at a campsite in Morocco.	**False**
2	Paul did not tell his parents that he wanted to explore the desert.	**True**
3	When Paul left the hotel, he met his parents.	**False**
4	In the distance, he suddenly saw an oasis.	**True**
5	When the scorpion bit him, he felt terrible pain.	**True**
6	When Paul woke up, he saw a man and a woman.	**False**
7	The men promised to take him back to the hotel.	**True**
8	Paul's parents were already waiting for him when he came back.	**False**
9	Paul thought that next time he would listen to his parents.	**True**

145
1 Paul's hotel was surrounded **by desert**.
2 His parents thought that there were **dangerous animals in the** desert.
3 Paul pretended to **have a headache**.
4 Paul did not go back to the hotel because he saw **an oasis** in the distance.
5 One of the men who found him said that the **scorpion was not dangerous**.
6 When Paul was back in his room, he was **tired and went to bed**.

146

1	The headmaster wants to close the library because it is too expensive.	**False**
2	Barbara doesn't know that the library might be closed.	**True**
3	Barbara wants to organise a meeting to inform the teachers.	**False**
4	Girl 2 wants to start a petition.	**True**
5	Boy 3 wants to organise a protest march.	**False**
6	Barbara says they should get into groups.	**True**
7	Only a few people come to the protest march.	**False**
8	The headmaster doesn't have to close the library.	**True**

147

1 She is upset because the headmaster wants to close the library (and all her friends go there).
2 He needs more space for new classrooms.
3 Yes, she does.
4 They decide to inform their fellow students.
5 The first group organises a protest march.
6 The second group prepares a petition on Instagram.
7 The third group writes an article for the school magazine.
8 The school gets an additional building.
9 und **10** individuelle Lösungen

148

L: Hi Ruby! How are you? Haven't seen you for ages. What have you been up to?
R: Hi Liz! I am fine. Guess what! Last Saturday I was at the Ed Sheeran concert in London.
L: Really? Wow, that's so cool! Did you enjoy it?
R: Yes, it was great. He was brilliant!
L: Was it the first time you saw him live on stage?
R: Yes, it was. He sang all my favourite songs like 'Shape of You', 'Thinking Out Loud' and 'Photograph'. I was dancing to the music the whole evening.
L: Who else went with you?
R: I went with my cousin, she is also a great fan of Ed Sheeran. The only bad thing was that there were so many people. I couldn't even buy anything to drink, because there was such a long queue.
L: Okay! Next time you go to a concert you have to tell me.
R: I promise! See you!
L: See you! Bye!
(151 Wörter)

149

Dear Mum and Dad,
How are you? I must tell you that my trip to Germany is terrible! The youth hostel is old and dirty. We don't even have our own bathroom, we must share it with all the other people on the floor! It's horrible! The food is disgusting, too. It's the same every day: fatty meat and rice, no vegetables, no potatoes … Luckily there is a burger place nearby, but it is very expensive.
Not even the weather is nice, it has been raining since we arrived.
Can you please come and pick me up? I don't want to stay here for another three days!
Yours, …
(108 Wörter)

150 London – A City You Shouldn't Miss!
I have always wanted to go to London. This summer, my dream has finally come true. Those of you who haven't been there should go there as soon as possible. London is definitely worth a visit.
There are so many fascinating things to do and see, but I have decided to tell you about my favourite ones. First, you must take a ride on the 'London Eye'. The 25-minute ride gives you the best view you can get. But make sure that the weather is fine. To avoid the long queues, I would recommend booking the tickets in advance.
Not far from the 'London Eye' is the 'London Dungeon', which is an absolute must. Some people find it scary and you should not be afraid of dark and small rooms. I liked the actors most who tell you about the dark history of London. It's so fascinating!
What you definitely shouldn't miss is 'Chinatown'. There you get the best Chinese food in the world!
London is great! I can't wait to go there again.
(180 words)

151 *G:* Hi Jacob! How are you?
B: Hi Julie! I'm fine. What's this? A new book?
G: Yes, it's really interesting. It's about superstitions from all over the world.
B: Cool! I don't know anything about superstitions. Can you tell me something about it?
G: Sure. There is one I really like. In Turkey people say that if you give a knife to someone, then you'll have a bad argument with her or him.
B: Oh gosh! That sounds weird!
G: Yes, it does. And in Austria, people believe that if you break a mirror, you'll have bad luck for seven years.
B: That's so interesting. Can I borrow the book?
G: Of course!
B: See you! Bye!
(121 Wörter)

152 I am lucky because there are not so many rules in my family. My parents are not strict at all. There are just two things I am not allowed to do. Firstly, I am not allowed to go out after 9 p.m. Secondly, I am not allowed to watch horror movies, which I think is bad. All my friends watch them.
But what I really like is that I am allowed to use my mobile phone whenever I want to and that I am allowed to invite my friends to my place almost every day. Actually, I wouldn't change anything.
(100 words)

153 SAVE OUR LIBRARY!
- Only when we work together – we can change something!
- Everyone is important!
- Join our protest march!

WHEN: FRIDAY, 9 p.m., in front of the SCHOOL
- Like our petition on Instagram!

WE COUNT ON YOU!!!!!

154 Hi!

How are you? I hope your holidays are as great as mine! I'm in California, at an international language school. I am staying for three weeks. My cousin Anna is with me, but we don't stay with the same family so that we can improve our English.

California is so cool! The language school is in Los Angeles, but I have already been to many other places, like San Francisco and Monterey. I like San Francisco best, especially the Golden Gate Bridge is gorgeous!

What I love about Los Angeles is Venice Beach. I often go there to watch the skateboarders. Yesterday, I even saw Brad Pitt!

Tomorrow we are visiting the 'Universal Studios'. I'm really looking forward to seeing where some of my favourite movies were made.

The only thing I don't like about California is the weather. It's so hot!

See you soon and enjoy the rest of your holidays!

Love, …

(154 Wörter)

155 The first thing I heard when I woke up in the morning was my mum's voice. "Andy, it's time to get up! It's already 7 o'clock!" "Oh no!" I thought when I jumped out of bed. "I'll miss the bus!" When I looked out of the window, I saw that it was raining. But it was too late for the bus, so I had to go by bike. What a terrible morning!

When I left the house, Mum said, "Be careful! Don't go too fast! The roads are slippery!" But what she did not know was that we had to write a Biology test in the first lesson. So I just could not be late. I stepped into the pedals. Unfortunately, the first traffic lights were red. But I did not see a car and so I rode on. Suddenly there was a big van right in front of me. I tried to stop but it was too late! I crashed into the car and fell down. The first thing I could remember was the face of a woman. She looked really worried. "I'm so sorry, I didn't see you! Are you hurt?" she asked desperately. I tried to stand up but my leg hurt. Then I started to cry because I felt miserable. In the meantime, some other people had called the ambulance. It arrived within five minutes. "Don't worry," a man said, "we'll take you to hospital. You'll be fine!"

Luckily, only my leg was broken and I could go home on the same day. My parents picked me up. They were so happy that nothing worse had happened. "You were really lucky, young man," the doctor said. "Be more careful next time!"

(283 words)

156 Dear, …

Thank you for inviting me! I've already booked the flight tickets. By the way, you don't have to pick me up at the airport, I'll take the 'Heathrow Express'. Could you just tell me your exact address? Do you live in a detached or semi-detached house? Maybe you could describe it, so that I'll find it more easily.

Should I bring any souvenirs from Austria?

Is there anything you already miss?

Looking forward to seeing you!

Love, …

(79 Wörter)

157 *A:* Hi Andy! How are you?
B: Not so good to be honest.
A: Oh no! What's the matter?
B: I have to write this really difficult English essay.
A: Okay. My English teacher always says that I am the best essay writer in class. Maybe I can help you.
B: Wow, that sounds great! The problem is that I don't have much time, I must hand my essay in by tomorrow.
A: No problem! I've got time. Let's start!
B: Thank you so much!
(78 Wörter)

158 Hi!
I want to tell you about this new Italian restaurant in town. You should definitely try it out! The food is delicious. I had the best lasagne ever and my brother had salami pizza. It tasted like the ones you only get in Italy.
But make sure that you are really hungry because you must try the tiramisu as well. It is soooo yummi!
My family and I also liked the atmosphere there. The cook and the waiters all come from Italy, so you get that real holiday feeling!
Maybe we can go there together next weekend!
See you!
Yours, …
(100 Wörter)

Test 1 – Schularbeit 1

159
1 Tom **was throwing** a piece of paper into the trash.
2 Gina **was talking** on her phone.
3 Mel **was yelling** at Lucy.
4 Lucy **was crying**.
5 My best friend **was smiling** at me.
6 Jim **was calling** out my name.
7 A girl in the front **was reading** a book.
8 Tom **was singing** a song.
9 Two boys **were listening** to music on their phones.
10 I **was thinking** about leaving the classroom and going home.

Transcript mit Lösungshinweisen
Tom was throwing a piece of paper into the trash. He likes doing that.
Gina was talking on her phone. She has a new boyfriend.
Mel was yelling at Lucy. It was something about not being a good friend.
Lucy was crying. She looked very sad.
My best friend was smiling at me. She is always friendly in the morning.
Jim was calling out my name. He wanted to know if I had done the homework.
A girl in the front was reading a book. She always reads in the breaks.
Tom was singing a song. He always sings when he is bored.
Two boys were listening to music on their phones. They had headphones so they couldn't hear anything else.
I was thinking about leaving the classroom and going home. I wanted to go back to bed.

160
1 The 'Donauinselfest' takes place every July. **False**
2 There are performances on eleven open-air stages. **True**
3 It first took place in 1982. **False**
4 You can listen to various genres of music there. **True**

161
1 About three million people visit it every year.
2 It first took place in 1983.
3 There are eleven open-air stages.
4 It lasts for three days.

162
This morning I **looked** for my bus pass everywhere, but I **couldn't** find it. I usually **keep** it in my school bag because I **need** it every day on my way to and from school. But when I **checked** the bag this morning, the bus pass **wasn't** there. I **told** my mum, and she **helped** me to look for it, but we **didn't find** it. But then I **remembered** – I sometimes **put** it in my jeans pocket after I've shown it to the driver. So I looked there, and there it **was**.

163
1 Max likes ice cream. He doesn't like chocolate cake.
2 All my friends listen to rock music. They don't listen to folk music.
3 For breakfast we have tea and toast. We don't have ham and eggs.
4 In the morning, Dad drives to work. He doesn't take the bus.

164
1 When I came home from school today, my mum **was preparing** lunch.
2 When we left the house this morning, the sun **was shining**.
3 When I took a photo of Emily and Sophie, they **were smiling**.
4 While the boys **were waiting** for the bus, it started raining.
5 Ben and I **were watching** TV when Ben's phone suddenly rang.
6 At the concert last night, Susan and Tom **were singing** and Brian **was playing** the piano.

165
1 *(b)* **After** Dad comes home from work, he watches the news on TV.
2 *(b)* At weekends, my brother and I play games **until** midnight.
3 *(b)* **By the time** we got to the train station, our train was gone.
4 *(b)* They showed two or three trailers **before** the real movie began.
5 *(b)* Julia and James were dancing **when** the lights went out.
6 *(b)* Somebody ate my sandwich **while** I was talking to a friend.
7 *(b)* My parents saw a ghost **during** their stay at a castle in Scotland.

166
1 Brenda's flat **isn't as big as our flat**.
2 Barbara **is as tall as Jimmy**.
3 Air **is not as heavy as wood**.
4 Patrick **is as clever as Michael**.

167
My favourite pop star is Elton John. I know this is very unusual for my age, because he is a really old man, but everyone in my family likes him. He is a brilliant singer.
Elton John was born on March 25th, 1947. He comes from Great Britain and he is one of the most successful singers in the world.
My favourite songs are 'Don't go breaking my heart' and 'I'm still dancing'. But I also love the song he sang at Lady Diana's funeral. It's called 'Goodbye England's Rose'. It is so sad that I must always

cry when I listen to it.
Last summer, my biggest dream finally came true and together with my parents I went to one of his concerts in Graz. It was amazing!
For me, Elton John is an outstanding musician because he has been successful for so many years.
(149 words)

Test 2 – Schularbeit 2

168 Hello, Susie. Welcome to the neighbourhood. I know you **haven't lived** here very long but I hope you'll feel at home very soon.
We **have already been** here for about ten years, so I can tell you everything about our neighbours. Mrs Jason **has lived** on this street for ever. She is a very sweet old lady. She always gives me candy when I visit her and I'm sure you will quickly learn to like her. She is nice to everybody and **has always been** a very friendly person.
Mr James, who lives just down the street, **has always liked** to have a beautiful garden since I've known him. Make sure you don't step on his lawn or trample his flowers or else he will get very mad. I**'ve never thrown** a ball into his garden before and I don't want to or else he won't give it back.
Mr Johnson, who lives at the end of the street, is always in a bad mood. I**'ve never seen** him smile. I don't think he even knows how to smile. I always try to walk on the other side of the street to avoid his house.
Ms Jakelyn is a very active person. She **has always gone** jogging in the morning for as long as I can remember. I often go jogging with her at the weekends. She **has been fit** for as long as I**´ve known** her.

169

1	Nora was a clever woman.	**True**
2	One day she invented a new mobile phone.	**False**
3	Nora invited her whole family to show them her new invention.	**False**
4	Nora took a photo of Corina, her boss.	**True**
5	Nora's invention was a real success.	**False**

170
1 She invented a camera that makes you prettier.
2 She was nervous because her boss was very critical and got angry easily.
3 The picture was bad.
4 She got angry and fired her.

171 1C, 2E, 3A, 4G, 5D, 6B, 7H, 8F

172
1 If you **are** nice to others, they **will be** nice to you.
2 Nothing **will happen** if you **do** what I say.
3 If we **don't go** now, we**'ll miss** our bus.
4 If I **tell** you the whole story, you **won't like** it.
5 You**'ll catch** cold unless you **put on** a sweater.
6 Unless you **try on** these jeans, you **won't know** if they fit you.
7 Nobody **will leave** the room if it **doesn't stop** raining.
8 This smell **won't go** away unless you **open** the windows.

173
1 This picture **has been** in our family **for** many years.
2 Martin and Ellie **have known** each other **since** they were children.
3 Dad **has had** his computer **since** before I was born.
4 I **haven't spoken** with Cathrine **for** two months.
5 My team **hasn't won** a game **since** the beginning of the season.
6 Alex and I **have built** two model planes **since** his birthday.

174
1 Look, **I've bought** new sunglasses. I **lost** my old ones during the summer holidays.
2 Dora **went** shopping an hour ago, but she **hasn't returned** yet.
3 Grandma **gave** me three DVDs for Christmas, and **I've already watched** two.
4 Gina **sent** me five emails yesterday, but I **haven't answered** them yet.

175
My best friend's name is Cathy. She has been my friend since my first day in primary school. I was really excited on that day because I did not know anybody, but then there was this little girl with curly red hair. She smiled at me and asked if I wanted to sit next to her. Since that day we have been like sisters. We do everything together. We like the same movies, we have the same taste in music and we also wear the same clothes. We both love horses and so we meet at the stable almost every day. Cathy is a very special girl because I can tell her everything and she always understands me. I hope we will be best friends forever.
(128 words)

Test 3 – Schularbeit 3

176
(1G), 2J, 3A, 4H, 5C, 6E, 7I, 8B, 9F, 10D

Transcript mit Lösungshinweisen
1 The Mennonites are a religious group that was founded by Menno Simons.
2 He claimed it is important to concentrate on family, faith and friends.
3 Mennonites live without electricity, machines or telephones.
4 They live in houses which they build themselves and eat food which they make themselves.
5 They spend much time praying and talking with friends and family.
6 In a Mennonite family, the women cook and clean and the men work in the fields or build houses.
7 The system is old-fashioned but many young people decide to stay with the group.
8 When the children are old enough, they can choose to become a part of the group for ever.
9 But first they leave for a while and go out into the world to do anything they want to do.
10 This is called 'rumspringa' and when they come back, they make their final decision.

177

1	Tobias lives in Wiener Neustadt.	**True**
2	This is a very small town in Lower Austria.	**False**
3	The only thing Tobias misses about Wiener Neustadt is a cinema.	**False**

178
1 The population of Wiener Neustadt is about **50,000**.
2 In Wiener Neustadt there is **a cinema**.
3 Tobias is allowed to **go out and meet friends**.

179
1 Wiener Neustadt is a wonderful town where you can do a lot of things.
2 He walks the dog every second day and unloads the dishwasher twice a week.
3 You should not cheat and talk back to the teachers.

180
1 You're not allowed to smoke in a restaurant.
2 Children are allowed to bring their toys to school.
3 Nobody is allowed to leave the room during a test.
4 You aren't allowed to park your car here.

181
1 My sister never **lets me wear** her T-shirts.
2 They **didn't let us see** the photos because they were terrible.
3 In the holidays, my parents **let me stay up** late.
4 The police **did not let the men go** after the fight.
5 I always **let my friends use** my school things.
6 Mr Jones **doesn't let us play** in his garden

182
1 If we switch off all the lights, we **will be able to** see the stars in the sky.
2 Last night, I **wasn't able to** fall asleep because I was too tired.
3 What's wrong with Richard? We **haven't been able to** speak with him for days.
4 The burglars tried to get into the house, but they **weren't able to** open the window.
5 You **won't be able to** answer my questions if you don't listen!
6 Mike has wanted a camera for a long time, but he **hasn't been able to** buy one yet. They're all too expensive.

183
1 Mum **has been working** for Smith & Company for six years.
2 You **have been learning** English for three years now.
3 It **has been snowing** heavily since Monday.
4 The neighbours' dog **has been barking** for half an hour!
5 The girls **have been practising** their dance for weeks.
6 I **have been dreaming** about going out with Julia since I met her.

184
A: Hi Matthew! How are you? Did you have a good time in California?
B: Hi Robert! Yes, I did. It was great! I really miss California.
A: So what did you do there?
B: We visited many places. The first three days we stayed in Los Angeles, at a really nice hotel with a big swimming pool. We went to the beach and to Universal Studios.
A: Wow! That sounds cool! What did you like best about Universal Studios?
B: Definitely 'The Harry Potter World'. It was amazing!
A: Did you also go to the 'Walk of Fame'?
B: Of course we did. I took a picture of the paw print of Lassie because I love that dog!
A: And was there anything you didn't like about California?
B: Some places are a bit dirty and there are many poor people. But our hotel was really nice.
A: Ok! I have to go now. But you must show me some pictures next time! See you!
B: Sure! Bye!
(158 words)

Test 4 – Schularbeit 4

185

[6] Suddenly there is a huge wave coming towards them.
[1] Yesterday I watched a film about a tsunami that suddenly hit an island.
[4] Before it does, the air is extremely quiet and everyone looks up into the sky.
[12] She calls for help and crawls a long way to find her family again.
[9] Her body circles around and it takes a while for her to get out of the water.
[7] When the wave hits, the mother is swept away.
[2] In the film, a family is on holiday on this island.
[11] When she looks around, she sees a car stuck in a tree.
[3] They are relaxing by the pool when the tsunami hits the island.
[8] She is pushed under water and cannot get up.
[10] It takes a while for her to understand what is going on.
[5] Many birds start flying away and making terrible noises.

Transcript

1 Yesterday I watched a film about a tsunami that suddenly hit an island.
2 In the film, a family is on holiday on this island.
3 They are relaxing by the pool when the tsunami hits the island.
4 Before it does, the air is extremely quiet and everyone looks up into the sky.
5 Many birds start flying away and making terrible noises.
6 Suddenly there is a huge wave coming towards them.
7 When the wave hits, the mother is swept away.
8 She is pushed under water and cannot get up.
9 Her body circles around and it takes a while for her to get out of the water.
10 It takes a while for her to understand what is going on.
11 When she looks around, she sees a car stuck in a tree.
12 She calls for help and crawls a long way to find her family again.

186

1 When Joanna woke up, she did **not know what had happened**.
2 In her area, earthquakes **were nothing unusual**.
3 Joanna's parents soon realised that **they were in danger**.
4 The whole house **collapsed**.

187

1 She heard a strange noise and the house was shaking.
2 The door was blocked.
3 Joanna's mum opened the kitchen window and they crawled outside.
4 Five minutes later the whole house collapsed.

188
1 340,000 cars **were registered** in Austria in 2018.
2 German **is spoken** in almost 10 countries in Europe.
3 Today, most computers **are made** in Asia.
4 In 2005, New Orleans **was destroyed** by hurricane Katrina.
5 The 'Indiana Jones' films **were directed** by Steven Spielberg, …
6 … and Indian Jones **was played** by Harrison Ford.
7 The London Dungeon **is visited** by thousands of people every year.
8 Olympic Games **are organised** in different cities every four years.

189
1 If Simon was here, we**'d listen** to some music.
2 Grandma would visit us more often if she **lived** closer.
3 If Joe **had** enough money, he would buy a bigger TV.
4 You**'d get** better grades in your tests if you studied more.
5 If Dan **wasn't** my best friend, I would be angry with him.
6 We **wouldn't go** to bed if the film wasn't so boring.
7 If you lost your keys here, you **wouldn't find** them again.
8 Bill would have more friends if he **didn't bully** everybody.

190
1 You ~~will be~~/**would be** fitter if you did more sport.
2 If the sun **doesn't shine**/~~didn't shine~~ tomorrow, we'll stay indoors all day.
3 Dad would not like it if we ~~are~~/**were** late again.
4 If they see us, they **will catch**/~~would catch~~ us.
5 Joey ~~won't tell~~/**wouldn't tell** the teacher if I copied his homework.

191
1 We're going to meet a famous musician after the concert.
2 Who is going to clean the blackboard?
3 I'm going to visit some art museums in Paris.
4 Are you going to tell your parents about the school trip?
5 Sally isn't going to like this book.

192
Dear xxx,
I was really shocked when you told me about your problem. I cannot understand why you didn't tell me earlier. I think that you must tell your parents about it. These pupils will never stop bullying you. Don't be scared, your parents can help you. They have to inform the police and then these boys will stop punching you and asking you for money.
Another possibility would be to ask some friends of yours to come with you on your way home. They could help and protect you.
You could also tell one of your teachers about your problem. I'm sure they will help you, too.
If you don't want to tell anybody, then I can do it. But you can't solve this problem alone!
I hope I could help you!
Yours, xxx
(135 Wörter)

1. Auflage (2020) – Entspricht der Rechtschreibreform 2006.

Auf umweltfreundlichem Papier gedruckt bei: siehe https://produkt.veritas.at/45712#additional
AutorInnen: Franz Zach, Nicole Eisinger-Müllner, Julie Eiwen
Lektorat: Klaus Kopinitsch
Bildredaktion: Raffaela Schuster
Umschlaggestaltung und Layout: Kathrin Schager
Herstellung: Sandra Reinhardt
Illustrationen: Sven Aring, Paderborn
Satz: FACTORY punkt Werbeagentur GmbH, Leonding

ISBN 978-3-7101-3776-1